FUNDRAISING THE DEAD

SHEILA CONNOLLY

WHEELER
CHIVERS

This Large Print edition is published by Wheeler Publishing, Waterville, Maine, USA and by AudioGO Ltd, Bath, England.
Wheeler Publishing, a part of Gale, Cengage Learning.
Copyright © 2010 by Sheila Connolly.
A Museum Mystery.
The moral right of the author has been asserted.

LIBRARY OF CONGRESS CATALOGING-IN-PUBLICATION DATA

Connolly, Sheila.
　Fundraising the dead / by Sheila Connolly.
　　p. cm. — (Wheeler Publishing large print cozy mystery)
　ISBN-13: 978-1-4104-3381-7 (softcover)
　ISBN-10: 1-4104-3381-1 (softcover)
　1. Antiquarians—Fiction. 2. Murder—Investigation—Fiction.
　3. Fund-raisers (Persons)—Fiction. 4. Large type books. I. Title.
　PS3601.T83F86 2011
　813'.6—dc22　　　　　　　　　　　　　　　　　　　　　2010048903

BRITISH LIBRARY CATALOGUING-IN-PUBLICATION DATA AVAILABLE
Published in 2011 in the U.S. by arrangement with The Berkley Publishing Group, a member of Penguin Group (USA) Inc.
Published in 2011 in the U.K. by arrangement with the author.

U.K. Hardcover: 978 1 445 83682 9 (Chivers Large Print)
U.K. Softcover: 978 1 445 83683 6 (Camden Large Print)

Printed and bound in Great Britain by
the MPG Books Group.
1 2 3 4 5 6 7 14 13 12 11 10

ACKNOWLEDGMENTS

W.C. Fields once said, "I'd rather be in Philadelphia." Of course, he was talking about an epitaph for his tombstone, but Philadelphia is a *lot* better than dead. It's a great place, with something for everyone — culture, sports, history. I've spent a big chunk of my life in and around the city, and that's why I set my new series there.

This book is based on an institution in Center City where I worked for several happy years, and where I met some wonderful, dedicated people. Let me assure you that no character in this book is based on any employee there, past or present, living or dead, and the crimes in the story are my own invention. There has never been a murder there, to my knowledge.

There was, however, a real crime that was discovered while I worked there. That event and its aftermath inspired this story, because it became painfully obvious how easy it is to take advantage of both the trust and the shortcomings of such a venerable cultural institution. In that case the culprit was caught quickly and prosecuted successfully, thanks to the FBI. As for the rest, the descriptions of the outstanding collections, and the ongoing efforts to digitize catalogs and make the collections more widely available to the public, are all true. And like many peer cultural institutions in Philadelphia and throughout the country, this place suffers from chronic underfunding, which contributed to my decision to make my protagonist a fundraising professional (that and the fact that I was one), one of the people who fight to keep the doors open and the lights on so that the public can enjoy the collections.

Of course my thanks go to Jacky Sach and Jessica Faust of BookEnds, who made this book possible, and my patient editor, Shannon Jamieson Vazquez, who has shepherded this through more than one revision, making it stronger each time. Carol Kersbergen, a colleague of mine at the museum, reminded me of a number of details about how things really worked behind the scenes. And as always, the ongoing support of the generous members of Sisters in Crime, and particularly the Guppies, has been essential.

I hope this story gives you something to think about the next time you visit a museum. And please do visit — collections are meant to be enjoyed!

CHAPTER 1

The sight of Marty Terwilliger charging into
my office with fire in her eyes was never a
good thing, but it was particularly unwel-
come right now, as I was trying to put the
finishing touches on the grand gala planned
for this evening. Tonight was a big event, a
really big event, and I was in charge of making it happen. The venerable Pennsylvania
Antiquarian Society in Philadelphia was
celebrating its 125th anniversary as the
guardian of the historic treasures of Philadelphia and the surrounding counties. We
were expecting nearly two hundred people,
which would set a new record for a Society
event.

Our famed vaults housed at least two million books, documents, and ephemera, rang-
ing from manuscript letters signed by William Penn and George Washington, to
advertising flyers from late nineteenth-
century hatters, to financial records for

several of the long-defunct companies that had put Philadelphia on the map of the commercial and industrial world. And that's not including our fairly respectable collection of paintings, silver, clothing, and some truly weird artifacts (like a horse's hoof made into an inkwell with silver fittings). The Society's stately neoclassical building had been constructed to reflect the seriousness of its purpose, and loomed over a neighborhood that had seen many transitions, both good and bad, and had weathered them all.

I'm Eleanor Pratt — Nell to my friends — and I'm the director of development for the Society. If that job title means nothing to you (I get a lot of blank looks), it means I'm a fundraiser. I'm the one who writes those begging letters you get from nonprofit organizations every couple of months. It's not my name at the bottom — oh, no, it's the president's, or, if your bank balance runs to seven figures or you're sitting on your great-grandfather's priceless library of Americana, the president's *and* the board chair's. But I'm the one who writes the letter, and also makes sure that there is a current address and the correct, intimate salutation on each one (*Dear Binkie,* et cetera), and that there is enough of the good stationery to print them all, and that the president actually gets around to signing them (well, most of them — my staff and I usually end up doing a bunch), and that they get into the mail, with postage on them. I'm the invisible person who keeps the money flowing.

I'm also the one who, when I say I'm a fundraiser, you run screaming from, your checkbook tightly clutched in your hand. Why would anyone go into fundraising? What starry-eyed college student ever said, with a gleam in his or her eyes, *Gee, I want to beg for money when I grow up?* Well, my answer is simple: I was an English major in college. Need I say more? I had drifted into development after a few years of trying to find an academic job, and then discovered that I liked the work. I've been at it for more than a dozen years now, and at the Society for the last five of them. In addition to sending out endless mailings and grant proposals, and currying favor from potential donors, party planning is one of my responsibilities. And finally, after many, many months of agonizing over the theme of the evening, the perfect font for the invitations, the menu selections, the arrangement of the tables, and dozens of other details, here we were, just hours away from the anniversary gala.

Now, however, instead of talking to the caterer just one more time to be sure he had the head count right; instead of counting the wine bottles that the liquor store had just delivered; instead of supervising the tables and plates and glassware that were at this very moment being off-loaded in the back alley, I pasted on what I hoped was a sympathetic smile and welcomed Martha Terwilliger, aka Marty.

"Hi, Marty. What brings you here so early? The party doesn't start until six." It was barely past three, though I needed every minute between now and then.

Martha Terwilliger was a board member — actually, a third-generation board member; her grandfather had been president of the Society in the distant past, and her father had grudgingly accepted a board position as an inheritance — and she took it quite seriously. She was fiftyish, with a brusque, wry manner and a sharp intelligence, and related to half of Philadelphia. Following the disintegration of her third marriage, she had decided that she needed some focus in her life, and she had adopted the Society with a vengeance. Her father, upon his death several years earlier, had

12

bequeathed to the Society his vast collection of family papers — records that went back to the original Terwilliger settlers, in the early eighteenth century, and included one of the great leaders of the Revolution, Major Jonathan Terwilliger, as well as a host of lesser dignitaries and movers and shakers of Philadelphia political, economic, and social life. The collection was huge, a true treasure trove, and it was quite literally priceless.

Marty's father had also left an endowment to support the daunting undertaking of cataloging the Terwilliger papers. Unfortunately, the endowment had produced only enough income to cover a cataloger's pay for a couple of days a week; as a gesture in recognition of the importance of the papers, the Society was underwriting another day or two, bringing the position up to bare full-time status. A few months ago we had hired Rich Girard for the position, fresh out of college, and he had barely scratched the surface. Marty, annoyed at the glacial pace of progress, had decided to step in and get to work herself. Luckily, she was smart and persistent, and it was possible to visualize an end to the project . . . some five or ten years down the road. In any event, Marty was now bearing down on me with a full head of steam.

"Nell, I need to talk to you. We've got a problem," she said curtly. "It's about the Collection." Whenever Marty spoke about her family's papers, you could see the capital letters: The Terwilliger Collection.

"I'm sorry to hear that, Marty. Please, sit down and tell me what I can do," I said, far more calmly than I felt.

Marty looked at the piles of books and papers on my sole guest chair and remained standing. "I was in yesterday, looking for a folder of papers, an exchange of letters between Major Jonathan" — she seemed to be on a first-name basis with all her dead family members — "and George Washington. I know I saw them a few weeks ago. But they aren't there now."

Great: a collections problem. Why was she talking to me about this? I did *not* need to hear about a collections problem at this moment. What was I supposed to do? Drop all the gala preparations, take a flashlight and go hunting through the file boxes in the stacks?

"Are you sure that Rich didn't take them to his cubicle to catalog them?" Rich was a sweet boy, but he could be absentminded.

"No," Marty said with conviction. "He was the first person I asked. He hasn't gotten up to the 1770s yet, and he hasn't seen them."

"Maybe they were just misfiled?" I parried. *Please, let there be a quick solution to this so I can get back to putting out event-related fires,* I prayed.

Marty was not about to back off. "Well, if they were, they aren't in any of the adjacent boxes. No, I know I saw them just a couple of weeks ago. I was checking where the major spent Christmas in 1774, for the family history" — of course she was also working on a family history, and had been for several years, although no one to my knowledge had seen even a page of it — "and they were there then. But they aren't there now."

"I'm not sure what I can do, Marty. Why come to me, rather than to someone in collections, like Latoya?" Latoya Anderson, our vice president of collections, was the most likely person for Marty to talk to about any items that might have gotten misplaced.

"Because we've worked together in the past, Nell, and I know you can get things done," Marty said curtly. "Latoya will just give me the runaround. I need answers."

"Marty," I said in my most pacifying tone, "I can understand your concern, and their absence is very troubling. But there must be some simple explanation. Why don't you and Rich and I get together tomorrow and see if we can track them down?" I smiled hopefully. Tomorrow: the day *after* the event.

She still looked miffed. "I suppose. But let me tell you, if those letters are really missing, there will be hell to pay. Do you have any idea what they're worth?"

I didn't, but I knew that whatever insurance we had wouldn't be enough. To be totally honest, I didn't even know if we *had* insurance for the collections. But I smiled even more brightly. "Marty, of course I know how important they are. And I'm sure we'll find them." I stood up, hoping to urge her out the door. "I'll tell Rich, and we'll meet you in the lobby at nine tomorrow morning, before anyone comes in, all right?" I came around my desk and moved toward the hall, and Marty grudgingly followed. "And you'll be back for tonight? It's going to be a wonderful evening. I'm very pleased at the RSVPs." I mentally reviewed tonight's guest list, which included at least six of Marty's cousins, and those were only the ones I remembered offhand. Marty took her board obligations seriously, and I knew she would be at the gala, no matter how annoyed she might be at the moment. I continued my progress toward the elevator, with Marty trailing behind.

"All right, nine A.M. sharp tomorrow. And of course I'll be here tonight," she said tartly. "This party had better be good. The Society can use the money."

As if I weren't well aware of that. I kept the smile glued to my face as the elevator doors closed behind her, but it faded immediately once she was out of sight. Just what I needed, one more problem — and I didn't like the sound of this one. I took a quick look at my watch and cursed silently. There was too much to do in the time I had left, and now Marty had just dumped a whole new problem in my lap. One which I was hardly equipped to deal with, since I had very little working knowledge of the vast collections in the building. Still, I could probably start the ball rolling, and then I could tell her that I was making progress when I saw her at the party. Our registrar, Alfred Findley, the person who'd be most helpful right now, had absolutely nothing to do with the party, so unlike the rest of the staff, at least *he* wouldn't be running around like a headless chicken.

Alfred's cubicle was only fifty feet from my office, but today was no ordinary day, and I was stopped twice en route with questions that absolutely, positively had to be answered immediately.

My membership coordinator, Carrie Drexel, was the third. "Nell, did you want to use the sticky name badges? You know the guests complain when they have to pin something on."

"Good catch, Carrie. They're in the supply closet outside my office. We ordered a huge batch after the last members' meeting."

"Oh, right. Thanks!" She turned and dashed back the way I had come.

I made it another ten feet before the next interruption: Felicity Soames, our head librarian, emerged from the staff room at the back of the building, a mug of coffee in her hand. "Hi, Nell," she began. "How's the __"

I held up a hand. "No time now, Felicity. See you at the gala?"

"Of course. It'll be grand, don't worry."

I turned and all but ran to Alfred's lair.

CHAPTER 2

As registrar, Alfred Findley was in charge of the minutiae of recording and organizing the Pennsylvania Antiquarian Society's collections. Alfred had come to the Society some fifteen years ago, had fallen in love with the place, and had never left. In appearance, he was short and sort of doughy — you had the feeling that if you poked him, the dimple would linger for a while — and he was also very pale, as if he never saw the light of day, which may have been true. The bare description made him sound rather like a fungus, but he was a really sweet guy. It was rumored that he was gay, but since he said very little about his personal life (in fact, we weren't sure he had one outside of the Society, and some people whispered that he actually lived somewhere deep in the stacks), no one knew for sure. But it was clear that the collections at the Society were the one true love of his life, and if anyone knew where something was, it would be Alfred. He had been lobbying the other staff members, and what board members he could bring himself to approach, for upgraded computer systems and more support for a full recataloging of the collections. He and I had been on great terms ever since I found funding for his new, state-of-the-art computer system and cataloging-software a couple of years ago.

Our collections management procedures could certainly use the electronic assistance. Together, the books and manuscripts in our collections total about two million items, which is rather mind-boggling when you think about it. I should add, we *think* it's two million — it depends on how you count. I mean, are five pieces of paper in a folder one item or five? It'd been counted both ways, as far as we could tell. So we just used the figure two million and hoped for the best. It was at least that and possibly quite a lot more.

And although our original mandate is closer to that of a library — focusing on historical books, manuscripts, and other documents — over the course of the Society's century and a quarter, we'd also somehow accumulated paintings, furniture, and other memorabilia. Many of them arrived in the early days, over a century ago, when the Society was grateful for anything. Some came lumped in with estates or bequests, and how could we say no? The problem was, we were fast running out of space. Worse, our handsome building was never set up for the storage of articles like these. And some things, like paintings, could be rather finicky. They liked the right conditions, such as certain temperatures, humidity, exposure to (or avoidance of) light, and so on. If you don't treat them nicely, the paint tends to fall off the canvas, which leaves you with a mess. But selling or otherwise getting rid of these gifts could be tricky, so we compromised by putting the best examples on public display and keeping far more odds and ends stuffed into dark and dusty corners, unused spaces, wherever they would fit, for a very long time.

Bottom line: we have a whole lot of stuff, and it could be anywhere in the building. It was Alfred's job to try to keep track of it — and he was the first person the Society had ever hired to do that specific job. It wasn't easy. In theory, each item had an identifying number, which would tell you when the item came in, but that number had to be linked to some sort of map, which would tell you where it was right now. I shudder to think what this process was like before the advent of computers. Still, Alfred handled all of it with good cheer. He massaged his computer programs and made them sing. He prowled the dark corners, and he had unearthed some unexpected treasures in his wandering. He was the man I needed to talk to.

Alfred and his machines lived in a cubicle constructed of modern movable partitions, which gave limited privacy — not that it seemed to bother Alfred, even though it meant that everyone had to pass by his cubicle to get to either the restrooms or the coffee room. Inside his cubicle, he had two desks, one where he worked and one that housed his computer and a scanner-printer; behind him loomed a massive array of filing cabinets holding all the earlier paper records, which he was slowly transferring to electronic format. Luckily, Alfred was extremely conscientious about the transfer process. Though it made a slow job slower, he took very little on faith, usually insisting on seeing the item and verifying its number and current location, before entering it into his precious database. He estimated he'd completed perhaps ten percent of the total to date. Barring any disasters, Alfred could count on doing exactly what he was doing now for the next twenty years, before retiring at seventy or so.

I poked my head around the corner of his lair. "Hi, Alfred."

"Hello, Nell. You need me?"

"Alfred, what I need is to pick your brain. Do you have a minute?"

"For you, sure."

I slipped around the corner of his partition and sat down, allowing myself a small sigh of relief. "I don't have much time before the gala, but I need to ask you about something. Let me give you a hypothetical. Let's say I'm writing a heart-wrenching appeal letter about Dolley Madison's boot scraper, given to the Society in 1883 by her great-grandniece four times removed, detailing how the poor boot scraper will disintegrate into a pile of rust if we don't buy a mink-lined box for it immediately. Are you with me?"

Alfred gave me a shy grin. "All the way."

I went on. "And I really want to take a smashing picture of the boot scraper to send out with the letter. How do I locate it?"

Alfred looked thoughtful. "Do you have the accession number?"

I shook my head. "No, I have a lovely note in my file — copperplate hand, mind you, but at least there's a date on it — that says that the donor hopes we will treasure Aunt Dolley's boot scraper. That's it."

Alfred was warming to his task. "Was it a single item or part of a larger collection?"

"No clue."

"And you're sure it was a boot scraper, and not a snaffle bit or a peach pitter?"

"Well, the great-grandniece thought so, but we have no idea what Dolley did with it. Maybe she beat her children with it. Did she have children?"

"Can't tell you. Okay, so we have an unknown object, possibly a boot scraper, with an accession number that should begin eighty-three something or other. Type: object, not paper. I punch those facts into Cassandra here . . . and voilà, a list of possibilities."

"Cassandra? That's your computer?"

"Yes. She's often issuing predictions of dire catastrophes, when she isn't crashing altogether. Somehow it seemed appropriate, especially since I usually ignore her and plow on regardless. But don't worry, I back things up all the time, just in case."

"Right." I was not reassured, though I did chuckle at the appropriateness of Alfred naming his computer system after a Greek prophetess, who, if I recalled correctly, was doomed to be always right yet was never

24

believed.

"Then we look at our list . . . and we see that *Metal Objects, Miscellaneous,* are housed on the fourth floor, northeast corner, shelves eleven-A to twelve-G. So that would be a good place to start. Unless, of course, the thing weighed fifty pounds or more, in which case it would be on the floor someplace, so nobody gets brained trying to get it down off the shelf. You would go up to the fourth floor and look for it." Alfred sat back and beamed at me, clearly pleased.

"What about if the great-grandniece also donated her diaries? How would I find books and documents?" I pressed on.

"Well, you know the card catalogs downstairs, right?"

I nodded sagely, even though I was fairly clueless, knowing that Alfred wouldn't understand how someone working here might not be intimately familiar with our catalogs.

"They give you the call number for the book, but sometimes we move books, or even whole collections, so we have to cross-reference in Cassandra here, so we know where the books actually are," he said.

"You keep all this up-to-date?"

"As far as possible. That's just the bare-bones version. I've only been working with it for two years, so the data are kind of limited. Everything that's come in since I started using Cassandra is in here, or anything that I know has been shifted, but the earlier stuff, not so much. I'm working on it."

"And how much of a lag time is included in that *possible?*"

Alfred almost blushed. "A couple of weeks? Depends on the scope of the shift, or the backlog."

I contemplated the poster behind his desk. It was a picture of the Old Library at Trinity College in Dublin, where it looked as though no book had been moved for at least two hundred years. Comforting, that. "All right, Alfred — here's the sixty-four-thousand-dollar question. What if the item is not where Cassandra says it is?"

He looked at me bleakly. "Well, that's actually a multipart question. One, I might not have gotten around to entering the details of the move into Cassandra. Two, it's been misplaced, or put back on the wrong shelf. Or, three" — he paused and swallowed — "it's gone missing."

A thick silence fell and lasted for about five beats. Alfred looked around him; he stood up and peered over the panels that made up his cubicle. Then he sat down again, rolled his desk chair closer to my chair, and leaned forward conspiratorially.

"Have you heard something?" he whispered, sounding worried.

I stared at him. "Should I have?" Our eyes locked for several seconds, until I roused myself. After all, the party clock was ticking. "Alfred, I have the feeling that there's something you want to talk about. Something about the collections?" I said, my tone coaxing.

He nodded. "I just don't know what to do. At first I thought, well, the files were incomplete, or some files had been archived. And then I began to wonder if I was getting sloppy, misplacing things, forgetting things . . ." He had picked up a piece of scrap paper from his desk, and he was folding and unfolding it, making and unmaking a fan. He wouldn't look at me, keeping his eyes on his hands.

"Alfred," I said firmly, "you are the most organized person I know, and the most conscientious. You're worried about something. What is it?"

Finally he looked up at me, with something like fear in his gaze. "I don't want to make any trouble. I mean, I love my work, I love the Society, and I'd hate to think that there was anything wrong, but . . ." He swallowed, and I resisted the strong urge to shake him, to hurry the words out of him. "You must know that a lot of what I do is very repetitive. Some people would say boring, but that doesn't bother me. I'm happy doing what I do, even though it seems very slow. But even I like a little break now and then. So, over the years, I've devised a sort of reward system for myself. I'll do however many regular entries, or a single collection, or some specific batch of processing, and then I'll treat myself to something special. I'll save the really nice pieces until I need a little boost, and then I'll check their tracking history and go visit them, just to make sure everything is right. You know, there are some wonderful things in the collection — real stars — and a lot of people, even staff, don't even know they're there. But I do."

"I completely understand, Alfred — I do the same thing myself sometimes. Go on," I urged.

He gave me a wavery smile, but it faded quickly. "Well, recently, I've found that a number of items aren't where they're supposed to be. At first I thought, oh, they're just misfiled, moved to a different shelf. Or someone had decided that they were important or valuable and had moved them to a safer place, without making a note in the record. That certainly does happen, even in the best-run places. When you've got a century's worth of sloppy cataloging, of course some things have slipped through the cracks." Maybe he was trying to convince himself, but Alfred didn't look very certain.

"And you were beginning to get worried?" I prodded gently.

"I was afraid that I'd messed up something or that there was a bug in Cassandra. So I started double-checking. And I couldn't find a number of these things, even in unlikely places. They're just not in the building."

Alfred and I stared at each other for several seconds. Then I said carefully, "What kind of things are we talking about?"

He considered. "Books, prints, letters, and some artifacts. Not just one group. Not just one period, either. But they all share something: they're what you might call *valuable* to a collector or on the open market."

"You mean worth a lot of money?" Alfred put monetary value far down the list of criteria when evaluating the worth of a historical item, but others might not feel the same way.

"Well, for example, I was at an auction at Freeman's last year, where there was a

Jefferson autograph letter that sold for twenty thousand dollars. Just out of curiosity, I checked our records after the auction, since I knew that we should have had one a lot like it. But that was one of the things I couldn't find." He lapsed into a glum silence.

My mind was churning furiously, turning over alternatives. Finally, I said carefully, "Alfred, let me ask you this: do you think this is the result of long-term carelessness — no, I don't mean you — or are you saying that you think that these things have been deliberately removed from the Society?"

He looked positively miserable. "I don't know. At first, as I said, I thought it could be human error or just bad record-keeping. But as more and more things turned up missing, and I looked at them as a group, I realized that they were important items — the type of things that someone would be likely to take for gain or for the sake of owning them. They're definitely desirable. So, to answer your question" — he took a deep breath — "yes, I'm afraid someone has been stealing from the Society."

We both sat back in our seats. I was stunned, though of course there were a million things I wanted to ask. I decided to start cautiously. "Alfred, have you discussed this with anyone else?"

He looked at me with a mixture of guilt and trepidation. "No. At first I didn't want to believe it. And then when I did, I was afraid someone would blame me. I've been trying to avoid thinking about it at all."

"All right, Alfred. Let's step back a moment. Walk me through the process. When you think something is missing, you do a very thorough search first." When he nodded, I went on. "And when you don't find it and decide it is officially missing, what do you do?"

"I fill out a missing-item form and put it in the file. Oh, and in Cassandra, now."

I gazed at him with no little incredulity. "And that's all? You don't report it to anyone else?"

"Like who?" He eyed me curiously.

"Latoya, to begin with." The vice president of collections was his immediate supervisor. "Or the president, or the board. Or the police."

Alfred looked horrified. "The police? Why would I tell the police?"

"Because it could be theft, Alfred, and that's a crime. But let's take this one step at a time. Do you report missing items to Latoya?"

He gulped. "Yes. I give her a monthly status report that lists items processed in the month and includes items not found."

I reflected on that. "So, in an average month, what do those numbers look like?"

"Oh, a few thousand input, in a good month — and usually there are maybe ten or twenty that turn up missing. But that could just mean I can't find them, not that they're really gone."

"I understand. But it's safe to say that the percentage of missing items is very small, right? And that the numbers here fall within the normal range for a place like this?" He nodded. "Do you identify the missing items?"

"Sometimes — it depends on what they are."

I knew that Latoya would report those results, in condensed form, to the president at monthly staff meetings, and then they would be passed on to the board at their quarterly meetings. But both the lack of detail and the repetition each month would dull the impact — it was just another piece of standard information to be checked off a list at the meeting. In addition, board members were seldom museum professionals, so if the Society's leaders told them not to worry, they wouldn't.

"All right. Is there any way for you to determine how long these things have been missing? Even very broadly — say a century versus a year?"

He shook his head. "No, not really. It depends on when the item was originally cataloged, or if it's been accessed since. In some cases, the more notable things have been used by scholars in publications, or they've been loaned for an exhibition somewhere else. We're always careful to keep close records of cases like that, and keep copies in the file. You know, for copyright issues or insurance questions. But those would be pretty much the only instances when there would be intermediate evidence of where something is, between its first entry and now."

Items flowed into the Society, had been flowing in for more than a century; they were assigned a number, and then wandered around the building — or, quite possibly, *out* of the building. Any number of people could have laid hands on these things, both staff and outsiders such as researchers and board members. Any number of these people could have slipped a rare and valuable item into a pocket or bag and just walked out the door. And we had little or no way of knowing who, what, or when.

Damn — I did not need to hear this now, with the gala less than three hours away. I was definitely getting a headache.

Alfred's voice interrupted the spinning in my head. "Nell? Why are you asking this now?"

I glanced at the clock behind Alfred's desk and cut to the chase. "Marty Terwilliger came to me today and wanted to know where the letters between Major Jonathan and George Washington from the Terwilliger Collection were. She'd seen them recently, so she knew they were there. But apparently they aren't now. So I said I'd look into it." And I was beginning to regret that I had. I should have just dumped this into someone else's lap and run screaming. But now I knew about it, and what was worse, I was beginning to understand how much could go wrong with our system. But what was I supposed to do about it? Alfred was still looking at me nervously.

I sighed. "Alfred, can you give me a list of all the things you think are missing? And any other information that goes with them?" From what he'd said, it could be quite a few items, but I wanted to see them all together before I made any assumptions — or any decisions about what to do, like what to tell Marty. "It would be a big help to me."

He nodded. "Sure, no problem. When do you need it?"

"Tomorrow's fine. You weren't planning to go to the gala, were you?"

Alfred shook his head vehemently. "No way — too much noise and fuss. Not my kind of thing. But I can stay late and run out the report for you, so you'll have it when you come in tomorrow. That okay?"

I gave him a warm smile. "That would be wonderful." I stood up to head back to the next item on my multipage to-do list, but stopped at the edge of the cubicle. "Unfortunately, I don't think Marty's likely to let this go, unless we come up with a good answer for her. Or better yet, the documents themselves. So I think we'd better think about what to do next. But at least now I can tell her we're working on it, right?"

As I made my way back to my office, I congratulated myself. I'd started one ball rolling. Time to get back to all the other balls I was juggling. Only two and a half hours until the guests started arriving.

But there was one more thing I had to do first: talk to Rich Girard. Luckily the staff members who spent a lot of time in the stacks carried beepers, so I could get hold of him quickly. When he responded to my page, I said, "Rich, can you come to my office for a moment?"

"I'm up on four — I'll be right there," he responded.

Rich Girard was barely twenty-two, just out of Penn with a degree in history, and this was his first full-time job. He was trying to make up his mind whether he wanted to go on in history in graduate school or get a library science degree or do something totally different. He had been hired specifically to work on the Terwilliger Collection, which worked out for everyone: the collection got a dedicated staffer, the materials he was working with would serve him well if he applied to either graduate school or library school, and because he was young and inexperienced, we could pay him a miserable pittance and tell him that he was gaining valuable experience. Still, he was smart, conscientious, and hardworking, and seemed really excited about the work.

When he showed up three minutes later he began, "Hey, Nell, what's up? I mean, aside from the obvious party stuff." He slouched in the chair, all angles and legs.

I had no time for chitchat, with the gala looming. "Have you talked to Marty lately?"

"Yeah, she asked me how far chronologically into the collection I'd gotten to by now. Why?"

I went on. "She came to me to say she couldn't find something she was looking for in the collection, something she knew was there earlier. I said I'd ask you if you had set anything aside to work on."

He looked perplexed. "No, I had a couple of boxes out so I could catalog them to folder level, but I put those back over a week ago. I told her that. What's gone missing?"

"Something from Major Jonathan, apparently. But she's coming by tomorrow morning, and I said I'd help her look. Can you join us?" I was being polite, since I was a senior staff member conveying a board member's request, and he would *have* to be there unless he came down with malaria. Or maybe smallpox.

"Sure, no problem. There's some other stuff I wanted to ask her about anyway." He seemed unworried.

"How's the project going overall?"

"Oh, great. There's some amazing stuff in there — the Terwilligers were definitely pack rats. That's good and bad from my point of view. I mean, there's all this fascinating material, but it's all jumbled together, sort of loosely grouped by date. So you can find a letter from Benjamin Franklin thrown in next to somebody's nineteenth-century shopping list. I'm having a lot of fun, but it's a long, slow process."

"You've been here for four months now, since, what, July?" He nodded. "How much do you think you've covered?"

He looked up at the ceiling while he considered. "Lessee. I decided to approach this chronologically, so I started at the beginning, and there's less stuff there . . ." I knew that the Terwilligers had arrived in Philadelphia early in the eighteenth century and had set themselves up as bankers and merchants and done extremely well for themselves, all the while reproducing and establishing their offspring in businesses in Philadelphia and beyond. "I'd guess I've finished roughly twenty percent in terms of volume. Of course, that's just to folder level — if I was going to do it down to item level, it would take a lot longer."

"And where are you now?" I asked.

"Just before the Revolution."

That's what Marty had said. "Marty was looking for some correspondence between Major Jonathan and George Washington — have you gotten to that yet?"

He looked nonplussed. "No. You know, she said something about that the last time she was working on the papers, but like I told her, I haven't gotten up to the war years yet."

"Hey, don't panic, Rich. I know you're doing a good job. But Marty's got clout, and she says they were there the last time she looked and that they're not there now, so I told her we could all go look for them together. Okay?"

"Sure. Maybe they're just misfiled. Heck, maybe *she* put them back in the wrong place — she's always poking around in there." He was all too right: Marty seemed to continue to regard the collection as her personal property rather than the Society's. While the Society's stacks were in theory off-limits to the public, there were some people like Marty — a triple threat board member, donor, and researcher — who felt quite free to come and go in the stacks as they chose. How many other people might have had the same idea? Did we have a list somewhere, and how up-to-date was it?

"You may be right. Let's hope so." I sent him on his way. I didn't really think he had been careless, but I had to check. "We'll meet her in the lobby at nine tomorrow morning, okay?"

"I'll be there," Rich said, and ambled out.

CHAPTER 3

Nothing is going to go wrong! I told myself firmly. I hoped I was listening to myself.

I stood at the top of the grand staircase and surveyed the scene of organized chaos below me. Standing on the handsome staircase with its massive mahogany rails and slate stair treads, I gauged the mob below. A newly installed exhibit on Philadelphia's theater history adorned the display cases in the catalog room — which was also the location of the open bar. Dinner would be served in the main reading room, with its soaring ceilings and brass railings, the usual massive reading tables lugged to the bowels of the basement in order to allow circular dining tables to take over for the night.

From my elevated vantage point, I could see that the flower arrangements looked handsome, the coat-check system seemed to be functioning, and the pile of name tags had dwindled nicely as arriving people picked them up. Senior staff members had all received a memo from the president commanding their presence at this important event, to help if and as needed, and they had turned out in force — and were actually talking to guests, not just to each other. A few board members had even managed to remember the date — several were lawyers whose offices were nearby or academics whose time was flexible. I counted the members of the press, including the ladies from the suburban newspapers who were hovering near the doors hoping to catch any of their local stars for photos to appear in the next weekly, as well as a reporter from the *Philadelphia Inquirer* who kept looking at her watch.

All was going according to plan. Even the weather had cooperated, the October evening crisp and cool and blessedly dry. It was time to jump into the water and get my feet wet.

I continued my descent of the staircase, largely unnoticed, even though I'd made time to put on a dress and heels. I'm used to not being noticed: I waved good-bye to thirty-five a few years ago, but am fighting forty; I'm carrying ten extra pounds (all right, fifteen) that I would gladly give to someone who deserved them; and my features could best be described as pleasant, and apparently easy to forget. But I like my job, and I'm good at it, so I don't worry if people's eyes pass right over me — as long as they sign their checks.

The Society was a good place to work, especially now that our previous president had been pried out, kicking and screaming, by a board that felt that her priorities were "not consistent with the board's long-term vision for the institution" (according to one highly confidential memo). Three years ago she had retreated with what dignity she could muster after her termination, to write a book about her experiences. Then the board had turned around and, after a highly publicized search, hired a person as diametrically opposite as they could find: Charles Elliott Worthington.

Where our late unlamented president had been plain and dumpy, Charles was tall, suave, and elegant; where his predecessor had had all the tact of a bulldozer and refused to listen to any idea that was not her own, Charles oozed charm from every pore (if he even had pores) and when speaking to you one-on-one, possessed the ability to make you believe that you were the only other person in the world. He radiated charisma, and his indefinable moneyed accent — British? Old New England? — didn't hurt. Those of us who had seen his résumé knew he'd actually grown up in Ohio, but why quibble? He was photogenic and had made himself a highly visible part of the Philadelphia historical scene in short order, if the society pages in the *Inquirer* were any indication. Exactly what the Society needed, and I for one was thrilled, since that charm translated directly to dollars for us.

Charles had used that charm to win over the staff as well as donors. The budget deficit was in the double-digit range, and the staff turnover had been approaching fifty percent per year. Starting salaries were laughable; most of the new hires were innocent babes struggling to find the restrooms, never mind the collections. Charles hadn't been able to turn the financial picture around yet, but he made it known that he was working on it, with the implicit promise of salary adjustments (there hadn't been any for years), more specialized staffing, educational programs, and improved health care benefits. If I really thought about it, I had to admit that it would be a long time before all of these things materialized — if ever — but somehow he convinced people to stay on and keep working.

Why was I still here, when I could probably be making better money somewhere else, especially with the musical-chairs scene among Philadelphia fundraising staff? Curiosity, at least: I wanted to see how this played out, see if Charles really could turn things around (with a little help from me, of course). Most of the people on the staff were great and really cared about what they were doing. Plus, I loved the solidity of the 1900 building, the heady scent of the old leather and paper in the stacks, the incredible wealth of *history* in this one building. I'd always been a bookworm and a history nut, so I put up with a lot of garbage for the opportunity to sneak off into the stacks during my lunch hour and actually hold something that had once belonged to Ben Franklin, or to attend a meeting with my (very respectful) elbow on the same mantelpiece that Thomas Jefferson had leaned on while writing the Declaration of Independence. Heady stuff.

And it didn't hurt, either, that Charles and I had been seeing each other socially since shortly after his arrival.

It was time to get down to business and start working the crowd. As I came down the stairs, careful not to trip in the stiletto heels I wasn't used to wearing, I again scanned the gathering below me. In a corner a delightful if superannuated city council member, an ex officio board member, had snagged our youngest, blondest female employee and was spinning tales while leaning over to enjoy her cleavage. I spotted Membership Coordinator Carrie Drexel smiling up at another board member, chatting brightly, and Rich hovering nearby. And out of the corner of my eye I saw Alfred slink into the room, looking uncomfortable — I wondered briefly what had changed his mind. Our venerable head librarian, Felicity Soames, headed for him quickly and started talking to him, gently leading him out of the corner where he had scuttled. I wondered briefly if Alfred was looking for me, but whatever it was could wait. I had other fish to fry.

I reached the bottom of the stairs, took a deep breath, and pasted my social smile on my face. *Here we go,* I thought, as I waded into the fray. From the volume of chatter, things were going well, helped by the generous free drinks that the bartender was pouring. I nodded encouragement at our newest staff member, a shelving assistant who was taking coats from the latecomers. Then I forged my way through the crowd into the catalog room, which was even more packed.

I'd been on the job long enough that I no longer needed to read name tags — I recognized the major players. It was a good turnout, not only in numbers, but the right people, the ones we needed the most. The ones whom we were courting, flattering, cajoling, wheedling, massaging — you name it, we had tried it on each and every one of them. And it seemed to be working. I finally spied Charles at the far end of the room, surrounded by a fawning crowd. I stopped to study him in action.

He looked every inch the distinguished leader of an important institution: tall, slender, with discreet touches of grey at his temples. His three-piece suit had clearly been made for him, and he always wore the vest. His shoes gleamed with polish. An antique signet ring glinted on one hand. His tie was a marvel of luxurious restraint. He cocked his aristocratic head to listen patiently to an anecdote from a doddering lady in dirty diamonds; he laid a firm and manly hand on the arm of a tweedy academic type standing next to him, who I happened to know had just published a critically acclaimed book; he made a self-deprecating joke that had the circle around him laughing.

Oh, he was good. Though it remained to

be seen whether his obvious skills would translate into long-term help for the Society. Based on what I had seen in my years here, the place seemed to chew up and spit out directors: the most recent disaster had been exiled; her predecessor had fled to Vermont and refused to answer any communications, written or oral; the one before that had apparently succumbed to a lengthy wasting illness attributed to the stress of the position — or maybe some evil fungus that lurked among the old books. But I had a feeling that Charles was going to put them all to shame, and what was more, he seemed to enjoy his role.

Time to remind him to make his formal welcome. I wove through the crowd and touched his arm. He turned quickly, and seeing me, unleashed one of his high-voltage smiles. *Sorry, Charlie, I don't have any money to give you,* I thought. *Save it for the paying guests.*

I leaned close to speak, savoring his subtle aftershave. "Charles, you should welcome our guests now. I'll tell the caterer to start serving in fifteen minutes, but it's going to take some time to move everyone in to dinner."

"Of course," he responded, sotto voce. He made his apologies to the group he'd been speaking with, then moved toward the center of the main wall to pose against the array of portraits of past presidents and board members, cleared his throat, and waited for the din to subside. Which it did promptly. Not for the first time, I wondered just how he did that.

"Ladies, gentlemen, I am delighted to welcome you this evening to celebrate the first hundred and twenty-five years for the Pennsylvania Antiquarian Society, as we take our first step toward a greatly enhanced future. It is gratifying to see so many old friends and supporters here, because we face some daunting challenges in the days ahead. But with the assistance of our able board and the valuable input from our architects and planners, we have developed a strategy to meet the challenges of the future, all the while preserving the best of the past. For that is our mission: to preserve and to protect our treasures, so that future generations may benefit from them.

"As you know well, our primary goals continue to be: to create the best possible physical environment in order to maintain our world-renowned collections; and at the same time, to create a place that welcomes scholars and visitors, that provides a suitable setting in which to learn and explore.

We strive to marry these two goals, and we must work together to forge an institution that will be a credit to this wonderful city. Please help us both to honor our past and to celebrate our future."

I had to admire the way the words rolled off his tongue as though they were spontaneous, which I knew they weren't, because I had written them for him. And of course that last line was a delicate hint to those present that they should take out their checkbooks.

I sneaked a quick look at the audience, which appeared well lubricated. Time to begin herding people toward their tables — no easy task, even though elegantly hand-lettered place cards had been carefully distributed by Carrie, after days of soul-searching over seating charts. With my eyes I gathered the junior staff's attention: they moved promptly to the double doors into the reading-slash-dining room, armed with fresh copies of the seating charts so that they could steer the guests in the right direction. I joined Charles at the dais and addressed the throng.

"Thank you, Charles. Let me add that I am delighted to see so many familiar faces here, and even more delighted by the new faces among you. You are the heart — and the backbone — of the Society, and none of this would be possible without you. Now, ladies and gentlemen, in a few minutes we will begin serving dinner. If you have any trouble locating your table, just ask one of the staff members stationed by the doors, and they will be happy to help you."

I gave the assembly a bright smile, which was lost on the majority of them as they surged in the opposite direction toward the bar for a final refill.

Charles leaned forward slightly to speak softly in my ear. "Nell, you've done a magnificent job, as always. I don't know what I'd do without you." His breath was warm against my neck as I continued to beam brightly at the crowd, alert for any glitches. He went on, even more softly. "Will I be seeing you later?"

Without turning, I replied in the same low tone, "Of course — we can do our own celebrating. But I'll have to stay until the caterer's wrapped things up, so it'll be late."

"And worth waiting for, my dear." With that, he moved purposefully toward a late-comer, a senior board member who had just come in and was wrestling with his coat. "Ah, Arthur, I'm so glad you could make it."

I watched Charles cross the room, admiring the elegant cut of his jacket, and the elegant back it covered. Then I squared my shoulders and went to supervise the dinner seating. My staff was ready and waiting at the doors. Alfred, I noted, had not moved from where Felicity had parked him, but he had been accosted by one of the more inebriated guests, who looked to be haranguing him about something. Poor Alfred — but I didn't have the time to rescue him now.

Those lucky souls who have never had the privilege of planning a major event such as a wedding are probably unaware of the hair-pulling and hand-wringing that goes on among the people who have to arrange seating. Since this was, for us, a major event, we had begun well in advance; unfortunately the process continued as people walked in the door. The staff scuttled around, swapping place cards, eliminating those for the no-shows, and strategizing all the while, trying to seat the right people together and keep others apart. And then, of course, the guests themselves often messed it all up by deciding that they absolutely, positively had to sit with somebody else entirely. Or they simply sat down at the first place they came to and refused to budge. Or they brought along guests of their own — usually nonpaying — and expected us to juggle everything to make room for them. Which of course we had to do, because the point of the whole game was to keep the guests (that is, the donors) happy so that they'd continue to love us and write us big checks.

Marty Terwilliger knew all this, but she still surged into my line of sight accompanied by someone I didn't recognize. "Okay, Nell, where'd you put me? And I need a seat for Jimmy here — he's my guest."

I looked at Jimmy. More precisely, I looked up at Jimmy, who towered over me by several inches, despite my heels. But the height was nicely balanced by the breadth, although I might've said that his tweed jacket was a little casual for the occasion. However, when I made it as far as his eyes, they were anything but casual. Even in a few brief moments, I got the impression that he didn't miss much.

"It's a pleasure to have you here, uh, Jimmy. Marty, let me check the seating chart, but I'm sure we can work it out. Would you excuse me a minute?" Tall Jimmy nodded once, then headed for the bar, while Marty waited near the door. I snatched a seating chart from one of my minions. Luckily I usually planted a staff member or two at each table, someone who could be discreetly withdrawn under just these circumstances, to open up a table space. I ran my eye over the list and turned back to Marty. "Ah, here we are — table twelve, at that end." I waved vaguely in the right direction, then accompanied Marty toward the door, where she paused to wait for her companion. Dropping my voice, I said, "About that matter we discussed earlier, I've asked Alfred Findley to look into it."

Marty fixed me with an odd look, but I didn't have time to think about it as Jimmy came up beside us, his hands clamped around a pair of glasses, one of which he handed to Marty. "That's all well and good, but I still expect to see you and Rich in the morning," Marty said firmly. "Come on, Jimmy, we're over there somewhere." She grabbed his free arm, but he turned briefly to say, "Nice to meet you," before he was hauled away.

I'd done all I could for the moment, and I had more immediate issues to attend to. While I and my elves had arranged for a truly delightful dinner menu, complemented by some outstanding wines, I didn't expect to have the opportunity to enjoy it, since it was my job to make sure that everyone was where they were supposed to be, that the caterer was on his toes, that the glasses stayed filled, that the microphone at the head table worked, and that nobody dribbled wine (or worse, threw up) on any of the valuable collections that lined the perimeter of the room. I allowed myself a few brief seconds to admire the handsome room, filled with happy, noisy revelers. I wondered if the room had ever experienced such a noise level in its staid existence. I patted myself on the back, figuratively: *Job well done, Nell — and it'll all be over in another couple of hours.* This warm glow of self-satisfaction lasted no more than half a minute: I was interrupted from my reverie by one of the caterer's assistants, who was yammering on about a tripped circuit breaker in the kitchen, and I followed her to the back of the building to quench yet another crisis. The work of a professional fundraiser is never done.

CHAPTER 4

The last guests trickled out the door after eleven, helped into their waiting cars or taxis by the security manager. It was nearly midnight when the caterer loaded the final crates of dirty dishes into his truck, and I handed him his hefty check and thanked him profusely, even as I noticed that his assistants were still folding chairs and rolling tables toward the loading dock. He'd done a good job, and we might want to use him again. The edible leftovers were stowed in the staff refrigerator for tomorrow's lunch. The maintenance manager and a couple of helpers were busy moving the library tables back into position for the readers who would be arriving in ten hours. I thanked him for his help and headed out myself.

The cool and bracing October night air cleared my head. It was only a few minutes to Charles's house off Rittenhouse Square, and by day I would have walked, but it was late and I was wearing heels . . . so I treated myself to a taxi. It pulled up in front of the brick-fronted townhouse, and I dragged myself out. I lingered briefly on the pavement, looking up at the building's façade, before ringing the bell. Even in the dark, Charles's place was exquisite: early nineteenth-century glass in the multipaned windows, original door frames and window sashes, all meticulously maintained, gleaming with fresh paint. The street was quiet, lined with similar elegantly appointed houses. It more than suited Charles, who had outstanding taste in all areas, as far as I could determine. Including women, I reminded myself. Charles had been married once upon a time, and he and his wife had produced a brace of smart, quiet children, now in their teens, who lived in another state but visited at wide intervals to dutifully troop around the significant sights of the city. Their mother had agreed to an extremely amicable divorce, and having family money, had made few demands on Charles since their split. He reciprocated by diligently remembering the children's birthdays, travelling to attend the major milestones in their lives, and generally ceding all responsibility to his amenable ex. Everyone seemed very happy with the situation, including me.

I'd been married once myself, a million years ago — a college sweetheart, and we did the big wedding thing and lived happily ever after for about three years, at which point we decided we really didn't have anything in common. When he was offered a good job in California, I think we both sighed with relief for the excuse to split up. He still sends Christmas cards, and I see him when I'm on the West Coast, which is almost never.

After the divorce, I decided that I needed some stability in my life, so I bought myself a charming (that is, tiny) converted carriage house that sat behind one of the grand old estates west from the city on the Main Line in Bryn Mawr, where the power players of Philadelphia had moved when commuting by train was still new and exciting. I like to think of those upper-crust types having been delivered to the Victorian train stations — which somehow cling to precarious life — in carriages driven by their chauffeurs, or later in motor cars, greeting each other on the platform as they went off for another day of dabbling in banking and lunching at the club.

But back to my carriage house: the grand house in front has long since been broken up into smaller units, and at the moment I think it houses a group of psychiatrists — the tenants seem to change every few years — but my little place is completely separate. When I bought it, it was barely livable: two rooms upstairs, two down, with minimal plumbing, antiquated wiring, and no insulation. The kitchen was nothing but a jumble of secondhand appliances shoved behind a screen in one corner. In the ten-plus years since I bought it, I've added a real kitchen, upgraded the plumbing, heating, and wiring, and filled it with funky, homey semi-antiques, the sort of stuff found at upscale yard sales in Bryn Mawr. Which is exactly where most of them came from, since after paying for the mortgage, and the second mortgage to cover the improvements, I didn't have a whole lot left over. Small non-profits don't pay very well. But the little house was mine, and I loved it. And I loved being able to walk to the train station, since I took the train into the city most days (when I didn't have a special event or other engagement to keep me in Center City), and I loved being able to leave the city behind at the end of the day and come home to the cool, leafy green suburbs, to the elegance of a bygone day (if you closed one eye and squinted).

Which is not to say that I didn't enjoy spending time at Charles's house. It was everything that mine was not: elegant, tasteful, clean (thanks to a series of cleaning personnel who came and went invisibly). He kept his immaculate black and white kitchen (dark granite counters, glossy white tile, halogen lights tucked out of sight so that the light seemed to emanate from the walls and ceiling) well stocked with delightful and expensive goodies, and there always seemed to be a bottle of champagne lurking at the back of the stainless-steel refrigerator. Sometimes it was hard to believe that a real person lived there, since it looked almost like a movie set — what some California director thought an upper-crust Philadelphia row house should look like. No matter: it was like playing dress-up for me anyway, only I was putting on a fancy house rather than fancy clothes.

I rang the bell, and Charles opened the door promptly. He had been home long enough to divest himself of his jacket, vest, and tie, and his still-crisp white shirt was open at the neck, which for him was the height of casual. He stood courteously aside to let me come in, but as I passed by him, he lifted my hair off my neck and kissed my nape. I shivered, and not from the cold. He moved on to the kitchen, and I followed.

"Champagne?" He had already pulled a bottle out of the refrigerator and was peeling away the gold foil, twisting off the wire cage that held the cork. "I thought that went very well. Several of the board members said that they were going to write us nice checks — in fact, several did, and I had them left on your desk." He mentioned that one new local CEO whom we had been courting for some time, who had come as the guest of a board member, had hinted at six figures, as long as we put his name on something. "Actually, I think it's his wife who's pushing him — thinks he needs a bit of class, now that he's established here. I'm sure we can accommodate him." He poured two glasses of champagne and handed me a flute threaded with lacy trails of minuscule bubbles — only the best French champagne, of course.

"No problem. Let me know what he's interested in, and I can work up a proposal. This tastes wonderful," I said, sipping the wine, savoring the delicate tingle on my tongue. "God, I'm tired — it's been a long week, and it's going to be an early morning tomorrow with the staff meeting at eight." I wandered toward Charles's living room, then slipped off my party shoes and wiggled my toes happily, sinking them into the lush carpet.

"Not too tired, I hope," he countered. On anyone else, the look Charles gave me could best be described as a leer. On him, it looked like aristocratic passion. Intense, brooding, lascivious — what was it about Charles that made me want to multiply my syllables?

"Not hardly, sir," I responded flirtatiously. "Shall we go up?" Charles was already leading the way up the narrow but highly polished walnut staircase.

"Would you like to use the bathroom first?" he asked.

"You, sir, are a gentleman." In his bedroom, I stripped down to my slip and made my way to the pseudo-Victorian bathroom. To an inexperienced eye, it would have looked exactly like an 1880 bathroom, which was the intent; to someone like me, who had put in many hours refinishing my own period bathroom, searching for replacements, stripping, sanding, and so on, it was clear that everything was a modern reproduction. But the ensemble drew on the best of the old and the new, and it worked. I washed my face and decided I could wait until morning for a shower. "Charles, where's my nightgown?" I usually left one

— an absurdly expensive Victoria's Secret silk number that I devoutly hoped made me look slinky — hanging on the hook in the bathroom, where, tonight, it was not.

"Hmm? Perhaps Maria moved it." Maria was the latest of his cleaning women, who all seemed to be called Maria. "Check in the drawers in the guest-room chest." I padded down the short hall, barefoot, and found the nightgown neatly folded in the third drawer I checked, along with my toothbrush. Apparently this new Maria had issues with unmarried ladies spending the night.

I returned to Charles's bedroom, suitably clad, or rather unclad, to find him comfortably ensconced in the king-size bed with a plethora of pillows, reading glasses (which he was far too vain to wear in public) perched on the end of his aquiline nose, reading a weighty tome. He put down the book as soon as I entered.

"I see the lost is found — just in time to lose it again," he said, carefully removing the reading glasses and pulling me to him. There followed a pleasant interlude. Well, more than pleasant. Charles approached sex the same way he approached all other aspects of his life: with grace, elegance, and charm. We were well matched in bed, and we both knew it. That was one area I didn't question, although sometimes on a dark night, I wondered what he saw in me — I was smart and competent but not exactly young, nor exactly svelte or hard bodied. Charles professed to appreciate my maturity, however, and what he labeled "the opulence of my flesh." Who was I to argue?

It seemed to be enough for both of us. We didn't harbor false expectations. I wasn't looking for a husband, and if I had been, I'm not sure he would have been on the short list. If I was totally honest, I suspected I might be more enamored of Charles's image, his lifestyle, what he represented, than the man himself. We were discreet about the relationship, whatever it was. But we shared an unvoiced feeling that it would be frowned upon at the Society if it were known that we were seeing each other, so we had been silent about it. Again, that suited me. I liked keeping work and play separate. Our attraction was not of the sort that would send us panting into each other's arms in the stacks, overcome with lust. No, we were adults enjoying an amiable, low-commitment relationship, and that suited both of us just fine.

And when we were finished with our inventive and completely satisfying bedroom activities, we would each retreat to our respective sides of the bed and sleep, to be ready to face another day of strenuous fund-raising, arm in arm.

But tonight there was that one niggling worm of doubt. Before I could drift off to my well-earned rest, I nudged Charles. "I need to tell you about something Marty Terwilliger said to me today."

Charles's hand caressed my hair. "Sweet Nell, you worry far too much about your work. I'm sure it will keep until morning. Won't it?"

I fitted myself against his lean body. "I suppose. But remind me in the morning, will you?"

I don't think he heard me, because he was already asleep, and in minutes so was I.

CHAPTER 5

The day started badly, and there was no time to talk to Charles about missing collection items. Charles had neglected to set the alarm (could he have been distracted?). Luckily I woke up early anyway, then collected my scattered garments and showered and dressed in the change of clothes I'd brought with me, as quietly as I could. Charles stayed in bed, serving as an admiring audience.

"Must you go so soon?"

"Yes, I must, and you know why. We've got the wrap-up meeting early, and I wanted to pick up some goodies for the gang — you know they're always friendlier when you feed them." Following any major event, we always held a before-hours staff meeting in the morning at eight, so that everyone could unload whatever gossip they had heard or overheard while it was still fresh, and review the event as a whole — what had worked, what needed improvement before the next one. Besides, if I was going to demand that people show up early, the least I could do was to dangle some yummy carbohydrates in front of them, and there was an excellent French patisserie on the way to the Society. "And then Marty's coming at nine — oh, shoot, I didn't have time to tell you about that. I'll fill you in later, okay?"

"If you think it matters." He looked all too comfortable in his high-thread-count sheets, reclining in state against his many pillows. But I had to move if I was going to pick up pastries and get to the Society in time to start the meeting.

By seven thirty, laden with goodies, I climbed the timeworn stone steps of the Society building and let myself in with my key. I didn't linger in the dark and quiet lobby, but I could tell that there was no evidence of the past evening's revels — the cleaners had done their job well. Instead, I crossed the catalog room and pushed the button for the building's sole — and antique — elevator. I could hear it lurching into action from somewhere in the bowels of the building, and when it deigned to appear, I inserted my key in the wall panel and pushed the button for the third floor, where all the administrative offices were. I stepped out into the dark hall — no lights meant that no one else was in yet, which didn't surprise me. I made for the nearest wall switch, outside the education director's office, which took me past the door to the stacks. When the lights flickered to life, I noticed a dark red stain in front of the door. *Damn,* I thought, *somebody spilled wine up here last night.* While this floor was off-limits, plenty of people had access — staff, board members, researchers — and maybe one of them had brought someone up to show off some of our treasures. Was it a turn-on to fondle a letter from one of the Founding Fathers? Maybe it worked for some people. But nobody was supposed to bring their wineglasses up here.

But as I approached the door, I began to wonder . . . That didn't look like wine; it looked like . . . blood? *No, Nell — that's ridiculous. You're tired, and you're imagining things.*

I bent over to look more closely. It still looked like blood. I stood up and took a deep breath. Maybe someone had had a nosebleed. Maybe someone fell and cut themselves. *Maybe you should open the door and find out, you wimp.* I laid my hand on the doorknob. It turned, but when I tried to push the door open, it stuck — against something on the other side. Not good. I released the doorknob and thought about what to do. There was no other access on this floor, but if I went to the floor above, there was a spiral iron staircase that led down to the stacks on this floor. With great deliberation I fished out my keys from my bag, went back to the elevator, and ascended one more floor. It was equally dark and deserted, so I headed for the stacks door, turning on lights as I went. Lots of lights, so I'd be able to see . . . whatever I found.

The internal staircase was located in the front corner, and I grabbed the spindly handrail and climbed down cautiously. The door that had stuck was right around the corner, beyond the next tier of shelves. With another deep breath, I crept around the shelves, then stopped. My worst fears were confirmed: the reason that the door wouldn't open was because there was someone lying against it. I took a shaky step closer.

It was Alfred Findley, lying in a pool of dark blood, his eyes staring blindly at his beloved books. Books and papers lay scattered around him on the floor, and the splintered remains of an old wooden step stool lay a few feet away. It looked as though he had fallen while trying to reach something. I didn't need to touch him to know that he was dead; his peculiar grey color and the amount of blood around him made that clear.

I backed up until I could lean against the adjoining bookshelves — solidly built a hundred years ago, and perfect for holding up a woman whose knees had just turned to jelly. I was seeing stars — a whole firmament, swarming in a lovely lime green color. I blinked a few times, but that didn't help, so I tried closing them and breathing deeply until my eyes, and my brain, started working again. *You are not going to pass out, Nell. No, you are going to proceed calmly and address this problem.* Unfortunately the employee manual did not, to the best of my recollection, have a section on dealing with dead bodies found on site. I'd have to make it up as I went.

But it wasn't just a dead body, I thought, as I tried to control my breathing. It was Alfred — poor, sweet, shy Alfred — who was lying there in front of me in a pool of his own blood. What a tragedy. And what a loss to the Society: he was the only person in the place who knew where everything was.

Nell, you can mourn later. All right, what now? I needed to report this to the police.

But for that I needed a phone, and my cell phone was in my bag, on the other side of that door, and there were no phones in the stacks. Therefore I had to leave the stacks, locate a phone, and call 911. Oh, good — a plan. I could do that. And, I realized dimly, I had better do that pretty soon, before other people started arriving and all hell broke loose. I retraced my steps, up the staircase, into the fourth-floor hall, then down to the third floor again, where I headed straight to the nearest office and punched in the three digits.

I was operating in a fog, but I think I managed to give my name and where I was, and the person on the other end of the line said they would send somebody ASAP, and told me to stay in the building. That part was easy, since I wasn't sure my wobbly legs would take me very far. I hung up and tried to jump-start my brain. I had to get out of the chair I had fallen into and go downstairs to wait for the police to arrive. Let them deal with the body. That wasn't my business. I'm a fundraiser. I don't handle dead bodies. People would be arriving soon for the meeting that obviously wasn't going to happen. *Okay, Nell, stand up and go downstairs to the lobby and keep everyone together.* I didn't want anyone else to see the blood pool or . . . Alfred.

I shifted my brain into neutral and went down the stairs to stand in the lobby. I was trying to come up with a good reason to give staff members for staying away, when there was a determined pounding on our massive metal front door. Too late — people were already arriving. No peephole, of course — that would mar the historical integrity of the door. Luckily the next thing I heard was, "Police! Open up!"

I did, gladly. On the other side of the door I found three police officers: two husky uniformed male officers, one black, one white, and a short woman who bore a distinct resemblance to a bulldog. She was in civvies and introduced herself sharply. "I'm Detective Hrivnak. You the one who called?"

"Yes, I'm Eleanor Pratt, and I'm the one who called you."

The detective held up a hand, shutting me up. "What've we got? You said a body?"

"Yes, on the third floor. But he's lying against the door, so you have to go to the fourth floor and come down again — there aren't a lot of entrances to the stacks . . ." I was dithering and I knew it.

"Show me. You — Johnson — stay here and keep anybody else from coming in. You

71

— Williams — you come with us." She turned back to me. "You touch anything?"

I shook my head. "No. Well, the elevator buttons, I guess, and the phone, and the doorknob, before I knew there was anything wrong, and the staircase inside the stacks."

"Right. Now, what is this place?"

"The Pennsylvania Antiquarian Society."

Detective Hrivnak all but snorted. "Library? Museum?"

"Both, sort of. We have a lot of collections, and we're open to the public."

"You got people coming in soon?"

I glanced quickly at my watch. "Well, we're supposed to have a staff meeting at eight, so the employees will be arriving any minute now. We don't open to the public until ten."

"Not today. How many employees?"

"Uh, about forty. Not all full-time. I came in early to set up for the meeting." For a moment I thought wistfully of the lovely pastries, sitting in a box upstairs . . . not far from the blood pool. I lost my appetite again.

"Who's the boss?"

"Charles Elliott Worthington. He should be here soon — he was coming to the meeting."

The detective was making a few notes in

her pocket-size pad. "You see anybody else this morning?"

"No, and there were no lights on when I came in. I don't think there's anyone else here." At least, no one alive.

"You know the victim?"

"Yes, he is — he was an employee here. His name was Alfred Findley. He was the registrar, and he's worked here for years."

Detective Hrivnak made a final note, then snapped the pad shut. "Okay, let's go see him."

I led the small procession back to the elevator and pushed the button. The detective was looking around at the soaring ceilings, the rows of card catalogs. "What time did you close up yesterday?"

The elevator put in its leisurely appearance. "We had an event here last night, after normal hours. I left just before midnight, but there were still some staff around, moving tables and stuff." We got on the elevator, and I inserted my key into the fourth-floor slot.

"When did you last see the victim?"

"I saw him briefly at the party last night — maybe around eight? But I didn't talk to him then."

The elevator doors opened, and I led Detective Hrivnak and Officer Williams to the staircase. They went down first, which was fine with me, because I didn't want to see Alfred again. Unfortunately they waited for me at the bottom of the stairs, so I pointed them toward the body and followed slowly, looking at anything but the floor.

Detective Hrivnak stood looking down at Alfred, who didn't look any better than he had the last time I saw him. "Dead, all right. Probably about eight, maybe ten hours — blood's pretty much dry. I'll let the ME decide."

Poor Alfred. That meant I'd been herding caterers and lingering guests out of the building while he was quietly bleeding to death upstairs. And the party had been so loud that no one could possibly have heard him fall all the way up on the third floor. I was startled out of my thoughts by Detective Hrivnak's no-nonsense voice. "Okay. Williams, call the ME's office, get someone over here to pick him up. You — Ms. Pratt? You go to your office. That's on this floor, right? And wait for me. As soon as I get this end sorted out, I need to talk to you. And then we can decide if I need to talk to anyone else."

"Right. Sure, fine." My mind spinning, I hurried out. Once I escaped from the stacks, I took another deep breath and tried to figure out what I had to do next. The detective had said stay put, but there was no way I could do that just yet. The staff would be arriving at any minute, if they hadn't already. Step one, rig up a sign to keep the public out. Step two, figure out where to put the staff members. The old conference room on the ground floor would do; the police might want to talk to them, so I should keep them there. Step three, talk to Charles, who should be on his way here now. *Right, Nell. Make a sign, then go downstairs and herd the staff aside, and then let Charles deal with the rest.*

CHAPTER 6

Officer Johnson was down in the front hall, looking bewildered. I took pity on him. "Officer Johnson? I thought I would put up this sign" — I waved my hastily crafted piece of paper at him — "to keep out the rest of the world. I suggest we tell the staff members to wait in the conference room over there." I pointed around the grand staircase; the old conference room was tucked away beneath it, but it had plenty of chairs and would be big enough to hold all the staff members. "Is that all right?"

Officer Johnson looked relieved. "Yeah, sure, good thinking. Staff have ID, so I'll know who's who?"

"Yes, they do. Let me just put up the sign, then." I hauled open the heavy metal door and came face-to-face with Charles.

"Good morning, Nell," he said, in case anyone was listening. "Are we all set for the meeting?"

I grabbed his arm, pulling him back outside and letting the door slip shut behind me. "Charles, we have got one large problem. Wait here a sec." Scanning the still-empty street, I went down the steps and taped my notice over the placard on the iron railing at the bottom. I had tried to be discreet — somehow *Closed due to death* did not seem like the appropriate wording, so I had settled for *Closed for emergency repairs. We apologize for the inconvenience.* The word would get out quickly enough. If it was a slow news day, Alfred might even rate a mention on the nightly news. I felt a pang again: poor Alfred. What a sad way to die. Although at least he had gone surrounded by the books and documents that he loved.

"Nell?" Charles said impatiently from his place at the top of the steps. He did not like to be kept waiting, and the wind was biting.

"Right. Sorry." I waited until I stood next to him and could speak quietly. "I found Alfred Findley in the stacks when I came in — dead. I called the police, and they're upstairs now."

"Oh my God! How horrible."

For a moment my sarcastic inner voice wondered what he thought was horrible: that Alfred Findley had been murdered, that

I had found him, or that this would mean negative publicity for his beloved Society, and thus, indirectly, him. Not that it mattered much, and all were true. "Yes, it was. There was . . . a lot of blood." Another note to self: who was supposed to clean up the bloodstains? Our custodial staff, or did the police have people for that? "The detective in charge is upstairs now. She asked that we keep the staff away from the third floor until this is sorted out, so I figured we could send them to the old conference room."

"Excellent idea. Well, then, I suppose I should go introduce myself to this detective and see what the story is. What is her name?"

My mind went blank for a moment, then my fundraiser mentality kicked in. "Detective Hrivnak. By the way, she's never been here before and doesn't know who or what we are, so you can fill her in." *And turn on the charm,* I added silently. I had the feeling Detective Hrivnak didn't like me very much, and she certainly hadn't seemed too impressed by the august Society.

"Thank you for the heads-up, Nell. Shall we?"

I rapped on the door, and when Officer Johnson opened it, I introduced Charles. "This is Charles Worthington, the president of the Society. I'm sure the detective will want to talk with him, so I'll just take him upstairs to her. All right? But you can keep anyone else who comes downstairs here. You shouldn't get any patrons this early, so just direct everyone to the conference room." Without waiting for an answer, I took Charles's elbow and all but dragged him toward the elevator.

Once the doors had closed behind us, Charles asked quietly, "Do they know when this happened?"

"Hrivnak guessed before midnight, probably during the gala. Look, you go sweet-talk the detective, and I'll talk to the staff downstairs. Heck, we can even go ahead with the debriefing." Yeah, right — like people would want to talk about who said what to whom at the party, when there was a dead colleague lying two floors above.

The elevator doors opened, and I stepped out to be confronted by an angry Detective Hrivnak. "You, Pratt — I told you to wait in your office. And who's this guy?"

"I'm sorry, Detective, but I thought I should tell your officer downstairs where to direct people, and I put a sign outside to keep patrons out — I assume you would want that? And this is Charles Elliott Worthington, our president."

Charles stepped forward smoothly. "Detective — Hrivnak, is it? I can't tell you how horrified I am by this event. Alfred Findley was a valued employee, and a very pleasant person. He will be missed."

I wondered uncharitably if Charles would have recognized Alfred if he met him in the hallway. But Charles turned on his carefully calculated smile, combining just the right mix of sorrow and sympathy, and the detective softened.

"Yeah, well, he's still dead. Look, I've got to talk to Ms. Pratt here, since she's the one who found the body. And I've got my people coming to handle the body. So maybe you should just wait downstairs with the rest of your staff until I get to you."

Under different circumstances I might have been amused by the sight of the mighty Charles Elliott Worthington being told to wait by someone so . . . uncouth. But this was serious business, and out of the corner of my eye I could still see the dark pool of blood. Charles's ego would have to take it.

"Of course. I'll be available when you need me. You'll be all right, Nell?" When I nodded, he went on. "Then you'll find me downstairs." He beat a dignified retreat, leaving me alone in the hall with the detective.

"Okay, where's your office? Shouldn't take long. This looks pretty clear-cut."

"This way." I led her down the hall and into my office, turning on the lights as I entered. I gestured toward the visitor's chair and went around the desk to my own. There were a few envelopes on my blotter that hadn't been there before — presumably the checks that Charles had mentioned — so I shifted them to my in-box and faced Detective Hrivnak. "All right — what do you need?"

"Tell me again exactly what you did this morning."

I went through the steps, adding more detail as more came back to me. The detective took some notes but mostly watched me, sneaking an occasional glance around my none-too-neat office. When I had finished, she asked, "Give me a time line for this shindig last night."

I complied, giving her the rough schedule for the event. Afterwards, she said, "Right. So let me see if I've got this right. There were a couple of hundred people milling around downstairs last night, and nobody could have heard this guy fall?"

"That's about it. It's a concrete-reinforced building, built around 1900, so it would be impossible to hear anything even if the place were empty."

"Who was there?"

I tried to think of a way to describe our guests. "Philadelphia society, plus some newcomers who can help us."

"You mean rich people?"

"More or less. And *society* doesn't mean the same thing here, inside these walls, as it does in the gossip columns. There are a lot of names that go back a couple of centuries, and they may or may not have money."

"Noted. Any of them have any connection to the dead guy?"

"Not that I know of, but there's no reason why I would know."

"What can you tell me about the dead guy?"

"Alfred? He's been here longer than I have — at least fifteen years. He loves his work; he's happiest with his computer and with the collections. He's never said an unkind word to anyone, in all the time I've been here. Of course, he tries not to see anyone at all — he's really not comfortable around other people." I realized I had slipped back into present tense again. This was going to be a hard adjustment to make.

"Family?"

"I can't really say. I mean, I knew him, but I didn't know him outside of work. I

82

can't remember him mentioning anybody. You'd have to ask our personnel director, who's probably downstairs now."

"Anybody else here close to him? What about his boss?"

"Not that I know of. His immediate supervisor is Latoya Anderson, the VP of collections. She's been here about four years, and from what I've seen, they had a fairly formal relationship, strictly business. Is there anything else? The staff should be gathering downstairs by now. What can I tell them?"

"I think I've got all I need. You can tell them there was an accident."

"Did he fall?"

"Looks like it. Hit his head on the concrete floor, cracked his skull, split his scalp open — that's why there was so much blood; head wounds bleed a lot. You might want to keep your staff behind closed doors until we get the body out. I'm gonna go find your boss."

The detective was out the door before I realized that I'd been dismissed. But for a moment I couldn't move. I knew the people waiting downstairs needed to know what was going on, but I wanted a moment to myself before I tried to talk to them. Alfred, dead. I'd just talked to him yesterday.

I felt a chill. We'd talked about theft from the Society. But that couldn't mean anything. The detective had said it was an accident. It had certainly *looked* like an accident, an unfortunate fall. Too many hard edges and creaky equipment in this building, and Alfred had put his foot wrong, or that old step stool had crumbled beneath him. It was very sad, but that was all.

I was going to have trouble erasing that scene. Even if and when the bloodstain disappeared from the hall carpet, I'd still remember seeing it there. And seeing Alfred, motionless and grey. At least no one apart from me and the police would have to see the body and the blood in the stacks.

Still stalling, because I wasn't ready to face anybody, I riffled through the envelopes on my desk. If there were checks, they would need to be processed — entered in our database and prepared for deposit. Charles had said they were substantial, so it was important to take care of them quickly. I should remember to take care of that later today after the meeting.

One envelope was thicker than the others, and sealed. I slit the top and pulled out a sheaf of folded papers, which turned out to be a printed, single-spaced list several pages long.

Alfred's list of the missing items.

CHAPTER 7

In the lobby Officer Johnson stood squarely in the center, feet planted apart, pointing staff members toward the room under the stairs with the barest minimum of speech. I threw him a quick false smile and went to find the employees.

Inside the room most of the staff was sitting around the table, looking sleepy, dopey, grumpy, and in a few cases, hungover. And now they were trying out anxious and frustrated.

Charles wasn't there, and I wondered what the staff knew from Officer Johnson. Since it appeared that I was the only person in the room who actually knew anything, I'd have to be the one to tell them. I moved to one end of the conference table but not before laying the pastry box I'd snagged from upstairs in the middle of the table. "Sorry there's no coffee, but I figured you must be hungry." A number of people made a grab for the goodies, but their eyes returned to me quickly.

Latoya Anderson was the first to speak. "Nell, can you tell us what's going on?"

I cleared my throat. "I am sorry to tell you that Alfred Findley was found dead in the third-floor stacks this morning." There was an immediate outcry from the staff, and I paused until the hubbub died down. I saw that Carrie, my bubbly membership coordinator, looked ready to cry, and even our unflappable head librarian, Felicity Soames, had paled, shutting her eyes.

I took a deep breath before going on. "I found him, and I called the police immediately. It looks like he fell and hit his head." I decided to leave out the blood. "We don't expect to open to the public today, under the circumstances, and if you want to leave, that's all right, and you won't be penalized for it. But if you feel up to it, maybe we should just go ahead with our planned meeting, while everybody's memory is still fresh?"

For a long moment I wondered what they would decide, and I had to admit, it sounded pretty callous to talk about the party with Alfred dead upstairs. Luckily they seemed to welcome the idea of a distraction, and no one protested. And that made me wonder — had anyone even cared about Alfred?

"All right, then. Let me say first — great job last night, one and all. Definitely our best event in living memory — and that's saying something, given the average age of our guests." A few people laughed feebly at my joke. "Does anyone have any general comments before we review what the attendees said? Any problems, issues?"

I looked around the table. Nobody was evading my eye, so I had to assume there were no major complaints in the offing. Or maybe they were all in shock.

We worked our way through the guest list. Various people had had conversations of various durations with various guests, and we picked through them, looking for any hints about that person's current opinion of us. The ones who seemed happiest, we would tap for a larger role in the organization: board membership, sooner or later; a volunteer committee; or a bigger donation. The unhappier ones I would have to sound out and try to placate. Then there were always the chronic whiners, the ones who never thought that they were getting the attention they deserved. Usually they were getting exactly what they deserved, which was the same courtesy we extended to everyone, if a bit more saccharine, since we had all long since pegged the whiners as permanently discontented. Still, that was the way things worked in this business, and at least they had paid for their seat — well, most of them had, anyway.

Felicity, her composure restored, said, "I had an interesting conversation with one woman — it seems her great-uncle has just passed away, and she remembers that he had some interesting collections. She hasn't seen them for a long time, but she thought there were quite a lot of old books. I said we'd be happy to send someone over to help her sort through the books."

"Good catch," I said. "Give her a call in a day or two, to follow up. Do you want to go, or do you want to send someone from collections?"

"I can do it — I could use a field trip."

"Great. Anything else?"

Carrie spoke up. "Mrs. Bennington didn't pee." There was general laughter. Poor Mrs. Bennington must be eighty-five if she was a day, and she had trouble remembering where to find the restrooms. On one memorable occasion, she had sought directions from a staff member, then said brightly, "Oh, never mind," as a puddle spread around her feet. We tried to keep an eye on her, since other than this little foible she was a sweetheart, but sometimes there just weren't enough people to go around. We were hoping we were mentioned in her will, and her estate was rumored to be substantial. Her father had been a board member in the 1920s.

The discussion faltered. Normally I would give a wrap-up of the financial side, mostly for Charles's benefit, but I didn't have any of my notes, which were still on my desk. Still, it was at least a bright spot. "This is still a rough estimate, but it looks like we should clear about thirty thousand, after we pay the bills." Polite applause. I went on. "Did everyone like the caterer?" Nods.

"Great desserts," someone added.

"Well, there are plenty of leftovers in the staff fridge, so enjoy. The caterer wasn't too expensive, so if he did a good job, I'd be happy to have him back."

Fred, the building supervisor, cleared his throat. "They were a little slow on the cleanup. I had to stay until they finished, to lock up, and it was close to one."

"Thanks for mentioning that, Fred. Next time I'll tell them to beef up the staff on the back end, okay? Sorry you had to hang around so late." He nodded, mollified.

Joan Sartain, our communications director, spoke for the first time. "Nell, I'll draft a public statement for Charles to approve. We should say something."

She was right, but I wasn't sure what we could or should say right now. "That's a good idea, Joan, but can you hold off until we know a little more? Maybe by the end of the day we'll have a clearer idea of what happened."

I had nothing more to add, and I was worried that the meeting was going to degenerate into questions about Alfred — questions I didn't want to answer even if I could. Luckily we were interrupted by a commotion in the hall. At first I could hear only the bass rumble of Officer Johnson's voice, alternating with a shriller and insistent female voice. Belatedly I realized it had to be Marty, arriving for her nine o'clock meeting, which had completely slipped my mind. Rich and I exchanged a glance; apparently he had reached the same conclusion.

"Excuse me," I said hastily to the staff, and rushed out to the lobby to rescue someone — and I didn't think it was Marty.

"What the hell is going on here?" Marty demanded when I appeared. "I show up, say that I have a meeting with you, but this officer here won't let me in, won't call anyone, just keeps telling me that you're closed. You'd better have a good explanation!"

I cast around desperately for a quiet place to talk to her. I couldn't take her back to the conference room, so the only choice was the catalog room, blessedly empty at the moment. I looked at Officer Johnson, and when he nodded, I grabbed Marty's arm and dragged her through the doors and around the corner.

"Marty, Alfred Findley was found dead upstairs this morning. It looks as though he died sometime last night."

I had expected my announcement to hush Marty's protests, but I wasn't prepared for the peculiar shade of green that she turned — and for the expression of distress that swept across her face. "Oh, my God, no," she whispered.

When I didn't get any further response, I said gently, "I think we need to postpone our meeting." When she made no sound, I added, "Marty? Are you all right?"

Color was creeping slowly back into her face. She drew herself up, and her eyes focused on me. "What? Oh, yes, of course. It was just a shock. Poor Alfred." She stopped before going on. "You're right — this is not the time or the place. But we still need to talk. You think you'll be here tomorrow?"

I shrugged. "As far as I know."

"I'll come back tomorrow morning." Marty's tone had regained its usual crispness, and she was thinking like a board member again. "And make sure Rich is here, too." She turned on her heel and left, with a withering glance at the officer.

Believing that the staff meeting was over, people were drifting out of the conference room, standing around in clumps and talking. After checking with Officer Johnson, I gave them permission to go into the reading room, where they wouldn't have to watch the people from the medical examiner's office cart out Alfred's body. I didn't want to see it, either, so I snagged Rich by the arm and dragged him in the opposite direction, to the microfilm room. Rich looked dazed.

"Are you okay? Did you know Alfred well?"

"What?" Rich's eyes focused on the present. "Not really. But, I mean, he was at the party last night, right? Then he died a couple of hours later? That's hard to take in. Hey, what's going to happen with the cataloging?"

I wondered if he was thinking about job prospects. He might be qualified for the position, but it was a little early to think about filling Alfred's shoes. "I have no idea, but that's something to worry about later."

He hung his head. "Sorry. That was kind of tactless, and I didn't mean it that way. Did you need me for something?"

"Actually, yes. Marty still wants to get together, about the Terwilliger Collection. I told her we'd be here tomorrow morning at nine. Does that work for you?" It occurred to me that I had no idea where Rich lived, or with whom. "I don't suppose you've had any luck finding what she was looking for?" I asked, nursing a small hope.

"Nope. I took a look at every place I'd been working on that stuff, and went over the shelves and the boxes very carefully. Those letters are *not* there, or at least, not where they're supposed to be." He hesitated for a moment. "You know," he began, "I've been having trouble finding some other things."

I didn't like the sound of that, especially after what Alfred had told me. "What do you mean?"

"Oh, things I wanted to look at, that I'd heard or read about — not in the T-Collection, but in others. And sometimes they just aren't there. Of course, maybe somebody changed the filing system and didn't make a record of it. You know, I may not be an expert, but there's a lot of room for improvement in the record keeping around here."

Just what Alfred had said, and now he wasn't even around to fix it. I sighed. "I know, I know. All it takes is staff and a lot of time. But staff costs money. We're working on it." Poor infant: he was going to have to learn about the realities of working at a nonprofit institution — low pay, limited staffing, and no money for interesting projects. But I didn't think I should share my concerns about any other missing items.

Rich seemed satisfied with my answer. "You think Ms. Terwilliger is going to blame me?"

"I don't think anyone's blaming anyone yet. We just want to see if we can find what's missing." Which could be far more than Rich knew, but maybe finding something would lead to finding other things. Maybe.

The day dragged on . . . and on . . . and on. Charles had retreated to his office, with the door firmly shut. It was noon before the gurney carrying Alfred's bundled body shuttled down the elevator and out the service entrance that opened onto the alley at the rear. There was only one news person hovering outside, and he had the savvy to

95

stake out the back door to get a good shot. How did the media know so fast? It occurred to me that I should touch base with Joan, our communications director, about the public statement she was working on. There was no way to cast this sad event in a positive light. Alfred had died alone, and no one had noticed. I wondered if there was anyone to write an obituary for him.

But instead I sent the staff back upstairs and I went to see Charles, breezing past his loyal assistant Doris Manning, who glared at me but said nothing, her eyes pink, a tissue wadded in her sleeve. Once inside his office, I shut the door.

Charles sat behind his handsome desk, looking appropriately sorrowful. I dropped into one of his guest chairs with a sigh of relief. "No more surprises?"

"This morning wasn't enough? No, the detective and I made nice noises, and I informed her that Alfred was a valued employee and a pleasant person. I'm not sure I ever exchanged more than ten words with Findley — he seemed to scurry out of my way every time he saw me."

"That sounds like Alfred," I agreed. "He really didn't like people much, but he was good at his job."

"You knew him well?"

"I got to know him a couple of years ago when I came to him for information I needed for a grant proposal I was working on — you know, how many widgets we had, and how many of them John Hancock had handled, that kind of thing. He always came through, and quickly. It will be hard to fill his shoes — especially at his salary level."

"Hmm." Charles seemed distracted. "I don't suppose we could divvy up his tasks among other staff members?"

"No," I said firmly. "You know that as well as I do. It takes a specific mix of skills to do what he did. But I'm sure we don't have to rush to advertise the position, at least until he's been properly buried." The Society's cataloging had waited years already, and another week or two wasn't going to make any difference. Unless that list he'd left me . . . no, I wasn't going to go there, not now. "We need to release a statement of some kind, and it should go out under your name. You want me to work with Joan to put it together?"

"Fine. I trust your judgment. What a tragedy." Charles lapsed into silence, and I studied him. He looked weary — and he had had more rest than I had.

"It is." I stood up. For a brief moment I wavered, wondering if I should tell him about Marty's concerns, but looking at his face, I decided it could wait until after I had talked to her and really scoped out the extent of the problem. If it was a false alarm, or if I could make it just go away, it would save wear and tear on everyone. "Well, let me get to work on that with Joan. She'll have a contact list — I don't know what the deadline is for tomorrow's *Inquirer.* Drat — she'll have to get something onto the website, too. And you should tell Doris to start contacting the board members — we don't want them to get blindsided by this."

"An excellent point." Charles, ever the gentleman, stood up to see me out. He laid a reassuring hand on my arm. "And, Nell? I am sorry you had to be the one to stumble onto this. I hope you're not too upset, because I need you to help me — help the Society — through this difficult time."

Well, it was nice that he had thought about it. But I had no intention of lapsing into a fit of the megrims, whatever they were. I would soldier on, and I would save any mourning for poor Alfred until later, when I got home. Which might be a while.

CHAPTER 8

The next day was Saturday. The Society was usually open to the public on Saturday, for benefit of those researchers who (heaven forbid) had normal jobs during the week. The staff had agreed that the sooner we got back to business as usual, the better. Generally only the library staff, not the administrative staff, was required to put in an appearance on Saturdays, but the story of Alfred's death had appeared briefly on the news the night before — "Tragic Accident at Local Institution Claims Life" — and I thought I should be there to help Joan deal with any inquiries from the public — and our donors. And there was a lot of follow-up for the gala that I needed to attend to: writing thank-you letters, paying the bills, summarizing results, and recording comments from the rather fragmented staff meeting. How long ago the event seemed, though it had been only two days! First, of course, there was the meeting with Marty, which I knew she wouldn't cancel. So I went in to work.

As I walked to the front entrance, I was relieved to see that everything looked completely normal. Rich was waiting for me in the lobby, fidgeting. We had barely exchanged greetings when Marty arrived, dressed in jeans, apparently ready for a hands-on attack of the stacks. "Hi, guys. Rich, Nell told you what we're looking for?"

Rich nodded diffidently. "I haven't seen the stuff, but I'll do my best to help."

Marty said crisply, "Okay, let's go." Then she took off toward the rear of the building, with Rich and me trailing behind. He and I exchanged a wry glance behind her back, then hurried to catch up. We headed for a room that had once been the heart of the Society — the fireproof vault, built in 1905 with a special endowment from a then–board member who was concerned about the vulnerability of our largely paper-based collections to fire and theft. At the time the room had been state-of-the-art. Now it was just a closely sealed room with metal doors, which made it marginally safer than some in the building. A newer fire-retardant system had been installed sometime in the last fifty years, but it would probably do more harm than good in the event of a fire.

One more item for the capital budget. The Terwilliger Collection took up approximately half the room, some four hundred linear feet of books, folders, boxes, and miscellaneous bundles.

Most people either love or hate old libraries. To some, a room like this — dim, high-ceilinged, dusty, smelling of old paper and crumbling leather — would be oppressive, a place to flee from in search of sun and air. To others, like me, it was a wonderful cave filled with unimaginable treasures and unexpected treats. I always found myself inhaling deeply when I entered the stacks, as if trying to absorb part of them into my bloodstream.

Marty, however, wasn't bothering with any romantic illusions, but instead headed straight for her family papers. She stopped in front of the first array of bookshelves, which stretched far over our heads, and turned to face us, arms akimbo.

"OK, the collection begins here, right?" She laid a hand on the shelves behind her. "And the earliest stuff is at this end, beginning around 1720?"

I looked to Rich and he nodded. "Right, with a couple of exceptions — some of the larger folio sizes we've had to move around a bit, to save space. But I did a quick pass through yesterday of all the file boxes and cross-checked what I found against the map I made for myself when I started, and this is where they start."

Marty went on relentlessly. "And the war materials start about here, right?" She pointed to the second tier of shelves. When Marty talked about *the war,* it could only mean the Revolution. "Now, you know that Major Jonathan Terwilliger and General George Washington began corresponding before the war was declared — before Jonathan was a major — and continued until Washington's death, right?"

I hadn't actually known, but I nodded anyway.

"I've seen these papers plenty of times, over many years. In fact, I grew up with them. Daddy used to show them to us when we were kids — he was really proud of our history, and he wanted us to be, too. *And* I've seen them since they came to the Society. They used to be on the second-to-top shelf here — I saw them there last month. But they're not here now."

She stopped, crossed her arms, and glared at us. I looked briefly at Rich, who said quickly, "As I said before, I haven't gotten up this far yet. I've been transferring some of the boxes to my desk for the more detailed cataloging — about a rolling cart's worth at a time — but the last batch I took came from those shelves back there." He pointed toward the far end of the shelves behind Marty, where there was indeed a gap about the size of a document box.

"Would anyone else have been looking at them?" Marty demanded.

I spoke up. "When Felicity comes in, we can ask if anyone has requested them — if so, they could still be down in the reading room, waiting to be reshelved. But I understand that the cataloging is still pretty sketchy, right?"

"Unfortunately," Rich said.

"So, in order to have requested them, someone would have had to know they existed," Marty pointed out.

"We don't let the public in here, wandering in the stacks and browsing. You know that — we've discussed access policies at board meetings," I said.

"Well, if they haven't been signed out, and Rich isn't working on them, and they're not on the shelf . . . they could have been stolen," Marty said bluntly. "Damn it, that's a whole box, not just a single letter. To do that, you'd have to have major balls — and inside help."

I could almost see Marty's thermostat rising. "Let's not jump to conclusions, Marty," I said in my most soothing tones. "There are several steps we ought to take before we say that. Let me check with the staff, ask if anyone has seen what we're looking for. Then we can do a more thorough search of the stacks, the reading room — maybe someone in-house decided to take a look at the letters and forgot to put them back, or put them in the wrong place. It happens. Please, give us a chance to sort this out, before you start crying *fire*."

Marty gave me a long, calculating look. "I'll give you a week, until Friday, to find them. And if you don't, there'll be hell to pay. I'll go to the board — and the press. I want those papers."

That kind of publicity was something the Society definitely did not need, especially coming hard on the heels of Alfred's death. "I hope it won't come to that, Marty. I'm sure there's some reasonable explanation, and I'll get to work on it immediately." As though I didn't have anything else to do. "I'm very glad you called this to our attention — clearly we need to look carefully at our procedures."

Marty hardly seemed mollified. "One week," she said again, then turned on her heel and marched out of the stacks. I exchanged another look with Rich, who was several shades paler than he had been a few minutes ago.

"If I weren't such a lady," I said, "I'd say we were in deep shit. We'd damn well better find the those papers." I took a deep breath, then let it out slowly. "Well, I guess I'd better start talking to the staff." I made my way out of the stacks, followed by poor Rich, who resembled a puppy who had just had his nose swatted.

Rich headed upstairs, but I found Marty waiting for me in the hall. "Did you need something else, Marty? I assure you I'll keep an eye on things."

She shook her head abruptly. "It's not that. Alfred's funeral will be on Tuesday. Will you let the staff know?"

Marty was handling Alfred's funeral? That seemed odd. "Of course. Can you give me the details? I'll send out an email blast right away. Why . . ."

Marty handed me a sheet with information on the funeral home and the cemetery. "Why'm I doing it? Alfred wasn't close to most of his relatives, and nobody else stepped up. Thanks for letting people know."

She turned away to leave, but I wondered if I had seen a glint of tears.

CHAPTER 9

I went back to my office, flopped down into my desk chair, and tried hard to think. Marty Terwilliger was important to the Society, not because she had a lot of money (which she didn't — the old Philadelphia families had run through most of their fortunes a long time ago) but because of her family's history with the place and because of her extensive and intricate connections with a whole lot of Philadelphia-area society. We needed them, as a group. Which meant that we needed to keep Marty happy, and that made fixing this mess my first priority.

That was the business decision. But I had this unsettling feeling that there were bigger issues involved: namely, how we kept track of our collections, how we fulfilled our obligation to the public and to all those, dead and living, who had entrusted us with protecting their historic treasures. From its inception, the Society had been run like a club. All the members knew each other, and it was a pleasant place to fritter away a couple of hours. It had been a trusting place then, but the world had changed and that trust was no longer justified.

At board meetings, staff and board members had debated about security on many occasions, as I knew well. Certainly the technology had changed, and various consultants had been called in to lay out high-tech options for strategically positioned video cameras, on-screen monitoring, sophisticated alarm systems, motion sensors — the list went on and on. But all of these glitzy systems cost money, big money, and we were barely able to keep the heat and lights on, not to mention pay staff salaries. Somehow electronic surveillance had been bumped far down the wish list, and no one had really protested.

But had we been wrong? Had we been too gullible, too innocent — and were we about to pay the price? I stared at the handsome framed etching on my office wall, but I didn't see it. What I saw was looming catastrophe. *Hang on, Nell, you're looking at the worst possible case.* Maybe somebody just moved the box to clean. *Ha,* I responded to myself, *when was the last time anyone had cleaned in the stacks?* Maybe the missing papers were on a cart, waiting to be reshelved. Maybe an inexperienced new hire had simply reshelved the box in the wrong place. Too many maybes.

Sometimes I regretted not having any sort of formal library training, and this was one of those times. I had a lot of questions, and I needed information. But I wasn't quite sure where to start. As I swung idly back and forth in my swivel chair, I saw two paths: first, I needed to review, for my own understanding, how we tracked items as they traveled within the building. Second, I needed to find out exactly what, if anything, was being done about the items that Alfred had been unable to find. For the first, I needed to talk with our head librarian, Felicity; I'd talk to Latoya second. Maybe that was backwards, since Latoya was officially responsible for managing our collections, but I'd known Felicity longer, and she was far more knowledgeable about what was where in the building than Latoya could hope to be. And, I reminded myself, I still hadn't given Charles the heads-up about the problem of the missing items; he wasn't in today, but Marty's complaint would demand his attention sooner or later — sooner, if I couldn't come up with an answer for her within the week. I decided to do a little digging myself first, but if I didn't come up with anything by, say, Tuesday, I'd have to tell Charles that we had a problem.

Before I headed downstairs to the reading room to find Felicity, I stopped to talk with Joan. She had been on staff less time than I had, and had been hired to replace a charming woman who'd been here decades but was completely oblivious to the changes that computers had wrought upon modern communications. "Hey, Joan — have you sent out that statement about Alfred's death?"

"Sure did, yesterday, once we got wind that the media were already on it. It was kind of generic, since I couldn't find anybody who knew him well. And before you ask, I also added something to the website."

"You are good, lady! Maybe you can put together a little more about him — you know, what he did, the collections he worked on, and so on — for the next issue of the magazine?"

"I'm on it. Poor guy! I don't know if I ever had a conversation longer than two minutes with Alfred, but he always gave me exactly what I asked for, and quickly. Let me know when you're going to advertise his position — I've got some ideas about where to post it online."

I could tell she was already way ahead of me. "Sounds good, and thanks. I'll leave you to it."

I stood up and headed downstairs. Felicity Soames, senior staff librarian, had been at the Society forever, and after Alfred, she was the best person to ask where things were — or where they should be. Briefly I wondered how she and Alfred had gotten along — hadn't I seen them together at the gala? She was of a certain age, as the French like to put it, had never married, and lived for the purpose of managing the unwieldy mountains of paper housed in the Society's building. Luckily, she also loved to help other people, in the often-futile hope that they would come to share her passion. A hapless researcher, fresh off the bus from Des Moines with two hours to spare, would be greeted by Felicity and inundated with stacks of books and promises of photocopies to come. They went away either glassy-eyed or starry-eyed, but it made no difference to Felicity. She was an incredible resource, and we were lucky to have her. Of course she was the first person I turned to in my quest.

I found her at her usual station: the elevated desk in the reading room, where she could survey her domain and keep an eye out for people foolish enough to use a pen rather than a pencil, or to think about bending a fragile book spine.

"Got a minute, Felicity?" I asked quietly (in a library, always quietly) as I approached.

Felicity scanned the crowd, though *crowd* was a rather loose definition, since it consisted of four people, at least one of whom was asleep. The room could hold a hundred easily. It didn't look like any murder-ghouls or newshounds had made it past the lobby, though, and I made a mental note to ask our front-desk attendant if he'd had to keep any at bay.

"I think so," she said.

"Privately, please."

She gave me an odd look, then said, "The new room, then?"

Perfect, I thought. The absurdly designated *new room* was another artifact from an earlier, more gracious age. Once it had been a comfortable sitting room for gentlemen — I had seen old photos showing overstuffed armchairs and brass floor lamps. Then it had been modified to house our collection of paintings, on specially designed vertical racks, but more recently it had been turned over to much-needed shelving, for those reference books we allowed the general public to access. I followed her there, making sure there was no one in the room. The chairs were long gone, so we retreated to the furthest corner and leaned gingerly against opposing bookshelves.

"What's up?" she asked. "Does this have to do with Alfred's death? Such a tragedy. He had a most meticulous mind."

I debated for about a half a second about whether to bring her into the loop about the missing Terwilliger papers, and then decided that she needed to know; she would be essential to figuring things out. "No, this is something else. We have a problem. I hope it's a small problem, just a minor mix-up. You know Marty Terwilliger?"

She nodded. "Of course. I saw her in the reading room earlier today."

"She came to me just before the gala and said she couldn't find a particular group of documents from the Terwilliger Collection, and she knows that they were there not long ago. Rich and I went with her to look for them again this morning, and we couldn't find them, either — at least, not where they were supposed to be. So, before we all fly into a panic, I wanted to check with you about the tracking procedure for a document in the building — you know, if somebody calls something up to use in the reading room, or if one of the staff takes it to look at, or if it goes out of the building for restoration, or something. Whatever you can tell me."

Felicity pinned me with a look that combined contempt and pity: *How could you be so ignorant?* her stare said. She cleared her throat. "Certainly we have procedures in place for any such movement within the building — and of course, items seldom leave the building, and then only under very carefully regulated restrictions. Here," she said, pulling a slip of colored paper from a small pile on the shelf behind her, "this is a tracking slip. When a book or folder or box — whatever — is removed from its place, the staff member who removes it fills out this slip, with the item's title, call number, and shelf location, and then signs it. It's a multipart form: one copy remains on the shelf, and the other is inserted into the article in question." She fixed me with an eagle eye. "Surely you've used these? I know I've seen items from the collections on your desk."

I tried to avoid her look. All right, I'd been guilty of sneaking a book out of the stacks now and then if I couldn't find the form, or I didn't have a pencil, or I was in a hurry and I was going to bring it right back . . . "Well, I always put things back," I said defensively.

She sniffed. "Actually, we prefer if people *don't* reshelve things on their own — all too often they end up in the wrong place." Oops, she'd nailed me again.

I threw up my hands. "Mea culpa, mea culpa. I'll never do it again, I promise. But in this instance, if something was removed legitimately from the shelf by an authorized person, there should be a multipart tracking slip — have I got that right?"

Felicity nodded. "Exactly. And when the book is returned to its rightful place, the two slips are stapled together and filed."

At last, a ray of light. "Could we check the slips to see if this particular item was requested anytime recently?"

"Of course. Do you have the call number?"

"I'll get it for you — if it exists. This collection isn't really cataloged yet, you know — that's what Rich has been working on. Oh, another question. If, say, this was a box full of individual documents, or folders of documents — would you sign out the whole box or just the items from inside the box?"

Felicity said primly, "The box, of course — or, if you requested such a folder to be brought to the reading room, the shelver would bring the whole box, not just a single folder. Again, it's far too easy to mislay a single folder, and often they are identified only in the broadest of terms. We're working hard to correct that, but there are many, many boxes, and a limited number of staff members. I had asked Alfred to pursue that, as time permitted."

My first attempt to track down the missing items had already revealed to me a major flaw in the process: keeping track of something depended on the good intentions of the person who took it — who would have to be scrupulous about leaving a paper trail. For anyone with less-honorable intentions, he or she could just walk away with the item, at least out of the stacks, if not out of the building. Assuming, of course, that the person was able to gain access to the stacks in the first place. And although such access was limited to staff, a select few researchers (whose credentials had been checked up one side and down the other), board members, and special friends (Marty fell into two or three of those categories and had free rein of the place), unfortunately it was not a short list.

"One last thing — didn't I see you talking with Alfred at the gala?"

"I spoke with him, yes. Actually I was surprised to see him there — I know how much he hates such events. I believe he was looking for you."

"Me? Did he say why?"

"No. I told him I hadn't seen you but I was sure you were around somewhere. So he never talked to you?"

"No. I was kind of distracted." Was that when he had left the list for me?

"If you have no more questions at the moment, I do need to get back to the desk," Felicity said.

"Go ahead," I responded. "I'll get you the call number on the box if I can, and I'll help you look through the slips if you want — I know how busy you are." While it sounded like sucking up, it was true: Felicity was one of the hardest-working people in the place, as well as a stickler for details. I really needed her as an ally in this search. "Thanks, Felicity. I appreciate it. And, I hate to say it, but the sooner the better, please. Marty's breathing down my neck."

"I understand, Nell. It's a fairly quiet day, so I'll see if I can find an answer for you."

Fairly quiet was an understatement: nobody had moved from their position in the room since we'd left. Maybe they were *all* asleep.

CHAPTER 10

My next step was to check in with Latoya Anderson, our vice president of collections, and the person charged with oversight for all collections. Latoya was a relative newcomer to the Society: she'd been on the staff just over two years, one of Charles's first major hires, and she was, in grant-writing terms, a "person of color." I always found it offensive to label any staff member based on race (or gender, sexual preference, handicap, whatever), but the reality was that a lot of the organizations that awarded grants gave extra points to your application if you could demonstrate diversity, especially if it was not just for show. Luckily for everyone, Latoya was extremely well qualified, with an undergraduate degree in history from Princeton and a degree in library science from Simmons in Boston, and we were very lucky to have her. We had snagged her not because of our shining status in the historical world (although we did all right in that department), or the magnificent salary which we could offer (we couldn't), but because the Society had an outstanding and largely unexplored collection of documents pertaining to slavery and the abolition movement in Philadelphia, and Latoya had been smart enough to negotiate for time to continue her own research, using those collections, while giving the Society four days a week.

I liked Latoya, or maybe *respected* was closer to the truth. She was smart and politically aware — which was more than could be said for many of the staff members. At the same time, I had a small but nagging doubt about her: she wasn't a risk taker, and was almost fanatical about maintaining the status quo. She did her job well and conscientiously, but she stayed strictly within the confines of a narrow job description — which I thought could have been broadened to greatly enhance the Society's standing within the academic world. Sometimes I wondered if she was giving one hundred percent to the Society. Or one hundred percent of the eighty percent she was committed to, anyway. Maybe I was biased because we didn't have a particularly warm relationship, but as far as I could tell she had remained aloof from most people at the Society.

I was pleased and surprised to actually find her in on a Saturday. I wasn't sure how many people had left as soon as they could yesterday, but if they had, they were here in force today. I rapped on her door. "Latoya?"

She held up one elaborately manicured hand and said, "One minute," her eyes never leaving the screen of her laptop. She added a few sentences, then sat back and sighed. She looked up at me. "Didn't want to lose the thought. What do you need?"

I made my way into her office. Unlike mine, hers was almost obsessively neat. All her books were lined up on her bookshelves. There were no stacks of papers sitting on any surfaces. There wasn't even any dust. Me, I've always subscribed to the theory that an empty desk is the sign of an empty mind. Let me tell you, my mind is very full. In any case, Latoya's visitor's chair was free of encumbrances, so I sat down facing her.

"I'm surprised to see you here. You didn't have to come in today."

Latoya sighed. "Alfred's unfortunate death means I have to attempt to reconstruct his methods. I'm afraid I'm not as well versed in his computer system as I should be."

Nor was anyone else. I was glad that she

was stepping up quickly. "I need to ask you something. I've encountered a, uh, situation, and you might be able to help me with it. And I could use a quick review on our cataloging procedures, at least as they apply to this."

I had her interest. "What's the problem?" she asked.

"You know Marty Terwilliger?"

"Sure. I can't say I know her well, but I know she's a board member and she does a lot of research here, and of course there's the Terwilliger Collection. Why do you ask?"

"She came to me and said that some things she knew we had in that collection of hers weren't where they should be, and she can't find them. She says it's an important group of items, and I believe her. Anyway, she's mad, and I said I'd look into it. She gave me a week to work it out."

"Hmm. Why did she come to you rather than me? Is she a troublemaker?"

"No, not at all. In general, she's one of our strongest supporters, and she has a right to be mad, I think. So I'm hoping that we find what she's looking for ASAP, and that it turns out to be some perfectly normal human error, or it was in transit somewhere in the building, or something like that." But why did I have this ominous feeling deep inside even as I gave Latoya all the possible excuses? Unfortunately, I have pretty good instincts. And they weren't telling me that the papers had been innocently mislaid. "When she brought this up, I realized I didn't really know a lot about the current status of our inventory, or catalog, or whatever you all call it. I write about it a lot, but mostly I just drop in the boilerplate on collections — the stuff that you and your staff hand me — so I don't really think about it. I have no idea if it's accurate or even what it means. It's pretty fuzzy."

The more I learned, the more I wondered if that language was deliberately vague in order to cover up some long-standing shortcomings of the system. Of course, I knew we weren't alone among our peer institutions in the dismal state of our record keeping. We were still struggling to make our way out of the nineteenth century (spidery brown ink on file cards), and here it was the twenty-first century. We'd been blindsided by the Internet, and had been scrambling for the past couple of years to try and keep an oar in the water while figuring out what it all meant and how we could possibly deal with it, with a budget that was already running a chronic annual deficit, and with a small — very small — endowment.

Latoya looked pained. "You want the short course on the state of our cataloging?" I nodded. She sighed. "Okay. You know the catalog room downstairs?"

"Yes," I said. Of course I did — I walked through it daily.

"That was state-of-the-art fifty, a hundred years ago. There are seven — yes, seven — individual catalogs, all on file cards. Books, manuscripts, music, photographs, maps, objects, ephemera." She ticked them off on her fingers. "And there are some subcategories for those. These are not integrated, but kept together as individual catalogs, all lined up side by side."

I interrupted. "You mean, if I'm looking for a particular person or a place — a cemetery, say — I have to look through multiple catalogs?"

Latoya nodded. "Yes. Now, as you know, we applied for and received a grant a couple of years ago to put our most heavily used collections into an electronic format, so they could be accessed remotely, viewed from the website."

I nodded encouragingly. That had been one of my proudest moments, and the grant had enabled us to take at least a baby step into the modern world. Alfred's new cataloging software had been part of that package. Though I was a bit ticked at her use of the word *we,* since she hadn't been around when the grant application had gone in — that had been *my* work.

I sighed inwardly. If we had lots of money available, we could do wonderful things, on-line and on-site. We could share our city's and our nation's glorious history with schoolchildren and the general public, near and far, and have them begging for more. All it would take was infinite resources, financial and human. But that wasn't going to happen, unless Bill Gates decided that we were his favorite institution in the whole wide world. I wish.

Latoya went on. "Then you know that grant covered only three of the seven collections, which in themselves amounted to only about forty percent of the total of the existing file cards. Those collections were chosen because they were the easiest to scan — they had the fewest handwritten entries, they conformed best to standard cataloging protocols, and so on."

I nodded again, with less enthusiasm. This was not encouraging.

"And that effort has been going on for over a year now, and while the bulk of the material has been scanned, translating that scanned material into new, consistent digital records and into an online format has been exceedingly slow."

I was getting depressed. Time to divert the flow of gloom. "So what you're saying is, we have modern cataloging for only a small percentage of our collections, and even that is incomplete?"

"Exactly."

I pondered for a moment. "All right, let me cut to the chase. Let's talk about the Terwilliger Collection, which I know is physically still maintained as a single collection. What state is it in?"

"We received that collection starting in, oh, 1967, I think. It came in several installments — the bulk of it when John Terwilliger moved out of his big family home and into a retirement community, and the rest upon his death. There was a catalog of sorts, but it was largely anecdotal, descriptive — nothing like a formal library catalog. I think some ancient cousin put it together a long time ago. It was better than nothing, but it was hardly specific. And if you've seen it, you know that the collection is massive, and we've only begun to scratch the surface. That's why Rich is here. You wrote the proposals to help fund him, so you probably know it as well as anyone here. Except me, of course. So Marty is worried?"

"Unfortunately, yes."

Latoya sat back and stared pensively at the ceiling for a long moment. Then she straightened.

"All right. Let me pull the files and get back to you. Later today?"

"Fine," I said as I rose to leave. And then I realized that neither of us had mentioned Alfred. Latoya had worked with him for nearly three years, but she seemed unmoved by his death. I stopped in the doorway. "It's a shame about Alfred, isn't it?"

"Yes, it's unfortunate. It won't be easy to replace him." Latoya turned back to her computer monitor: I was dismissed, and so, apparently, was Alfred. Or so I thought, until she said, "Will there be a service?"

"Yes, tomorrow. I'll send you the details." As I went out the door, I sent up a silent prayer: *Please, please let this all be a mix-up.* I didn't like what I was hearing. It would be interesting to see if Latoya's findings jibed with Alfred's, or if she even mentioned his reports.

I had started two hares, so to speak, and now I wasn't sure where to turn next. I went to my office and shut the door, which I never do. But I wanted a quiet minute to think, to try to put my thoughts in order. Unfortunately, what I *didn't* know about how the Society managed its collections far exceeded what I did know. It was embarrassing — how many years had I been working here? Why hadn't I ever asked anyone these things before?

I stared at the peeling paint on the ceiling for a while and decided to start with what I did know. Point one: some things might or might not be missing from the building. Point two: nobody could say for sure if they were missing, because most of our records were at least a half century out-of-date. Point three: if they *were* missing, the list of people who could have taken them was pretty extensive. Point three, sub (a): was it one person or lots of people? Point three, sub (b): was this recent or ancient history? Oh yes, this was going very well.

I decided to turn to the don't-know list. Top of that list: if we determined that some things — either the Terwilliger letters, or those and a whole lot more — had really been stolen, who was I supposed to tell? According to Alfred, Latoya knew that things were going missing, or at least she should have, if she had read Alfred's reports. She had apparently dismissed them as insignificant. Presumably Charles and the board knew, too, since Latoya had supposedly reported those findings at board meetings, at least in vague terms, but if she hadn't sent up any red flags, they wouldn't have worried.

But assuming the items had actually been stolen, who should be informed? The police? The FBI?

At that point I stopped cold in my mental tracks. Telling the police about the missing items would be disastrous to the Society, especially to me. How was I supposed to raise money if we went public with the fact that we didn't know what we had already or where it was? And that we seemed to be losing what we did have? That would not exactly inspire confidence among donors. A body in the stacks was bad enough, but losing documents — that was unforgivable; preserving and protecting them was our core mission.

I still had no proof that there was any crime involved, anyway. It could just be human carelessness. But somehow I knew in my heart of hearts that it was more than that. After all, if Alfred had been worried, there was probably a good reason. Alfred had dutifully told his superiors, and if we were lucky, Alfred had left his usual careful notes buried in Cassandra. I could only hope he had left adequate instructions on how to penetrate Cassandra's recesses.

At this point I laid my head down on my desk and wished I was dead. The gala had been so nice, after all our planning. And then everything had fallen to pieces, and I had the feeling there was more to come.

Focus on the documents. I was completely out of my depth when it came to assigning a value to the collections. It was a daunting prospect. We had things that had been accumulating for well over a hundred years. Some of them were garbage: Great-Aunt Tilly's pen wiper and that ilk. Some of them were unique: personal correspondence from then-presidents to the men who had shaped this city, this country, for example. The collections had grown and become increasingly unwieldy, as more and more was shoehorned into the same limited and antiquated space. Things were stacked in piles, and I had seen at least one suitcase used for document storage, somewhere in the stacks. We couldn't even identify half of the items, much less assign a dollar value to each one of them — a value that would change all the time because of shifting economic conditions, tastes and trends among collectors, et cetera, et cetera. Did we carry insurance? Yes, on the building and equipment, but not on the collections. They were, literally, priceless.

All of this was making it clear to me just how complacent we'd been. Things had always gone along just fine, managed by the local old-boy network for their own personal use. They were all gentlemen, and they all knew each other. I had seen documents from the early twentieth century that showed that there were only two or three employees running the Society, one of whom doubled as a security guard and lived in a small apartment upstairs. Who had needed more than that back in those days? And then there was the problem I had just run into: knowing what we had and where it was, at any given time. It was easier to assume that everything just stayed put. There had been some indefinable element of trust, a belief that the people who used a library or archive were honorable and sincere in their interest.

Well, the world had changed. We had visible evidence in the neighborhood around us: what had once been an orchard and gardens was now peopled by hookers after dark, and drive-by shootings were not unknown. And people had changed. Now there were street people who wandered in, looking for warmth or a toilet, and who had to be gently persuaded to leave. And not just the lobby, but the steps as well, where they would beg for change, scaring the little old ladies who made up a large portion of our users. The academic world had become more and more cutthroat, with everyone fighting to publish something new, something noteworthy. It was hard to believe, but professors and graduate students were not above spiriting away an essential document or slicing the relevant pages out of a book to keep it away from their competitors. And even the swelling ranks of genealogists had sticky fingers. When they found a will or a letter that some long-dead relative had penned, they thought, *Hey, this should by rights be mine* — and they would pocket it or stick it under their shirt. We had no way to search everyone who walked out of the building. What's more, only a full body search would nab a really determined thief — were we supposed to strip-search every patron in the lobby?

It was depressing. It might have been encouraging that technology had grown along with the problem, making it theoretically easier to keep an electronic eye on the stacks, to track who came in and left the building, who requested which documents. The problem I kept coming back to was that all that lovely electronic gear was expensive. Many of our sister institutions were chasing after the same pot of limited grant money for technology and security upgrades, and it wasn't happening very fast.

So, what to do? I couldn't come up with a solution, so I decided to turn the problem over to my subconscious and do something else instead. Carrie wasn't in today — not that I blamed her, for she was young, single, and not terribly devoted to her job — but I could check how many of the gala checks she had already processed. I was sure there were more, too, like the ones that had been left on my desk, which in the turmoil following Alfred's death I had neglected to hand over to her.

Which reminded me of Alfred's list, in the same pile. I pulled it out and smoothed it carefully on my desk. I made an effort to relax before running my eyes over the list. It was far longer than I had expected, and even I recognized the names attached to a lot of the items there. My heart sank. If anyone asked me — and I prayed they wouldn't — I would have to guess that someone with a fine eye and specific expertise had been cherry-picking the good stuff out of our collections. And had gotten clean away with it, for quite some time.

I needed time to think about this, and to think about what to do with what I knew. I lined up the papers and carefully returned them to their envelope. And then changed my mind, pulled them out, and headed for the copy machine. I wasn't sure who could re-create this list, with Alfred gone. I knew I couldn't. So it seemed prudent to make an extra copy and stash it somewhere safe. As I stood over the machine, its scanner lights moving underneath the copier cover, I almost laughed at my own cloak-and-dagger attitude. I was copying a list that nobody else knew existed, to protect it from — who? I had no idea. I just wanted to be sure Alfred's list had a backup.

Back in my office, I slid the original list in amongst the files in my desk drawer. It was highly unlikely that anyone would find it there, since I often had trouble finding my own files. The copy I stuck in my carry bag. Impatient now, I sifted through the stack of checks from the gala, made a few notes, then bundled them up to be input by Carrie on Monday and deposited to the Society's bank account. Better sooner than later, in case some donors had second thoughts after hearing the news of Alfred's death and decided to stop their checks.

But it was now late afternoon, and I'd had

enough. I was going home to put my feet up, chill out, and try to figure out just what the heck was going on at the Society. I was almost out the door of my office when I remembered one last thing: I had promised Marty that I would let the staff know about Alfred's funeral. I went back to my desk and wrote a brief email giving time and place, and sent it to all staff and board members. Then I shut down the computer, turned off the lights, and headed home.

CHAPTER 11

Returning to Bryn Mawr and my home always felt like going from one universe to another. Charles and I seldom got together on weekends, since he lived in the city and I lived in the Far West, and there was a great chasm between that I'd heard described as the urban-suburban split. The distance was no more than twenty miles, but to the denizens on either end, it could have been light-years.

My house was small, but it was all mine, and if I wanted to put on my grubbiest sweats and go barefoot, I could. I also had shopping to do, a new Nora Roberts romance novel by the bed, and a lengthy to-do list to work on. I enjoyed the endless small projects that an older house generated. With all the thinking and writing and talking I had to do at work, it was nice to go home to silence or music, and then make something, shape something — sand, polish, reweave, whatever — and have a tangible result to show for it at the end. I found it therapeutic.

I decided to let my subconscious mind gnaw away at Alfred's list while I did unrelated things, and went about my distinctly suburban business. I shopped, made myself an extravagant dinner on Saturday, and read most of the book. But the problem wouldn't let go of me. Things looked fine on the surface, but if the issue of the missing documents proved to be the tip of the iceberg, what would happen? I had to assume that there would be a lot of ass-covering and finger-pointing, which would be toxic in a small, tightly knit shop like ours.

Sunday night, I dreamt that I was searching for something in my kitchen cabinets and I kept finding random and illogical things, but not what I was looking for, except I really wasn't sure what I was looking for in the first place, or why it would be in my kitchen. In any event, I woke up out of sorts and restless on Monday morning. It was a dark, dreary day, and I had to rush to catch my train, which then kept stopping and starting, the garbled announcement over the tinny loudspeaker making the usual excuses about "signal problems." You'd think after more than a hundred years the commuter-rail system would have worked out their signals. Normally I enjoyed my commute, catching up on my reading, but today I was impatient. I watched the towers of Center City loom through the low clouds and wondered what unpleasantness I might find today.

Like many museums, the Society was closed to the public on Mondays, although the administration staff was expected to be there. Actually, Mondays were usually rather nice, since most of the building was dark and quiet, and there was a more relaxed feeling among the staff who were there. I doubted that today would be enjoyable, though, given Alfred's death and Marty's looming deadline. I knew she would hold me to it, and I was beginning to believe that she had every right to do so. I just wished I had better answers for her.

As one more delaying tactic, I stopped at the kiosk down the street for a double cappuccino. Maybe that would jump-start my day. Carrying the cup, I let myself into the building. The heavy metal door swung closed behind me with a reassuring click. The lobby was shadowed, and there were no lights on in the catalog room beyond. I made my way to the elevator and up to the third floor, to my office, without seeing anyone.

I turned on the overhead light in my office and hung my coat on the back of the door, then sat down with my coffee. I squared the piles of papers on my desktop, opened my coffee, sat back, and tried to think. What did I need to do first?

Since no one was around, I pulled out Alfred's list again and looked at it analytically. The missing items came from no single collection, had been stored all over the building, and represented all different kinds of media — manuscripts, books, letters, objects. But, as I'd noted before, they seemed to share one outstanding characteristic: they all appeared to be potentially valuable. Everything on the list could easily be disposed of on the open market. Or, more likely, on the so-called grey market — to collectors who were less concerned about the source of their acquisitions than having them in their possession. The Terwilliger correspondence between Major Jonathan and George Washington — which wasn't even on this list, since we didn't *officially* know the letters were missing — fit quite neatly into the group.

One other thing that Alfred hadn't included on this list: *when* these things had first gone missing — because Alfred had no way of knowing, beyond when he first noted their absence. One of those prove-a-negative problems; how do you show when something *isn't* there? These disappearances could have been going on for a long time, or they could have been recent, but we'd probably never know. That deduction did not help me much.

I sat there, rocking slightly in my swivel chair, contemplating doomsday scenarios. A thief in our midst. A public investigation. Humiliation in the eyes of the historic and arts community, locally, nationally. A poisoned fundraising climate (well, that *was* my job, and I had to think about it). Criminal liability?

The phone rang, jerking me out of my contemplation of disaster.

"Nell. Good, you're there." Marty's voice.

"Hi, Marty. Before you ask, no, I don't have any answers for you yet."

"I know that. But we've got to talk. Can you come over tomorrow, for dinner?"

"I probably won't have any answers by then, you know." In fact, all I was accumulating was more questions.

"Doesn't matter. See you at six."

She hung up before I could protest or even ask for instructions, but I knew where she lived — her address was in our donor database, after all, and it was only a few blocks away. Not that I'd ever seen the inside of her townhouse. We weren't exactly in the same social circle. I had to admit I was curious, both about her house and about what she wanted to discuss with me.

Turning back to the piles on my desk, I took care of several small business items, like writing thank-you notes to the committee members who had helped put together the gala — even those who had done nothing except make sure their names were spelled correctly on the program. I also wrote thank-yous for Charles's signature to the people who had sent particularly nice (that is, four-figure) checks or bought a table. I reviewed the calendar for grant application deadlines. I checked the status of the agenda for the next board meeting and made a mental note to ask Carrie when she would be mailing the meeting reminder.

That took care of most of the busywork. My mind kept creeping back to Alfred's list. Many of the items on it looked like high-dollar pieces — but what did that really mean? Not being a collector myself, apart from a few flea-market finds, I wasn't really tapped into the historic artifacts market, so I decided to do some homework on the Internet. Calling up Google, I started trolling for information on Americana, manuscripts, auctions, dealers — whatever looked promising and included real-world prices.

At the end of an hour, I sat back, a bit stunned. Looking only at the *name* items — things associated with dead presidents, for example, or other known and noteworthy historical figures — it was clear that the market was booming. And some single letters were going for five and six figures at auction. The Society's list of items known to be missing was over five pages long, and most of them appeared to be highly desirable, if what I was reading was an accurate view of the market. Take each of those missing pieces and multiply it by, conservatively, twenty-five thousand dollars, and . . . the total ran into the millions. Oh my God. We had a *big* problem here.

I allowed myself a moment of panic. The dollar value of the collections was one thing, but I also had to consider the Society's reputation. Hadn't there been a recent spate of news articles about someone stealing maps from multiple collections and getting away with it for years? If pieces from our collections were walking out the door, we would look like incompetent fools. And that wouldn't exactly encourage people to contribute money to us — money we depended on and sorely needed just to stay open. All my hard work, all the small advances we had made since Charles arrived — all trashed, if Marty went public with her suspicions about the Terwilliger Collection, which would lead to more scrutiny, which would lead to . . . disaster.

Reluctantly, I realized that there was another area I needed to think about: the legal aspects. I didn't feel like I could go to the Society's official legal counsel just yet because he was a board member, and I didn't want to let the board in on this until I was sure of my information. On the other hand, I certainly didn't want to contact some outside attorney, not only because that would cost money I didn't have, but also because it might tip off the wrong people that we had a problem, and I didn't want to bring that down on my head, either. So once again I turned to the Internet.

I had in the back of my head that there was a special category for the theft of items of historical significance, so that was where I started. Aha: Title 18, United States Code, Section 668: Theft of Major Artwork. "Makes it a federal offense to obtain by theft or fraud any object of cultural heritage from a museum. The statute also prohibits the 'fencing' or possession of such objects, knowing them to be stolen." From another source, "an 'object of cultural heritage' means an object that is over 100 years old and worth at least $5,000." Well, there we were, in the thick of it. I knew for a fact that we were legally defined as a museum in the Society's bylaws. And we could easily classify *all* of the missing pieces as at least a century old and worth over five grand.

I plowed on, glued to my screen. According to the FBI, ninety percent of all museum thefts turned out to be inside jobs. Not surprising, but not reassuring. There were sounds from the outer offices now, people arriving, exchanging greetings, bustling around. I sighed. I really didn't want to think that anyone on our staff had been systematically ripping off the Society. Most of them did have the expertise to choose what to take, and all of them had free access. But I'd worked with the people here for years. They were good people, knowledgeable, committed to history and its preservation, and to helping other people share their interest. They were willing to work for pathetic wages simply because they did care. And then that little voice inside me said, *Maybe somebody's gotten tired of the low pay and equally low respect, and decided to do something to make up for it. After all, it would be so easy . . .*

I shook myself. I was almost afraid to look, but I needed to know what the proper procedure would be to report such a theft. The FBI was kind enough to provide just such an outline on their website. One, do not let staff or visitors into the area to disturb evidence. Well, it was a little late for that. Two, notify the local police department. That clearly hadn't happened yet. Three, determine the last time the objects were seen and what happened in the area, or to the objects, in that time. Like that was going to happen — although, I realized, Marty could give specifics for the Terwilliger Collection. One more reason to keep her happy. Four, gather documents, descriptions, and images of the missing objects and provide to the police. Well, we had a start on that, thanks to Alfred. Five, follow up on police actions and investigations to ensure that everything possible is being done. Yeah, right.

So it looked like the police were the first line, and then they would call in the FBI, since this was clearly a federal offense. What wasn't clear was who from our end was supposed to report the problem to the police. Me, who had first discovered it? Latoya, as head of collections? Charles, as the president? The board, as the official managing body for the institution? Or Marty herself, as an interested outside party as well as a board member?

I felt sick. I felt scared. Right now I was sitting on a guilty little secret that Alfred had shared with me, but he couldn't help me now. Oh, and the thief — if there was one — probably knew about it, too. But I didn't see what I could do about it.

Charles. When should I tell Charles? This would devastate him. He had worked hard to identify himself with this institution and to make his way into the local historical community, and he had done it well. A theft like this, under his aegis, would be a serious blow to his professional standing, both locally and in the broader museum community.

OK, Nell, slow down. I gripped the edge of my desk and took a deep breath. *Take this one step at a time.* I believed the Society had a problem, thanks to what Alfred had told me. I had reported Marty's complaint to the next person in the chain of command: Latoya. She had dismissed Alfred's reports as trivial, or as a normal part of his cataloging procedures — of course there would be a few misplaced items among the thousands

144

he had looked at. Maybe we could just make it go away, hush it up, save our reputation. Why didn't I believe that?

Maybe she hadn't listened to him, but she was going to listen to me.

CHAPTER 12

I stood up and headed to Latoya Anderson's office. She was on the phone, but I summoned up my patience and waited. Finally she managed to extricate herself from the phone call and gestured for me to come in. I closed the door behind me, and Latoya's eyebrows went up a notch. She must have picked up on my unease — not to mention the fact that I'd closed the door. "What's going on now, Nell?" She folded her hands on her pristine desk blotter and waited.

I took a deep breath. "You remember I talked to you Saturday about the problem with the Terwilliger papers?"

She nodded, then said contritely, "Oh, and I promised to get you the files — it slipped my mind entirely. Let me hunt them up for you." She started to rise, but I held up a hand to stop her.

"Latoya, that's not the immediate problem. There's something bigger that we need to talk about. Something that Alfred told me about the collections."

She sat back and said, "All right. What's the problem?"

Here we go, I thought. "When Marty came to me with her question, I realized how little I knew about the maintenance of our collections, in hands-on terms. So I talked to Alfred, since he was more directly involved in the day-to-day management."

Latoya's expression was wary. "Go on."

This was the difficult part. "Alfred told me that there are a number of other items he had not been able to locate."

She sniffed. "I know — that was in his reports. That's to be expected in an organization of this size and age. You should know that."

"Yes, I do know, and that's what Alfred told me." I pressed on. "I think the problem is bigger than that. Alfred gave me a list of the items he knew of, that he hadn't been able to find. I looked at the list, and even to my untrained eye it appears that most of them are both historically significant and valuable."

"What are you suggesting?"

I drew myself up and said deliberately, "I think there is good reason to believe that there has been systematic looting of the

Society's collections."

There was silence in the room. I could almost see the wheels turning in Latoya's mind: where did her responsibility lie? "Alfred never mentioned anything like that to me. That's a very serious allegation," she said slowly, buying time.

"I understand that Alfred gave you regular reports on the status of his cataloging — and on the numbers of items that he has been unable to locate?"

She stared at me. "Yes, that's part of his job description — he provided monthly summary reports."

"And," I went on, "did you never see any reason for concern, in the reports that he gave you?"

"No," she replied stiffly. "He did not give me any indication that there was anything out of the ordinary. As I said, misplaced items are a fact of life in institutions like this."

I wasn't going to let her brush me off. "I understand that. But you were not worried about the extent or the nature of the disappearances?"

She waited before answering, even more stiffly, "No. And Alfred never made an issue of it. Perhaps I should have questioned him more closely, but I had no reason —"

I interrupted her. "Latoya, Alfred was a very careful man, and I'm sure he didn't want to make any claims until he felt they were substantiated. He was also rather shy and didn't like to make waves. That's probably why he never said anything to you. But I think the number and the quality of the missing items had really started to bother him. The question is, what do we do now? If you ask me, I think we need to get to the bottom of this very quickly, for all our sakes."

"Of course. Providing there is any substance to his concerns." Latoya looked as troubled as I had ever seen her. Maybe the message had finally hit home? "Who else have you talked to about this?"

"I asked Rich and Felicity specifically if they knew if any part of the Terwilliger Collection had been moved recently — they both said no. But I haven't spoken to anyone about the larger issue, the other things that might be missing. Alfred left the list on my desk before he . . ." I stopped, swallowed, then plunged on. "And now I'm bringing it to you. So, no one else knows — yet."

Latoya looked over my head, thinking. Finally she said, "Nell, thank you for bringing this to my attention and for being discreet about it. This certainly deserves a closer look. Let me handle it from here."

Was she dismissing me? Well, I wasn't done. "Latoya, Marty Terwilliger wants an answer about her collection in the next few days. She's not stupid, and I think she'll see through any phony excuses we might come up with. She's not afraid to make public noise about something like this, and she's extremely well connected in Philadelphia. She can make a lot of trouble for us, if she wants to." I paused, then looked her straight in the eye. "What do you want me to tell her?"

"Let me deal with Marty," Latoya said. "And I'd prefer it if you refer any more questions from her directly to me. Okay?"

Her request was reasonable, at least on the surface. After all, it was a collections issue, right? But Marty had come to me rather than to her, and I felt a personal responsibility to follow through. And I had a strong feeling that Latoya would act to cover her own derriere. Which most likely meant dumping the blame on Alfred. I wasn't going to sit here and let that happen.

"I'll be happy to let you deal with her, but she did come to me first. And what about the bigger issue?"

"You have a copy of the list that Alfred

gave you?" she said finally.

"Of course." I handed Latoya a new photocopy.

She scanned it quickly. "Let me look this over and think about it, and then I can decide what to do next."

I summoned up a smile. "That's all I ask, Latoya. Please let me know what you decide." I stood up. As far as I was concerned, the meeting was now over.

But Latoya was not finished. "You will keep this between us, won't you?"

She gave me another long look, and I felt a small chill. Who else did she think I would tell?

"Latoya, it would be unprofessional of me to do otherwise." With that, I swept out of the room, before things could get any more complicated.

All right, I had done what I was supposed to do about the institutional problem of the missing items. What next? No matter what Latoya thought, I felt I should talk to Charles; he shouldn't walk blindly into this situation, and he would need some time to consider all the ramifications, plan for a defensive strategy if necessary, to nip the issue in the bud, as it were. Maybe Charles would have some insights into how best to deal with this, too — after all, he was hardly a novice to administration, and he must have encountered difficult situations like this before. I felt a small lightening of my burden: maybe he could help. Heck, he *should* help — that was why he got paid the big bucks.

I squared my shoulders and took a deep breath, trying to organize my thoughts. I was just going to give him a friendly warning — nothing in writing, nothing inflammatory. I was taking advantage of our relationship to slip him this piece of information so that he could work out how he wanted to handle it. And, oh, how I looked forward to sharing the responsibility!

I strode to his office, nodding pleasantly at Doris, and knocked on his open door.

"Charles? Are you busy?"

He looked up from his desk. "No more than usual."

"There's something we have to talk about. Now." I walked inside and shut the door behind me.

He chuckled. "My, this sounds serious. And you, my dear, are looking positively drained. Tell me, what's so urgent?"

"Charles, I've encountered a problem that I think you should know about," I began.

"Go on — I'm at your service. Unless you'd rather talk over dinner?"

"I don't think this can wait." I decided to ease into it. "You remember I told you that I needed to tell you something that Marty Terwilliger had said to me? Well, she came to me before the gala and said she couldn't find something in the Terwilliger Collection — something that definitely should have been there. I told her I would look into it and get back to her. I didn't have time to talk with her on Friday, what with Alfred and all . . ." We both observed a moment of respectful silence, and then I went on. "But since then, I've talked to Rich, Felicity, and Latoya. Her missing documents are nowhere to be found."

Charles appeared unruffled. "Well, that's unfortunate but not unheard-of. Do you want me to talk to Marty, see if I can smooth things over?"

I shook my head. "At some point that might be a good idea. But, Charles, it's not that simple. You see, I asked Alfred about it last Thursday, and he told me that there are a *lot* of other things that don't seem to be where they should be."

Charles went still. "I thought we recognized that we had issues in that area — hence the new cataloging software. And a certain amount of inconsistency is to be expected in a mature organization like ours."

So everyone kept telling me. Still, I nodded. "Yes, but that's just made the underlying problem more obvious."

"And you think there is more to this than a century's worth of carelessness?"

I looked him in the eye. "Yes, I do. You see, Alfred gave me the list of missing items. If these, uh, disappearances were random, I would be more than happy to write it off to human error, and hope or assume that a number of the things will turn up eventually as we continue to catalog our holdings. But the items on that list are definitely all desirable, potentially high-value pieces." I swallowed. "I think we've been robbed." There, it was out.

Charles's face showed all the concern that I had hoped. "Oh, my dear Nell, I can see why you're worried. But we can't allow ourselves to leap to conclusions. Do you have any idea when this happened, or how long it has been going on?"

I shook my head. "No. Alfred gave me a rough list. Even he couldn't say whether it was recent or ongoing. I've just filled Latoya in on the situation — I thought she needed to know, since this falls under her purview. Look, I know how sensitive this is and how harmful it would be if it's true, and if it got out. Our reputation, and the goodwill of the historical community, are essential to our operations. I'm telling you now so that you won't be surprised when Latoya brings it to you, and you can begin thinking about how to address the problem."

I lapsed into silence. On some level, I felt relieved: I had discharged my duty, and it was out of my hands. I realized Charles had not yet said anything.

"Earth to Charles?" He gave a small start, then focused on me with a wry smile.

"I'm sorry. Thank you for bringing this to me — I know it must be difficult for you."

"And for you, too, Charles. I can only guess what kind of scandal might arise if this weren't handled properly. That's why I thought you should be involved as early as possible, if there's any way to resolve this quickly and quietly. Should we tell the board?"

"That seems premature. Let me see what Latoya can assemble, and make my own assessment."

"Of course," I said. "But . . ."

He cocked his head at me. "More problems?"

"It's Marty Terwilliger. She wants answers, and you know Marty — she's persistent. I don't think I'll be able to stall her. Perhaps if you spoke with her, off the record, it would help — or at least prevent her from making a large stink." *And informing the rest of the board personally,* I added to myself.

Charles nodded in approval. "An excellent idea. I'll call her in the morning and see if we can meet. Thank you, Nell — I truly appreciate your discretion. Not that I would expect anything less."

We smiled at each other as I stood up. Charles stood as well, then laid a hand on my arm. "Nell, are you sure you don't want to come over this evening? I know how upsetting this past week must have been for you."

I looked at him and softened. He was right. Finding Alfred Findley dead and then uncovering what might be a major mess in collections had disrupted my sleep and distracted me at work. It would be nice to have him pamper me a bit, but I needed time to think about what I'd learned.

"I'm sorry, Charles, but not tonight. But keep that thought in mind."

"Of course I will." He opened the door and ushered me out — carefully avoiding any physical contact in front of any staff members who might have seen. But as I passed Doris's desk, the expression on her face told me that we weren't fooling anyone.

As I made my way back to my office, I

wondered why I hadn't mentioned to either Latoya or Charles that I was seeing Marty the next night.

CHAPTER 13

I slept restlessly. When the alarm went off in the morning, I swatted it blindly, sending it halfway across the room. I dragged myself out of bed and made myself some coffee — strong — but it barely made a dent in the haze that seemed to surround my head. I went through the motions: brushed, washed, dressed, collected my stuff, stumbled out to the train station. Good thing I could operate on autopilot.

The world today was not the world of yesterday or last week. Poor Alfred Findley was dead under possibly suspicious circumstances, and today he would be buried. We were losing valuable materials from our precious collections, and nobody at the place wanted to hear about it, either. I felt like Chicken Little, declaring that the sky was falling, while all those around me kept patting me on the head and telling me not to worry about it. But I *was* worried. And, thank goodness, so was Marty.

The train made its slow way into Suburban Station, and I followed the herd up to the main station level, then to the outside world. I always enjoyed emerging from the low, dim tunnels below into the light, to be immediately confronted by the absurdly ornate bulk of City Hall. It was cheering, somehow — even if Philadelphia's government had seldom lived up to the grandeur of its house. I stopped for another coffee — large — before climbing the stairs at the Society and struggling with the heavy door.

The usual piles of things to be done sat before me on my desk, but I couldn't shake the nagging feeling that to draft yet another donor letter would be like fiddling while Rome burned. We could have a serious problem on our hands. I was definitely a supporter of the cool, calm, and collected approach to things, but it seemed that we should feel some sense of urgency now, even though the Society's normal response was to pull our head into our shell like a tortoise and hope it would all go away.

But this wasn't going to go away — not if Marty Terwilliger had anything to say about it. She was a board member, which gave her a fiduciary responsibility to act in the Society's best interests, and she also had a personal stake in the Terwilliger Collection. She had every right to be outraged if it was being plundered. She was also more perceptive than I had given her credit for being.

I jumped when my phone rang, interrupting my brooding.

"Good morning, Nell," Charles said formally. Speak of the devil. "I just wanted to alert you that Marty Terwilliger will be coming in this morning."

Well, that was fast. Was Marty that impatient?

"I'm glad to hear that, Charles. I think it's important that you speak to her. What time?"

"Elevenish. But, Nell? I think I should meet with her alone — you don't need to sit in."

Oh. All right. Keep me out of the loop. But I knew what was going on, *nyah nyah.* "Fine, Charles — whatever you think best. Please let me know what she has to say." I could play my role here. Dumb and ignorant.

"Of course." He hung up.

I sat back and stared at the phone. Maybe he would finally take this problem seriously. Well, let him try to work his magic on Marty, and then we'd see what the next step would be. I sighed and reached for the top pages in my in-box. Somehow the morning passed. I saw Marty arrive, headed for Charles's office; she didn't so much as nod in my direction. I kept myself busy, but I had to admit I was nervous. I assumed Charles would handle the situation with his usual tact and diplomacy, but I wasn't sure how Marty would respond. I wondered what Charles would say. Would he try to smooth things over, or even bury them? Make nice and hope it would all go away? He could be very soothing without being patronizing, but somehow I didn't think Marty would fall for snake oil. Would she play along, or would she force the issue and demand that Charles take action?

I decided to distract myself by writing up the financial summary of the gala — tracking down all the bills, making sure I had the documentation from the caterer, and running another summary of the income. It looked as though Carrie had finished inputting all the checks in our database system and left me a report, which was good. Then I drafted a spreadsheet with the information I had assembled. If I had it right, we had cleared more than the thirty thousand dollars I had originally estimated, after all the bills were paid — not bad, and definitely better than last year's results. Then I ran a quick and dirty analysis of how many new donors there were, how many repeaters, and how many people had fallen off the list this year. Again, the results were encouraging: we were definitely building our support base.

Or we would have been, if we weren't about to be derailed by news of Alfred's death and a major scandal. I clipped together my reports and stuck them in a folder — I would pass an abbreviated version on to Charles and then present a fuller version to the board at the next meeting, in less than two weeks' time. It would be welcome news, if it weren't for . . . other things.

Charles and Marty came out of his office, and he escorted her to the door of the outer office, in my line of sight. Their conversation sounded cheerful enough, so presumably he had managed to keep her calm. Charles made his polite farewells, and Marty turned to leave. But as she did, she caught my eye and winked at me, then left quickly.

A moment later, Charles's assistant Doris Manning stalked over to my office.

"Charles would like to have a word with you," she said curtly.

I got up and followed her over to his office. Charles waved me inside, and Doris went back to her desk. He motioned to me to close the door. I did, then sat in front of his desk.

"So, how did Marty take it?" I began.

"I managed to persuade her to give us a little more time to look into the problem — I said it might not be limited to her particular collection, and we needed more information before we could proceed. She thought that made sense, and she won't press immediately. But she did hold firm that we should have a summary of the possible missing items ready to present to the board at the next meeting."

I felt a sense of relief. "That seems fair enough. And it gives us more time to investigate. Did you tell her anything else about the scope of the problem?"

He shook his head. "No, I didn't want to get into that, especially given how preliminary our information is. But I assured her that this would take top priority and that we were taking her concern very seriously. I think she was mollified."

"Good. What would you like me to do?"

"I think you should let collections handle it. After all, this is not your area of expertise. I'll speak to Latoya, and we can review our records."

That was reasonable, although I felt a bit miffed at being shut out, since I was the one who had started this. Another thought occurred to me.

"Charles, should we be talking with our lawyers?"

He looked pained. "No, I think that would be premature. We still aren't certain that there is anything like theft going on. And you know how they bill."

"All right. Do we need to include anything about it in the board agenda? We'll be sending that out the end of this week."

He considered a moment, then said, "Why don't you just include a bullet point about security issues? That shouldn't alarm anyone."

"Will do. Oh, did Marty mention Alfred's service?"

"This afternoon? I'm afraid I've a prior commitment. You'll be there to represent us, won't you?"

"Of course." As I left his office, I stopped in front of Doris's desk. "Doris, what's the RSVP list for the board meeting look like?"

She gave me an icy stare. "I'll have to find it for you. It's still early, you know."

My, my, she was touchy. "Fine — whenever you have a minute."

She nodded without adding anything, then turned away to shuffle a pile of pages on her blotter, and I went back to my office, pleased that the administrative wheels had begun to turn.

After lunch I gathered up my coat and scarf to head out for Alfred Findley's funeral. I didn't run into any other staff members on my way out, but I was still a little saddened when I arrived at the funeral home and found only Marty Terwilliger there. Felicity Soames did slip in after I did, though. She was the only other person from the Society to attend. I hadn't realized that Alfred and Felicity were friends, although I'd seen them together briefly during the gala, and both had worked at the Society for many years. I wasn't surprised that Charles did not attend, although I assumed the tasteful array of white flowers at the front of the room had come from the Society.

The casket in the front of the room was closed, thank goodness — I really didn't want to see Alfred's face again. Marty was seated in the front row, her expression grim. I settled myself in a folding chair next to her. She nodded to me but then turned her eyes forward again. After waiting for ten minutes past the appointed time, the funeral director stood up and read from what was clearly a standard script, with Alfred's name inserted periodically. He'd clearly never met

Alfred. The room was cold, despite the pompous drapery swags and plush carpet. As the director droned on, I did my best to remember positive things about Alfred — shy, conscientious Alfred, who had never harmed anyone in his life. Who had loved his job. Who had trusted me. I felt that I owed it to him to make things right, and I was glad Marty was on the same side.

After the brief service, Felicity left without speaking to either of us. Marty went forward to lay a hand on the coffin, then conferred with the funeral director. Then she slipped her arm through mine and led me out to the front of the building.

"You don't have to go to the burial, Nell. I'll take care of that. Pretty sad turnout, wasn't it? Don't say anything — I know what they thought of Alfred at the Society."

I couldn't add anything. I wondered where the rest of Alfred's relatives were and why they hadn't attended.

Marty buttoned her coat. "Well, I'd better be off to see to Alfred. Thanks for coming, Nell. I'll see you at six."

We parted ways on the sidewalk: she went off to bury Alfred Findley, and I went back to work.

Felicity sought me out before the end of the day. She came into my office and perched on a chair, uncomfortable outside of her own kingdom downstairs. "I'm glad you came to the funeral, Nell. Alfred always liked you. And he really did care about this place. It may be hard to find that kind of loyalty again."

We shared a few moments of silence, in honor of Alfred. Then Felicity stood up abruptly. "I'd better get back downstairs. Let me know if you need any help in searching for his successor." And then she was gone.

I was not ready to think about that, not until I had a lot more information.

Marty Terwilliger's townhouse may have been within walking distance of the Society, but it was in a distinctly different neighborhood. She lived in a tall, narrow row house, on a shaded cross street that still retained a fair number of trees; a nice street, very old Philadelphia. I walked up the brownstone steps and pressed the polished brass doorbell. I could hear footsteps immediately, and then Marty opened the door.

"Nell. Glad you could make it. Come on in." I followed my hostess down her narrow hallway. She was wearing blue jeans and a sweatshirt; her feet were bare. As I looked around, the plainness of the house surprised me. I hadn't thought that Marty was the type to go in for Victorian gewgaws, but I hadn't expected the stark modernity of many of her furnishings and artworks. The high windows in the bay at the back were bare of curtains, and even this late in the day I could see trees at the rear and the twinkle of lights from houses the next block over.

"Here. Sit down. You want a glass of wine or something? Dinner's almost ready."

Why not? "Sure. You have white wine?" I was within walking distance of Thirtieth Street Station, and I really did want a drink.

Marty grinned. "Good woman. I hate to drink alone." With that, she disappeared toward the kitchen area, a large alcove tucked off to one side, and kept up a running commentary.

"I made a corn and cheese casserole — it tastes better than it sounds — and a salad. I'm not much into cooking." She clattered around the kitchen, finding a tray, plates, glasses. I decided it wouldn't improve things if I volunteered to help, so I stayed where I was and studied her furniture. Now that I'd gotten past the first impression, I noted a number of handsome eighteenth-century mahogany pieces around the room; overwhelmed by the modern stuff, they reminded me of timid wallflowers at a dance. Knowing Marty, those older pieces had probably come down in the family — whichever great-great having once bought them new, fresh off the ship from England.

Marty staggered in with a tray loaded with wine, glasses, and bowls of munchies. "Here, just clear that junk off the table."

I swept aside a stack of magazines and newspapers, and she set down the tray and sat down with a sigh of relief.

"There. Help yourself."

I was a bit at a loss. I felt as though I was there under false pretenses, because I didn't for a minute think that this was a polite social occasion. I decided to take the bull by the horns.

"Marty, I'm flattered that you want to have dinner with me, but I have to admit I don't really know why I'm here, and I'd rather be clear about that before we eat."

"Good for you — never break bread with the enemy, eh? Fair enough." She bounced out of her chair again to fetch something and a moment later returned with a large envelope. She reached in and pulled out a sheaf of papers. I recognized it as a copy of Alfred's list. Had he shared it with her? And why? She waved it at me. "You know what this is?"

For about a millisecond, I thought about denying it, and then I decided that it would be better to have Marty as an ally, given her clout with the board. "Yes. It's a list Albert put together of things he thought were missing from the Society. He left a copy on my desk, before he . . . died."

"Bingo." Marty threw herself into her chair, draped her legs over the arm, and reached for her glass. "I'm glad you're not going to play games with me — saves time. What do you know?"

I picked up my wineglass, stalling. "Let me ask first, do you think the missing Terwilliger papers are part of something larger?"

"I'm not sure yet, but there sure does seem to be some kind of pattern. You agree?"

"I'm afraid I do. But nobody else wants to believe it."

"Who've you talked to?"

"Other than Alfred? Well, I asked Felicity and Rich about what you told me you were looking for. But about Alfred's list, I went to Latoya, since she's head of collections."

"That it?" Marty fixed me with an eagle eye.

I debated with myself, then said, "I also told Charles that there was something going on and that he should expect to hear about it from Latoya."

"Pillow talk, huh?"

So she knew? I had hoped Charles and I had been discreet. All right, cards on the table. "Not that it's any of your business, but why do you ask?"

Marty pondered her answer. "If you and Charles want to fool around, that's no concern of mine, but I'm trying to work out who knows what. I guess I'm trying to figure out if I trust you. To be blunt, I was testing you."

With deliberation I set my wineglass back on the side table. "What do you mean?" I said.

"Oh, don't get up on your high horse. Look, I've known there was something funny going on at the Society for a while, but when it reached my family papers, it got personal. So I told *you.*"

"Wait a minute," I interrupted. "I wondered about that — why me? Why not go to Latoya or Charles or the board?"

"All in good time. I told you, this was kind of a test. I wanted to see what you'd do about it. And you did everything right — asked all the right people. Good for you."

I was really getting confused. "I still don't understand. Are you saying you don't trust the staff?"

"Nell, right now I'm not sure who to trust, now that Alfred's gone."

"You trusted Alfred?"

"Sure — he was a cousin, about three times removed. I'd known him all my life. And I got him the job at the Society."

Oh. That was interesting. I knew Marty was related to half of Philadelphia society, but I'd had no idea Alfred was one of her many relatives. At least that explained why she had taken care of the funeral details — and maybe a lot more. "So he was keeping you informed? That's why he sent you the list?"

"Yes. And he knew I'd be concerned about the family collection. I'm guessing he stuck that list in the mail to me the same time he left you a copy. I got it in the mail yesterday, but that was the first I'd seen of it — and the first I knew just how big this thing might be."

I looked at my wineglass. It was still full, so the confusion I was feeling was not due to the wine. "Marty, this isn't making any sense. If Alfred thought there was something going on, why didn't he just tell Latoya?"

"He did, at least by his terms. You knew Alfred — he wasn't very good at being pushy. He probably dropped a few hints here and there, but nobody paid him any mind."

"He did tell me he had included what he suspected were losses in the monthly reports to Latoya," I said slowly, "but according to Latoya, that level of missing items was to be expected. I don't think he ever told her straight out what he suspected."

"Latoya's right, up to a point — museum records aren't all that they should be, and that's true at a lot of our peer institutions. But Alfred was worried that somebody had sticky fingers, and that was good enough for me. I'm sorry to say, Alfred got ignored a lot. He was kind of negligible, may he rest in peace. And you need to know that he had another reason to keep quiet, at least until he was really sure."

"What?"

"I hate to speak ill of the dead, but to put it bluntly, cousin Alfred was a bona fide kleptomaniac. People with that problem take things, not because they need the money, but because they can't stop themselves. The place he worked before . . . he sort of *borrowed* some of their artifacts. He didn't sell them or anything, though, and all the articles were recovered, so I managed to keep it quiet with the help of a hefty donation. When I got him the job at the

Society, I asked Felicity to keep an eye on him. She'd check his cubicle now and then to see what he'd picked up, and he was the first person she'd ask if she couldn't find something. I'm guessing that's why he was reluctant to tell anyone about the missing items, knowing he'd be the prime suspect."

That explained why Felicity had been at the funeral. "So what made him tell me?"

"Well, I gather you were the first person who asked him about it directly. And I know he liked you — you actually took the time to talk to him. Most people ignored him. And looking at this list" — Marty held up the papers — "I think he started adding things up and got scared. This is serious stuff here."

"I figured that much out." I took a swallow of wine. "You saw Charles this morning — what did he say?"

"He said what you'd expect him to say. He was concerned, he was going to devote the full resources of the Society to getting to the bottom of this, and so on. The gist of it was, please go away and let us handle this — or not."

I wasn't surprised. "What else could he say? But I assume he and Latoya will put their heads together now. At least he's been alerted."

174

There was something else I had to ask Marty, even though I really didn't want to. "Marty, don't you think that the timing of Alfred's death is kind of suspicious?"

Marty sat back in her chair and cocked her head at me. "So that's got you wondering, too? Alfred stumbles on what might be major theft, then suddenly he dies? Yeah, frankly, it *does* seem suspicious to me."

I finished my glass and poured myself some more wine before responding. "So, Marty, do you think someone actually killed Alfred?"

"The police called it an accident. He fell off a stool and hit his head and bled to death. He was such an odd duck that nobody wondered what he was doing wandering around the stacks then. Right?"

"You didn't answer my question. Do you think Alfred was murdered?"

Marty's flippant expression melted away, replaced by a more honest sadness. "I'm afraid I do. You see, I happen to know that Alfred was afraid of heights. No way would he have climbed that stool. And no way could he have fallen hard enough from ground level to do that kind of damage — unless he had help. Did you kill him?"

"Good God, no! I found him, remember?"

"Plenty of people could have faked that."

"But why would I kill him?"

"Because what he found might put a real kibosh on your fundraising efforts, if the thefts were discovered?"

"Marty! You've got to be kidding. You really think I'd kill somebody so I could go on raising money? That's ridiculous!"

"Relax, Nell. I'm just pulling your chain. No, I do not suspect you of killing Alfred Findley. But I think someone did, and I'm betting it's someone who knows something about the thefts."

I felt almost nauseated. Alfred, killed? Deliberately? Because of some vague suspicions? "Have you told the police anything about this?"

"I don't trust the local cops to find their way out of a paper bag. They decided it was an accident, and I've got nothing that's going to change their mind. And as for the missing items in the collections, what're they going to do? Can we prove that anything has been stolen?" Marty challenged.

I wilted. "No. And any outsider would just say we were lousy at keeping records. Not that they'd be wrong. But if Alfred's list was a shopping list, then somebody knows exactly what he or she is doing." I sighed. "So who knows that we know? Are we in danger?"

"I don't think so. And you've told other people now — Latoya, Charles. Whoever's responsible may not know that I know anything, but the cat's out of the bag anyway."

Maybe I was tired, or maybe I was stupid, but I still didn't get it. "So what are we supposed to do now?"

"My grandfather made the Society what it is — or was, in his day — and my father was a part of it, and now I am. I don't want to see it go down the drain just because someone has a yen for bibelots and autograph documents. It's bad enough that there was a death in the place, but if there has been a series of thefts, and the news gets out, the Society is in serious trouble. And you of all people should know how precarious the financial situation is. Your donors lose faith in the place, and that's all she wrote. The current endowment will carry you maybe a year, and that's with layoffs and cutbacks. Nope, I want to figure this out before the proverbial shit hits the fan, and then you can spin it to make us look like geniuses and everyone will be happy."

I swallowed more wine, because I needed it. Last time I had checked, my job description had not included *sleuthing,* and I felt completely unprepared to start now. "What

177

the heck am I supposed to do?"

Marty's eyes gleamed. "You in?"

I didn't have to think long about that. If Alfred had been killed, I wanted to see this through. "Yes, I am."

"Hurray! Have another glass of wine. Look, what I need is someone on the inside. Sure, people know me, but they think I'm a meddler and a loudmouth. You, they'll talk to. And you're right there on the spot, and you have access — even at the highest levels."

I knew she meant Charles. "But, Marty," I protested weakly, "I don't even know what I'm looking for or how to find it. Can't the police do a better job? I'll be happy to work with them."

"Why would they listen to you? You're just a fundraiser!" Before I could protest, she held up one hand. "That's what *they'll* say — I know how important you are to the place. But don't worry — we have an ace in the hole."

"What do you mean?"

Marty looked at her watch. "Let's eat."

She hadn't answered my question, I noted, but I was hungry, and I didn't want the wine to go to my head any more than it had already. So I stood up, too, and followed her to the kitchen, where she handed me a stack of plates and cutlery, and pointed to a table. Three plates, which matched the three place settings at the table. There was another guest coming?

As if on cue, the doorbell rang. "Get that, will you?" Marty said.

I found my way back to the front door and opened it. On the other side was Marty's escort from the gala. "Uh, hello — Jimmy, isn't it?"

He entered the hallway with the ease of long familiarity. "James. Nice to see you, Ms. Pratt."

"Nell, please," I said automatically, and followed him as he went toward the kitchen.

Marty greeted him with an affectionate kiss on the cheek. "Hi, Jimmy. Right on time. Dinner's ready. Help yourselves."

Once seated with a plate full of food, James turned to Marty. "You talked to her?"

Marty nodded. "I did. All clear."

"Hello? I'm still in the room. You want to fill me in on what's going on?" I was beginning to feel left out.

"Sure. Nell, I'm not sure I introduced you two properly the other night — bad manners. This is my cousin, Jimmy Morrison. Or, I should say, Special Agent James Morrison of the FBI."

My mouth fell open. Cousin Jimmy was

an FBI agent? The FBI was responsible for investigating the theft of major artifacts. The lightbulb finally went on. "You've called in the FBI to investigate the thefts, which are a federal offense. He's *your ace in the hole!*" I finished triumphantly.

"I knew you were smart," Marty said. James raised his glass to me, without comment. Marty went on. "But Jimmy's just doing me a favor, at the moment. Since we don't officially know there have been any thefts, he can't officially investigate, right? And we're still trying to work out how we can get him invited to play. That's where you come in." Marty refilled my glass.

"What do you mean?" I forked up a large bite of Marty's casserole. Corn and cheese hardly described it — it had lots of butter and a dash of jalapeno pepper as well, and it was delicious.

James finally inserted himself into the conversation. "You know how the Society works, and who does what and goes where. And if you don't know, you can ask without raising any suspicions. We've got a delicate situation here. Most likely with Alfred's death, whoever is responsible for the thefts will go to ground, which will make it that much harder to ferret him or her out. But you can keep pressing for an inquiry into the thefts, quite innocently, and if you do it right, somebody up the food chain is going to have to ask my office to look into it. Maybe with a little nudge from Marty."

"Uh-huh." I picked up more food, chewed, swallowed. I was in no way prepared to play undercover agent. But Alfred certainly hadn't deserved to die, and even more frightening was the thought that if he had died because somebody was pilfering important historic artifacts, and trashing the Society's good name in the process, then that person might not stop at one murder. It seemed as though I really didn't have a choice, and I *was* already involved. I looked up to see both Marty and James staring at me. "I take it you're assuming the two events are connected?"

"Aren't you?" James countered.

I nodded reluctantly. "So what do we do next?"

CHAPTER 14

For the next few days it was business as usual — except I had the gnawing feeling that something awful was going to happen. It was like having a weird binocular vision: on the one hand (or did I mean eye?), everything seemed just as it always had, with people doing their jobs, visitors coming and going, meetings, minor crises; while out of the other eye, there were faceless people skulking around the corners, grabbing things and stuffing them into their pockets or down their shirts, and sneaking out the door — and nobody seemed to notice. And even though the puddle of blood had long since been scrubbed from the floor, I kept seeing it there.

It was unsettling. I had trouble believing any of our staff could be a thief — I wouldn't even let myself think of anyone as a killer — but I'd noticed them eyeing each other oddly, and there was a lot of whispering going on in corners. The atmosphere of mistrust was contagious and could do a lot of damage, and I wanted to nip it fast. But how? I didn't have any ideas.

There was no further word from Marty. There seemed to be nothing else I could do except worry, so I did that. I do it well.

I was heartily glad to see Friday roll around. I had no plans for the weekend, other than to be somewhere other than at the Society. Maybe a couple of days off would clear my head, give me perspective. Maybe. I ran through my list of household tasks and decided that I'd use this weekend to paint the walls and trim in my tiny second bedroom. I could put a CD on my little boom box and crank up the sound as loud as I wanted, paint the endless nooks and crannies of the Victorian moldings, and not think about the problems at work.

Saturday morning I was up early to buy paint, a creamy ivory that would be warmer and more cheerful than plain white. It was barely ten in the morning when I came back, swinging my heavy gallon of paint, to find Rich sitting on my doorstep. He bounced up when he saw me coming.

"Hi, Rich," I greeted him, trying to remember where he lived. "What brings you out here?"

"Hi, Nell. I wanted to talk to you, and I didn't want to do it at the Society. Do you mind? I'm sorry I just dropped in, but I couldn't make up my mind if this was a good idea or not. So I just came."

By now I was thoroughly mystified. "No problem." I unlocked my door and ushered him in. "You want some coffee or something?"

"Yeah, sure, coffee'd be great. Hey, I like your place."

I looked around at my comfortable clutter. "Thanks. Make yourself comfortable."

As I boiled water and ground coffee beans, I tried to figure out what Rich might need to talk about without being overheard. Maybe he was going to confess to taking Marty's documents? Or maybe he had found them? I could only hope. "You want sugar or milk?" I called out.

"No, black's fine."

I carried two filled mugs out to the living room and handed him one. I sat down in one of my armchairs and tried to look sympathetic and approachable. "What did you want to talk about, Rich?"

"It's about the Terwilliger Collection. Or, well, it's kinda more about the job, I guess." He took a deep breath. "Look, I really like working at the Society and handling all this

184

really great stuff. The Terwilliger Collection — it's like a peephole into Philadelphia history — heck, even American history. So you've got to believe that I wouldn't do anything to jeopardize this job — it's important to me."

"Okay," I said, wondering where he was headed with this.

"The thing of it is" — he swallowed — "when I was in high school, I was arrested once. It was really stupid — I took something dumb on a dare, and I got caught. Luckily I lived in a small town and the cops all knew my family, so I got off with community service, and when I turned eighteen the record was expunged or whatever they call it. So when I was applying for this job, I figured I didn't need to mention anything about a record, you know?"

"I wouldn't worry about that," I said, still mystified. "Why do you think it's important now?"

He stood up and began pacing around the room; with his long legs it didn't take him long to make the circuit. "Look, if the stuff from the collection really is gone, I didn't want anybody to look at me for it. I mean, sure, I know that a Washington letter would be worth good money, and anybody would think I could use the money, what with student loans and stuff. But I wouldn't do that, honest. And I wanted to tell you first, in case somebody said something. Do you believe me?"

In fact, I did. "Rich, I appreciate your telling me, and I don't think you had anything to do with this. I won't let anyone point a finger at you, if that's what you're worried about."

Apparently it was, because all of his joints suddenly seemed looser. "Thanks a lot, Nell. Look, if there's anything I can do to help find the missing stuff, just say the word. I've been looking everywhere I can think of, but so far there's nothing. Really weird, you know?"

Tell me about it. "Oh, I know. And thanks for coming all the way out here. I can understand why you wouldn't want to talk at work. Are you okay for getting home?"

"Oh, sure. Actually I'm doing a ten-mile bike ride today, so I thought I'd ride out this way. I'll get out of your hair now. See you Monday!"

"Right." I showed him out, marveling at the energy of youth. Ten miles on a bike? For fun?

After he'd left I changed into my grubby painter's pants and a stained T-shirt. I slapped a throwaway painter's hat over my hair (I have been known to add creative streaks, inadvertently, when painting), gathered my brushes, threw down my drop cloths, stirred, and dug in, with a CD blaring.

I had just finished two out of four walls when I thought I heard something, and turned down the music. Yes, it was my doorbell. I wasn't expecting any deliveries, and didn't have neighbors of the type who dropped in for a cup of sugar, so I had no idea who it could be. Two unexpected visitors in one day? I put down my brush, wiped the worst of the paint off my hands, and went to the front door.

It was Charles.

Now, this was a real shock. Charles had never been to my place in the more than two years that we had been seeing each other. Likewise, Charles never did anything unannounced — he wasn't a very spontaneous person. I took one despairing look at myself — paint-stained, baggy clothes, no makeup, unwashed hair — sighed, and opened the door.

"Charles," I said brightly, "what a delightful surprise! What brings you out to the wilderness?"

For a brief moment I swear he recoiled at my appearance, but he recovered quickly.

"Nell, my dear, may I come in?"

"Of course." I stood back, careful not to let him brush against my paint-covered clothes. I would've hated to sully the magnificent tweed jacket he had chosen for this expedition to foreign territory. He stepped into my tiny vestibule, then into the main room, which I laughingly called the parlor.

"What a charming place this is." His eyes swept the room, which was filled with my yard-sale finds, lovingly refinished and reupholstered, and my eclectic collections of prints and objets trouvés hanging on the walls. I hoped that he was ignoring the dust bunnies in the corners and the stacks of books and magazines that I never seemed to finish reading or put away.

"Thank you. I like it." I trailed after him as he wandered into the room, through the archway that set off the eating area (well, it did have a table and chairs), into the tiny kitchen. He did seem positively intrigued. Finally, I couldn't wait any longer.

"Charles, it's lovely to see you, but what are you doing here?"

He turned to look at me, then said, with touching concern in his voice, "I thought you might enjoy a diversion, after this past week. A friend of mine offered to lend me his car — it's a Jaguar — and it would be

188

wasted in the city. A car like that really needs an open road. So I thought of you, way out here, and took the chance that you'd be home, and free. Shall we go explore the winding lanes?"

How sweet. I beamed at him. "That sounds wonderful — if you'll give me time to clean up a bit?"

"Of course. I thought we could go investigate Chester County. I've heard there are some interesting antique places out that way. And perhaps we could finish up at a restaurant? I'm told the Dilworthtown Inn has an excellent cellar."

I, too, had heard of the Dilworthtown Inn, but my budget did not extend to trying it. Rustic it might be, but sloppy? I doubted it. I had better plan on changing into something a cut above blue jeans. "That sounds wonderful. Oh, and do you know the Brandywine Museum?"

He shook his head. "I've met the director, but I've never had the pleasure."

"Maybe we could start with lunch there — it has a wonderful view of the river."

"Isn't that largely a collection of Wyeths?" I could almost see a faint curl to his lip. Snob.

"Yes, Andrew Wyeth lived nearby. It's a

lovely place, and I enjoy the paintings." *So there.*

"Well, then, go perform your ablutions, and I will amuse myself until you're ready." He prowled around the room, picking up a book here and there, then settled himself in front of the window in a wing chair that had been my grandmother's. I took one last despairing glance around the mess that I called home and fled for the bathroom.

Half an hour later, scrubbed free of paint, powdered and primped, clad in my best country-casual outfit (which looked suspiciously like all my usual workweek outfits), we set off in Charles's borrowed Jaguar. I was navigator, and since I knew he was itching to get off the Lancaster Pike, which was filled with slow SUVs running Saturday errands, I pointed him toward the back roads and scenic byways. The car was a joy, purring along the rolling lanes, and I sat back in the leather upholstery and reveled in the engine's effortless power. The weather was perfect — the trees were already losing their leaves, but the cool autumn sun bathed the monochrome landscape with clean white light. It was, in fact, very much like being inside an Andrew Wyeth painting, and I stuck to my guns and insisted that we stop at the Brandywine Museum, which was one of my favorite small museums anywhere. After a sandwich there, watching the river roll by, we wandered for miles, stopping at antique stores when we felt like it. Charles picked up a few bits and pieces that caught his fancy, but mostly we enjoyed the process of looking, making snide comments about overpriced dreck, and occasionally haggling with a proprietor.

We finished up with an early supper at the Dilworthtown Inn, which lived up to its reputation. It managed to combine the best of colonial and modern: the small dining rooms, many with working fireplaces, were warm and intimate, and the wine cellar was impressive, even by Charles's estimation. I let him order, and sat and watched him play alpha male. He looked distinguished, even dashing, in the flickering light of the candles and the fire, and I managed to rise to the occasion, bantering with unaccustomed wit and charm.

The food was lovely, the wine rich and velvety, gleaming like old garnets in the glass. But even the best of nights must end. We departed the restaurant as the first wave of regular Saturday night diners began to appear and drove back to Bryn Mawr in companionable silence.

Charles pulled up to my carriage house

with a flourish. I looked over at him. "Do you want to come in?" I said, shoving aside thoughts of my unmade bed and the mess I'd left in the bathroom and the half-painted room.

"I think not. I should get back to the city and put this lady to bed." He patted the steering wheel affectionately. I sighed inwardly with a poignant mixture of regret and relief.

"Well, then, I'll see you Monday. And Charles? Thank you so much for today. You were right: I needed it, and it was lovely."

He leaned over to kiss me, a warm and lingering kiss. Then he sat back in the driver's seat as I opened the door. When I reached the path to my door, he pulled away with a brief backward wave of his hand, the motor nearly silent. I watched him go, then reluctantly turned back to my house with its unfinished paint and the usual mess. I felt a bit like Cinderella after the ball. *Back to the real world, Nell.*

CHAPTER 15

Monday I was still thinking back wistfully on Charles's unheralded appearance at my door. It seemed to me as though some undefined boundary had been crossed. Before now, our relationship had taken place exclusively on his home turf in the city. I could understand his need for room to let the lovely Jaguar prowl, but I wondered which had come first: borrowing the Jaguar or wanting to comfort me? I had no intention of reading too much into it, though. Besides, I had plenty to keep me busy.

After a week's worth of waffling, agonizing, and tweaking, we were finally ready to send a discreet and mournful letter to the entire membership regarding the unfortunate demise of a treasured employee, Registrar Alfred Findley. Of course, they'd likely have read about it in the newspapers already, but we needed to make a public statement of our own. Our spin was that there was no spin: Alfred had died. Period. No mention of the fact that he had bled all over the floor of our own stacks. We would just say that he had been a longtime employee and he would be missed. But that still meant printing out a couple of thousand letters and matching envelopes, and stuffing and sealing and stamping and mailing. And that would require the efforts of myself, underlings, and anyone else we could snag. As I said, I was busy.

In addition, there was the upcoming board meeting to worry about. The Pennsylvania Antiquarian Society's board of directors met four times a year, to manage the affairs of the institution. I doubt that it's a coincidence that *board* sounds like *bored,* which is what the participants usually are. But in case you've never been privy to this style of management, let me tell you that getting ready for a board meeting throws the entire staff into a tizzy. Board members are supposed to receive packets filled with useful and relevant information — attendance figures, acquisitions, state of the budget, and so on — a week or two before the event. That rarely happens — usually they get delivered a day or two before the actual meeting. Board members are supposed to have read and digested the two or three inches of information they receive in advance of the meeting — and that happens even more rarely. Of course there are some conscientious souls who do plow through the documents, making notes, and then come to the meeting and ask serious probing questions — while their peers all look blank, shuffle through the pages, and check their watches frequently.

Don't get me wrong. The board members are good people in most cases. The majority of them know history and collecting, as well as the ins and outs of the Society. A few others are chosen because of their public stature (political figures, academic leaders), and a few more are picked because they have money. No surprise there. Many of them have been on the board in some capacity for years, or in some cases decades. When their allotted term in one position (per the bylaws) is over, they shift to another one. As you might guess, a lot of these people know each other, both within and outside the Society. It's pretty typical of small nonprofits, and we seem to muddle along well enough, just as we have for over a century. Nominally there are twenty-seven members, with an average age north of sixty, although we do try to bring in some younger folk; more men than women; and very few minorities, although we'd been recruiting hard in that area. So when you sit down in a board meeting, you generally see a sea of grey flannel and grey hair.

The meetings usually followed a stately progression, more or less set in stone. There were munchies and even alcoholic beverages to grease the slides a bit, and then a welcome, a summary, and individual departmental reports. Faithful Doris took notes, with a tape recorder as backup for her impeccable shorthand, not that she'd ever needed it. The meetings went on for a couple of hours, and then the members scattered to the winds for the next three months. The only major exception was the annual meeting, open to all of our members (although very few ever come, even with the lure of free food), as required by our bylaws.

This time I was a bit on edge, even though I'd made sure that the notices and the information packets went out in a timely fashion for Thursday's board meeting. But there was no mention of Alfred's death in the meeting agenda, and I knew there would have to be some talk about that. And then there was the whole collections issue. It was a touchy subject, so I hadn't committed anything to writing, apart from Charles's suggestion to include *Security* on the agenda. At least I knew I had good news to report from the gala: our fundraising was marching along at an encouraging rate, and our membership was inching steadily up. Or at least it had been, before Alfred's death.

Since it was Monday, the building was locked tight, with only staff members around. Most of the lower floor was half dark, despite the tall windows overlooking the street. Actually I relished the quiet time: my staff and I could stuff all the member letters without interruption. The first inkling that something was amiss came when Carrie Drexel slipped into the room where we had spread out our stacks of letters and envelopes on a big table, and closed the door behind her. She looked positively giddy.

"You'll never guess who's downstairs."

"I have no clue. The mayor? The head of the Philadelphia Museum? Brad Pitt?"

Carrie sat down and pulled a stack of letters toward her. "Not even close. It was an FBI agent!"

I felt a distinct chill in the pit of my stomach. "How do you know it was an FBI agent?"

"Because Doris was hovering around the

lobby waiting for him, and he identified himself when he came in. Besides, he looks exactly like every FBI agent you've ever seen on television. I think they have a dress code. You know, wool topcoat, dark suit, shiny shoes, hair short but not too much — the whole package."

"What, no shades?" I was thinking furiously. Was it James Morrison, Marty's cousin? If Doris had been expecting an agent, he must be here to see Charles. Had Marty already blown the whistle and sent James into the fray? After all, her deadline for action had already passed. "Well, that's interesting. Maybe he's a history buff. Anyway, I'd like to get these lovely items" — I gestured at the stacks piled around the table — "into the mail by the end of the day, so let's dig in and get them done."

"But aren't you curious?" Carrie pressed. "Why would His Lordship be talking to an FBI agent?"

"I have no idea," I lied. "But I'm sure he'll tell us if he thinks we need to know."

With all hands at work, the letters were done quickly. Leaving Carrie to run them through the postage meter and bundle them for the mail pickup, I made my way back to my office and tried to make sense of what was going on. A knock on my door frame interrupted me. As I had so astutely guessed, it was none other than Cousin Jimmy, in his special-agent role.

"Ms. Pratt?"

I nodded. Was he being formal in case anyone was listening? Did he not want anyone to know that we had met before?

"I'm James Morrison, special agent for the FBI, Philadelphia office." He flashed some sort of credential, too quickly for me to see. "I've just spoken with your president, and I'd like to have a word with you, if it's convenient."

"Of course. Please, come in, sit down. Would you like some coffee or something else?" I could act the perfect hostess.

"No, thanks. I just wanted to ask you a few questions." He came into my office, which immediately felt much smaller. I nodded toward the door and raised my eyebrows, asking if he wanted to close it; his curt shake of the head indicated no. So this was to be a public conversation, one that could be overheard by all and sundry. I'd be willing to bet that Carrie was hovering just around the corner.

At Marty's house James Morrison had been wearing jeans, and at the gala, a sport jacket. But Carrie had been right: here in an official capacity, in his serious suit, he now looked like an Agent, with a capital A.

I realized he was studying me, too. He'd probably noticed that I had a run in my panty hose, and that there was a button missing on the cuff of my shirt. I thanked the stars that I had nothing worse than that to hide.

"I assume your mother read A. A. Milne? Are you 'commonly known as Jim'?" A little light banter to defuse the situation. All right — I was nervous. This was official; this was serious.

"James, James, Morrison, Morrison? Most people think of The Doors."

"Not my speed, I'm afraid. Now, what can I do for you?"

He sat down in my guest chair and took his time about answering as his eyes prowled around my office. "I'm here to investigate a possible theft of historic items from the Pennsylvania Antiquarian Society. Are you aware of any problems in this area?"

I stuck to the simple truth. "Yes. A board member — someone I know fairly well, who's done a lot of research here — came to me on the morning of our annual gala to tell me that she thought some pieces were missing from her family collection."

Mr. Agent Man had pulled out a small

pad and pencil, and was checking his existing notes. "That would be the event held a week ago Thursday?"

"Yes, that's correct. That same day, I spoke with the registrar to see if he knew where the missing items could be. You must know that the registrar was Alfred Findley, who sadly was found dead the morning after the gala."

"I was informed of that," he said.

We both paused for a moment, and then I went on. "I also spoke to our head librarian and to the employee who is currently cataloging that collection. When neither of them could shed any light on the whereabouts of the missing items, I felt compelled to communicate the problem to the vice president for collections and to our president. They said that they would look into it."

"I see." James checked his notes. "Did you speak with anyone else about this?"

"No. I felt that any official action should be taken by someone higher up the ranks than I am, and the president agreed with me. I'm not directly responsible for the collections. I merely reported what I had been told."

"Why would this board member come to you rather than go straight to the top?"

"We had worked together on some

projects, so she knew me. Maybe she didn't want to make a fuss and thought it could be handled at a lower level. Or maybe I was just the first person she came to. I really can't tell you." No one could say that I had had any sort of special relationship with Marty before all this came up.

"Your title is director of development. Is that correct?"

I nodded.

"What exactly does that mean?"

"I am responsible for raising funds to support the activities of the Society, through grants — government, foundation, corporate — and individual contributions. I also supervise the membership coordinator and the database manager. And I manage the public events, such as the gala. We hold a couple of major events each year, and a number of minor ones."

"And you have been here how long?"

"Just about five years."

"Who do you report to?"

"The president — oh, and the board, at least indirectly. If you look at our organizational chart, I'm below our vice presidents, but I *am* a department manager." This whole thing felt weirder and weirder. I was playing a role in a play, pretending this was the first time I had said anything about this, much less met Agent Morrison. If I were really clueless, what would my next line be? "Am I allowed to ask any questions here?"

James looked at me directly. "You can ask. I'll answer if I can." He didn't smile.

"Do you have reason to believe that there actually *are* things missing? That it's not just our own confused filing system?"

He stared out the window behind me, mulling over my questions. At least, I hoped he was mulling them over. For all I could tell, he was doing the times tables or trying to remember if he'd picked up his dry cleaning — his face certainly didn't reveal anything. Finally he spoke.

"I'd have to be more familiar with your internal workings to make a judgment about that. At this time, I am responding to a formal complaint from an interested party who appears to be credible."

"What happens now?"

"I'll speak with the staff, check for any criminal records among them, and review your collections management procedures. If I identify any items that are not where they should be, I would investigate beyond the confines of this institution."

"You, or a whole herd of agents?" The idea of expanding the search made me nervous. I wondered whether I should say something about Rich's disclosure to me about his past, or Marty's disclosure about Alfred's record, but I decided not to stir anything up. If he was a good agent, he'd already know about both, or would find out soon enough.

"Just me, for now. If I think I need help, I can call in others."

An awful thought struck me. "Is this public information? I mean, do you have to announce that we are under investigation?"

He looked at me curiously. "Why?"

"Because it would make my job a whole lot harder. I'm supposed to be raising money, remember? People have to believe that we're doing our jobs preserving their history — not letting it walk out under our noses or misplacing it." I restrained myself from saying *losing it.*

"I'll try to keep that in mind," he said. "Actually, until we determine that a theft has occurred, it isn't actually news. We'll just have to see."

I gave him a weak smile. "I guess that will have to do, right? Anything else you need from me?"

He stood up. "Thank you, Ms. Pratt. You've been most helpful. Your president suggested that you could provide me with a staff list and perhaps a brief sketch of individual responsibilities — who has access to what, for instance."

"Our VP of collections, Latoya Anderson, would have a better handle on that end of things."

Imperturbably he said, "Mr. Worthington thought you might have a better overview of the institution as a whole, and what roles various staff members play."

I wasn't sure if that was a compliment, but it was true. Since I wrote grants for all and any purposes, from building repairs to scanning equipment to staff salaries, I talked to almost everyone in the building on a regular basis, and I prowled the halls and the stacks. Far more than Charles ever did — he seldom ventured from his elegant office to mingle with the hoi polloi.

"Certainly. Will you be around for a bit longer? I can call up a staff list and add the sort of detail you might find useful. And do you need a tour of the building?"

"I would appreciate that. Why don't you take care of that while I speak with the collections person?"

"Of course," I said graciously. "I'll have it ready when you finish with Latoya."

He made a silent exit, and from the hurried scuffling outside my door I wondered just how many people had been listening to our conversation. But I had to assume that was Agent James's intent — and that word of the investigation would spread throughout the building with lightning speed.

CHAPTER 16

As soon as James left I swiveled in my chair and stared at the computer screen. All right, first things first. I decided I needed to talk with Charles, so I stood up and marched purposefully to the president's office. Doris was, as usual, standing, or rather sitting, guard.

"Is he in?" I said breezily, without breaking stride.

"No," Doris replied with a small smirk. "He said he had a meeting to go to, and he won't be back in the office today."

Interesting. In his place, the first thing I would have done after an impromptu visit from an FBI agent would be to call an all-hands staff meeting and give them a clue as to what was going on, and ask them to co-operate fully. There was nothing worse than a lot of half truths and rumors floating around a small institution like ours, and it didn't take much to poison the atmosphere.

I wondered why Charles seemed to have beaten a hasty retreat instead.

"If he calls, will you tell him I need to speak to him?"

"Of course. I always give him his messages." Doris turned away from me and resumed whatever it was she was typing. End of conversation, apparently.

"Thank you, Doris — I know you do." I made my exit.

I went back to my office and put together a staff list as requested, cutting and pasting until each person had a paragraph or so describing his or her responsibilities, then added a copy of the organizational chart — who reported to whom, oversaw whom. I was just squaring up the stack when James reappeared in my doorway.

"Perfect timing!" I greeted him. "Here's the material you wanted. Is there anyone else you were planning to talk to?"

"Not at this time. Let's walk through the place. You can give me a sense of the layout."

I stood up. "Fine. We can start at the top — we keep collections not accessible to the public on the third and fourth floors . . ." I kept up a running discussion as we walked to the elevator, got in, and I inserted my key in the fourth-floor slot. We stepped out on the top story. There were no lights on, but James laid a hand on my arm, and we stood still for a couple of seconds as he listened. No sounds of anyone moving around, either. It looked as though we were alone.

"Let's start at one end and work our way back, and you can tell me what's kept where," he said.

"I'll do what I can. As I've said, I'm not a collections person, so I have only a very general idea of how the collections are distributed. Let's start in the back corner, over there." I led him to the farthest point on the floor, a dim, dusty corner whose metal shelves were piled with large leather-bound ledger books from long-defunct companies. Then I lowered my voice. "Okay, do you really want the fifty-cent tour, or is there something else you want to talk about? Like why you're here?"

He leaned back against the wall and broke a smile for the first time. "A little of each. I do want to scope the place out, get some idea of security and who has access to what. But I wanted to talk to you, too. You did well with that little charade downstairs — good reactions. Think everyone heard?"

"Thanks, and probably yes. I assumed that was your intention, when you left the door open. It's a small place, and I'm sure those who weren't eavesdropping in the hall will hear soon enough. So Marty got tired of waiting?"

"She told me she set a deadline and she's sticking to it. By the way, your security sucks."

I sighed. "I know. But there's only so much money, and it doesn't go very far. So we all pretend we don't have a problem. But we do, don't we?"

"Oh, yes." He pulled out a sheaf of papers and waved it at me. "Alfred's list."

I nodded. "I bet he was surprised when he finally printed it out — when I first talked to him about it, I don't think he anticipated the length of the list, or the nature of the items, as a whole. That's probably why he sent a copy to Marty, too, in the first place."

"He hadn't communicated his concerns to anyone else? Before you, that is?"

I shook my head. "Not that I know of, beyond his regular monthly reports to Latoya. Alfred was a very thorough person, and I'm sure he wanted to be certain that the items had not merely been shifted. And he was probably afraid he'd be blamed." I wasn't sure if Marty had told James about Alfred's kleptomania — but if he was a cousin, he probably knew already. "I can't say when he would have pressed for action on his own, until Marty complained and I came to him and asked him directly." Did that mean that somehow Marty and I had pushed someone into killing him? I didn't like that thought.

"Hmm. How would you characterize the items on this list?"

"Remember that this is not my area of expertise. There's a little bit of everything here. *MSS* refers to manuscripts. Ephemera are things like advertising flyers, things that were originally made to be discarded. Some of these notations refer to condition or location. But I think you can see what kind of a mess the recording system has been. Alfred had made great strides in imposing order, but there's still a long way to go."

James said carefully, "This list goes on for pages, and even I recognize some of the names attached to items here. You're aware of the cumulative dollar value of the missing items?"

"I did a little research when I first saw the list, but I'm not really sure. We don't usually think in terms of market value for the collections we own. They're irreplaceable, for one thing, because many items are unique."

"Well, I had some of my people look at

the list yesterday. They said more or less the same thing you did, but for the purposes of our files, they suggested a total of roughly five million dollars."

So I'd been right, which didn't make me happy. Hearing it from an FBI agent made it seem all the more real — and shocking. I still had trouble getting my mind around the concept. Somebody had walked off with several million dollars' worth of items from our collections? How could that have happened?

James stared over my head at the piles of musty volumes. "Let me review the time line here. Marty came to you on the seventh. You spoke to Alfred that same day, and he set about preparing a list of items he believed to be missing. He left that list on your desk that night, but you didn't find it until the next day. By then, he was dead. He'd also mailed a copy to Marty. Is that accurate?"

I nodded.

"All right. What took place next?"

"Alfred died, which was something of a distraction, to put it mildly. And then I went to Latoya and described what he had told me, and then I told Charles. He said he and Latoya would handle it. That was Monday. He and Marty met on Tuesday."

"Do you have any idea why he did not report this possible theft of significant proportions to the managing board of this institution?"

"I imagine that he wanted to make sure of his facts first."

"I find it hard to believe that an institution that is based on collections has such a shaky grasp of exactly where its collections are."

"I hate to say it, but it's not unusual. I mean, think about it — we've been acquiring or inheriting things for over a century. The Society has gone through a lot of changes — the original building we occupied was replaced around 1900, and then there were additions after that, and improvements. It's an ongoing process. We've been trying to put the records for some of the easier materials online, so that both we and the public will have better access to them, but at the rate we're going, it'll be about thirty years before we're finished. And of course by then the technology will have changed again, and whatever we're doing right now will no doubt be obsolete."

"That's what Marty told me." He still didn't look convinced.

"I know it seems hard to believe that we could be so careless, but from what I've heard, it's to be expected. Look, we've got literally millions of items in our collections, and we're talking about a tiny percentage that aren't where they should be. Let me ask you: if you had to find a single piece of paper in your house, one that you hadn't looked at for, oh, five years, how easy would it be for you? Then multiply it by a factor of a million, and maybe you'll see our problem."

He smiled reluctantly. "Point taken. You know quite a bit about this."

"I know the general outlines. I told you — I write grant proposals to fund this sort of thing. And I know what the competition is like among our peer institutions. There are a lot of us in the same boat."

"You're not making my job any easier. All right, let's look at this from a different side. How do people get access to the collections?"

"Apart from staff, you mean? Well, we have members who pay for a varying number of on-site visits. But they don't get to use the stacks — they have to request the documents they need, and a staff member brings the material to them, in the reading room. The same goes for researchers, who pay by the day. And there is a paper trail for that; we know who has requested which items, so if they go missing, we know who to ask. That is, if they play by the rules — and we all know there are some people who don't. But there are also some board members like Marty who pretty much have free rein of the place and can go anywhere."

"Do you have much of a theft problem, day to day?" James seemed genuinely interested.

"To a small extent, but I don't think any of this comes anywhere near the scale we're talking about. That almost has to be an insider, doesn't it?" I stared at him bleakly.

He ignored my question. "Do you search people or their bags on the way out of the building?"

I shook my head. "We don't let them take their own bags into the collections areas, just pads and notes, and more recently laptops, but out of the case. We've talked about stepping up security at more than one board meeting."

James changed tack. "What's your staff turnover like?"

"This place has a good reputation, so a lot of people will work here for a year or two, to put it on their résumé or to help them get into grad school or library school. But they usually leave on good terms."

"You said earlier that you've been here,

what, five years?"

I nodded. "Yes, and that's pretty long for this place. There are only a few people who have been around for any length of time — like our librarian Felicity Soames. And Alfred."

"And your president has been here two years?"

I nodded again. "Going on three."

"And he brought in some people when he came?"

"Yes — he did some reorganizing, and he created a couple of positions, but nothing sweeping. He inherited a well-run place, and he didn't want to make changes just for the sake of putting his own stamp on it."

"No disgruntled employees who have been dismissed?"

"None that I can think of. Oh, we're not always one big happy family; there are people who complain, but that's normal for any workplace, isn't it?"

"Probably," he said noncommittally. He pulled himself away from the wall. "Well, why don't we finish our walk-through? What's the square footage on each floor?"

We talked of neutral things like shelving and HVAC and lighting, and I realized I knew far more about the building than I had thought. I was happy that he didn't seem critical, but listened with what appeared to be real interest. Or maybe that was just the official FBI manner, intended to elicit confidences. It didn't matter. I wasn't hiding anything.

I wondered if James noticed how empty the floor was. Of course, it was Monday, so there were no patrons downstairs demanding research materials, no staffers scuttling around with their shelving carts collecting them. The downside was that anyone could come up here and pocket whatever they wanted, without being observed — assuming they had access and knew where to look. As I had said: an insider.

I was startled by a scuffling, and then Rich emerged from behind a high tier of shelves, looking sheepish. "Hi, Nell." His eyes darted to James.

James stepped forward. "Special Agent James Morrison. And you are?"

Rich's eyes widened. "I'm, uh, Rich Girard. I work here."

"You're working on the Terwilliger Collection, right?"

I thought for a moment that Rich's knees were going to give out, and I couldn't say I blamed him for worrying. He glanced at me; I looked at James, who nodded. "It's okay, Rich. Agent Morrison is looking into the problem with the Terwilliger Collection, at Marty's request."

Rich looked relieved, which in turn made me feel relieved, even as I wondered just how much of our conversation he had overheard. "Hey, if I can help you at all, let me know," he said.

"I'll do that. Ms. Pratt, shall we go down to the next level?"

"Of course. Let's take the stairs."

We ended the behind-the-scenes tour on the third floor, where Alfred had died. My steps faltered, and James was quick to notice. "I'm sorry — this was where it happened?"

I nodded, fighting to control my voice. "Yes. He was lying against that door there. I couldn't open it from the other side."

James said nothing, merely looking at the space — the high ceiling, the tiers of shelves. It was peculiarly silent, and dust motes danced in the few shafts of light that penetrated the protective paint — and dirt — on the high windows. Finally he said, "Thank you. I think I've seen enough. We can reach your office through that door?"

"Yes, it opens onto the hallway." After another moment's hesitation, I moved forward and opened it, stepping over the spot where Alfred had lain. After James had followed me, the door swung slowly, heavily shut. We were back in the realm of lights and noise and people, and I sighed in relief and turned to him. "Is there anything else you want to see? The reading and catalog rooms?"

"Not at this point. I may be back. Thank you for your help and for the list of employees." He patted his jacket pocket.

"Then let me see you out. Security, you know." I laughed weakly at my own pathetic joke. Talk about shutting the barn door after the horse had escaped.

"Of course."

We didn't speak as we were going down in the elevator, through the dim catalog room, the brighter and shinier lobby. As he reached for the door I looked furtively around before saying, "I can't think of anyone here who acts like they've come up with an extra five million dollars over the past few years, or however long these thefts have been going on. I mean, we're a pretty low-key group — no fancy cars, no flashy vacations."

He considered that. "Maybe this person isn't doing it for the money or doesn't realize what the stuff is worth — he, or she, could be dumping it on the market for a fraction of its value. Or he could be a rabid collector, someone who just wants to have it, take it out, and look at it now and then."

"Do people do that?"

"Sometimes. Do you remember the Isabella Stewart Gardner job, up in Boston, twenty years ago? High-value artwork was taken, and it hasn't been seen since. Nobody could sell it openly, so you've got to figure that somewhere someone is enjoying a nice Rembrandt — very privately."

I digested that for a moment. "That doesn't make it any easier for you to find this person, does it? If the missing items are not going through traditional channels, or not being sold at all?"

"I'm not worried. We've just begun to investigate. Thanks for your insights — you've got a pretty good handle on the place." He hesitated a moment, then asked, "You like working here?"

I tried to answer honestly. "Yes, most of the time. There are a lot of good people here who work here because they love the job, not for the money or the glory. And the collections are extraordinary. I'll admit to visiting the stacks, just pulling out a letter from a president or a Civil War general or a Pennsylvania author, just to hold it. It's an eerie feeling, you know — making that direct connection to history." Then I was struck by a sudden thought. "But that doesn't mean I want to take it home and gloat over it — I want other people to be able to share that experience," I added defensively.

"Hmm. Well, I need to be going. Thanks for the help." As James held the door open, he paused. "Nell, be careful."

I looked up at him. "Why? Isn't it a little late? After all, the word is out — lots of people know. You know."

"That may be true, but don't say any more than you have to, to anyone. All right?"

"Fine. Let me know if you think of anything else you need."

"I will. And here's my card, in case *you* think of anything else that might be helpful."

I took the offered business card, and then he was gone. I closed the heavy door behind him and walked slowly back to the elevator, lost in thought. I was still reeling about the dollar figure that he had confirmed. That was serious money — and that meant serious motive. I shivered — what was going on beneath the slightly shabby surface of the Society?

Word of James's visit spread fast, and since a number of people had seen me with him, quite a few of them stopped by to find out what was going on. Carrie came first, plopping herself down in the chair in front of me. "So, dish. What did that yummy agent want with us?"

Yummy? "Marty Terwilliger asked him to look into the disappearance of some papers from the family collection."

Carrie's eyes widened. "You think they were stolen?"

"I don't know. I've asked the right people to look for them, and I'm hoping they turn up in the building somewhere." I didn't dare say more.

"Wow. Marty didn't have to panic, though. I mean, really — the FBI? Isn't that kind of over-the-top?"

"She cares a lot about her family's collection," I said.

"Yeah, I guess." Carrie stood up. "Is there going to be any formal announcement?"

"That's up to Charles."

"Got it. Thanks, Nell." Carrie went back toward her desk, and I wondered if she'd be able to keep this secret. Or if anybody could, for that matter.

Felicity was my next visitor, rapping on my door frame. "Do I gather Marty has, shall we say, turned up the heat?" she asked without preamble.

I sighed. "I'm afraid so. And right now I can't say any more. I'm sure Charles will make some sort of statement."

Felicity sniffed. "I do wish she had given us a little more time. Ah, well, too late now. Let me know if I can help you in any way."

"Thanks, Felicity. I appreciate it."

As the day dragged on, several more curious staffers stopped by, asking questions of varying directness, but I couldn't tell them much, and I was heartily glad when I could make my escape to the train station.

CHAPTER 17

After another restless night, I arrived Tuesday morning to see that Charles had taken official notice of FBI agents prowling in our midst: when I arrived there were signs posted at the entry doors and elevator announcing an all-hands staff meeting at nine o'clock sharp, before we opened the doors to the public at ten. I noted with amusement that Charles had avoided any use of the term "emergency."

I figured there wouldn't be time for a serious talk with Charles before the meeting, so I filed into the boardroom along with the rest of the staff. There was a low buzz among the crowd: a few people looked bewildered, but most looked worried. Charles was already in place at the head of the long table. He was, as always, impeccably groomed, and was wearing a sober dark suit designed to send the message that he was serious and responsible. He waited until most people had managed to find themselves seats — some had to go back out and drag in some extra chairs — and looked at the crowd. Finally he cleared his throat, marshaling everyone's attention.

"Thank you for joining me on such short notice," he began. "I'm sorry to disrupt your schedules, but there is a matter of utmost importance that I need to communicate to you before we open today. Yesterday I was visited by an agent from the Federal Bureau of Investigation, who told me that he had received a complaint about items missing from the Society's collections, and that the complainant suspected theft." He paused to let that sink in. There was a moment of stunned silence and then an explosive babble of voices.

Charles raised a hand, silencing them, then continued. "Of course I have implicit faith in the integrity of all of my staff members, but as you can imagine, any complaint of this nature must be investigated fully. The agent in charge of the case is James Morrison — some of you may have seen him in the building yesterday. I ask you to give him and his colleagues your fullest cooperation, so that we can get to the bottom of this charge and resume our normal operations. And I don't think I need to tell you not to speak of this with anyone outside the building — and that most certainly includes any members of the press. Adverse publicity would serve no useful purpose and could damage the reputation of the Society, which I'm sure no one of us wants. If you are approached by a member, a researcher, or an outsider with any questions about an investigation, please refer all inquiries directly to my office — Doris will see that they receive an appropriate response. But to the best of my knowledge, this has not been made public, and I sincerely hope that it will be resolved before we reach that state. Thank you all for coming."

With that, he stood and exited, ignoring the surge of questions. That left the rest of us seated around the table staring at each other.

"What the hell was that about?" asked one of the junior librarians.

I weighed my options. Several people already knew about the original problem, the missing Terwilliger documents. I could play dumb and do nothing, but that didn't feel right. I thought I owed my colleagues some small crumbs.

I cleared my throat. "As Charles said, a board member has claimed that some important documents have gone missing. We're hoping it's all just a mix-up in filing and we'll find the missing papers and be done with it. Our people are already working on it. We have nothing to hide."

"It's Marty Terwilliger and her precious family papers," Felicity Soames said. "Nice try at being discreet, Nell, but Marty's been making a stink for the past two weeks, and half the staff knows about it. But calling in the Feds? Isn't that a bit much?"

Latoya Anderson had been silent thus far but now said carefully, "Theft of historic documents is a federal offense and has been since 1994. The FBI *is* the appropriate agency to investigate."

That silenced everyone. Then one or two people looked at their watches, cursed, and headed quickly out the door: opening time loomed, and business as usual was the order of the day, at least until we were told otherwise. Latoya and I were among the last to leave.

"I have a bad feeling about this," Latoya said to me. "I can't think of *any* institution like ours whose practices look good under a spotlight, and we're going to have a lot to answer for. If only Marty had waited a bit, we would have had things in much better order." She didn't wait for a response, but turned and headed for her office. I watched her retreating back, wondering how many more pieces of the collections might have vanished if Marty hadn't said something and triggered my questions.

I still wanted to speak to Charles. I found him standing in front of Doris's desk, giving her instructions. She beamed up at him as usual, and I wondered how he could remain so oblivious to her adoration.

Charles saw me approaching. "Ah, Nell, just the person I need. Please, come in."

Doris glared at me as I followed Charles into his office. He folded himself gracefully into his leather-covered chair, his hand absently caressing the mahogany of his desk. I took a chair facing the desk.

"You certainly disappeared quickly yesterday," I began.

"Ah, yes — I had a previous engagement, and it seemed prudent to attend. I take it you met with Mr. Morrison?"

"Yes, he stopped by after he'd seen you, and I gave him a tour of the building. He seems competent. So Marty called in the FBI?"

Charles regarded me across the gleaming wooden surface. "When I spoke with Marty last week, I urged her to allow us to handle this in-house, at least as far as a preliminary review goes. Particularly in light of Alfred's recent death, which complicates our access to collections records. However, it is clear that she feels strongly about her family's papers, and that has made her a bit precipitous."

Yeah, sure, I thought. *She gave you a chance to act, and you blew it.* I wondered just how long Charles would have stalled if Marty hadn't acted.

Charles was still talking. "But I'm sure the matter will be resolved quickly in the capable hands of Agent Morrison." He straightened his Mont Blanc pen, the only item on his desk except for the phone. "In any event, I'm calling a senior managers' meeting for this afternoon so that we can review procedures and discuss how we want to handle this situation. I'll see you then — two o'clock?"

Apparently I was dismissed. "Of course."

When the senior staff met at two, nobody had any brilliant insights, and nobody confessed to the crime — or crimes. As I listened with one ear to Charles drone on in mellifluous tones, I wondered idly whether this was considered one crime, over a long period, or a whole series of separate crimes? Would the FBI file a report on each item? The paperwork must be daunting. Imagine trying to track down each item when there could be thousands of them. I tried to refocus on the meeting. Everyone was properly bewildered, shocked, hurt, confused, and so on. Charles repeated his earlier lecture on cooperating with the authorities and not speaking to anyone else about the disappearances. He also told Latoya to accelerate the cataloging process, although without Alfred I couldn't see what she could do right now. It would take time to advertise for his position and fill it, and to bring that person up to speed on the computer system. And would we have to disclose to that person just what a mess he or she would be stepping into?

I thanked the fundraising gods that there were no major grant proposals due before the new year, so I didn't have to craft any creative language to conceal the fact that we were getting robbed and we didn't even know how or by whom. I started fantasizing about writing proposals requesting support for a high-tech security system, using the documented disappearance of all those items as an argument that we really, really needed the system. Charles finally sent us on our way like a group of chastened school-children, and we went about our various chores in a semidaze. I felt frustrated, foolish, and stupid. How could we have been so blind, and for so long? And what was it going to mean for the Society?

I got home earlier than usual — I'd felt I could legitimately catch the early train, especially since I wasn't getting anything done at work — but it was still dark by this time of year. I'd forgotten to leave any lights on at home, so the house was dark, too. The world was conspiring to match my mood. *Get a grip, Nell,* I told myself. I hung up my coat, turned on lights in the living room and kitchen, and poured myself a glass of wine. I stood for a while in front of the open refrigerator, trying to find anything that looked like a potential meal. Inspiration did not strike, so I rummaged in my cabinet for a bag of dry tortellini and a jar of tomato sauce. I put a pot of water on to boil and went to my bedroom to change into something comfortable, a pair of old sweat pants and a matching sweatshirt. I took my wine along, and had seriously reduced the level in the glass by the time I was dressed.

When I came back downstairs the water was boiling, so I dumped in the pasta, then wandered aimlessly around my living room, picking up stray newspapers and magazines and tossing them into the trash. I was restless, and I had to admit I was upset. I loved my job, and I loved the Society. Yet someone had been rifling through its collections for his or her own nefarious ends, and thus threatening both my job and the institution. That made me mad.

I realized I was crumpling a week-old newspaper in my hands, and made a conscious effort to relax. Charles and Latoya were working within the Society to get to the bottom of this; Marty and James were working from their own end and had brought me in to bridge the gap. Things were under control — weren't they? I stared at my own little collection of treasured objects, arrayed on a shelf — things I had collected over the years from flea markets and antique stores, not for their value but because I liked them.

Then I took a harder look. Nestled among my tchotchkes was something I had never seen before, a charming silver snuffbox. I picked it up and looked at it: eighteenth century, I could tell from the hallmarks. Nice quality. And completely unfamiliar, unless I had already succumbed to early memory loss.

No, this was not mine. I thought for a moment, then began a systematic search of the rest of my house. After half an hour I had collected no fewer than six other items in various locations, all small and exquisite and no doubt valuable. And not mine.

I felt a queasy mixture of fear and anger. I carefully drained my pasta, heated the sauce in the microwave, tossed them together in a bowl, and sat down at my table to think, with the bibelots arrayed in front of me. They ranged from the silver snuffbox to a small printed pamphlet, its paper foxed, bearing a date of 1685, to a pocket-size leather-bound book whose contents were less interesting than the inscription inside — it apparently had been a gift from Benjamin Franklin to a friend.

Somebody had planted these pretty things in my house, I was sure. But who? And why?

Who had had opportunity to bring these items into my home? I had few visitors — except for Rich and Charles the past weekend. When Rich had arrived, I had gone to the kitchen to make him coffee; when Charles had shown up later, I had spent some time in the shower, scrubbing off paint so I wouldn't sully his borrowed Jaguar — which would have left either of them with enough time to plant the pretty antique trinkets I had found scattered through my house. All the suspicious items were small enough to have been concealed easily, and either one could have carried them into the house, just the way so many people tried to sneak stuff out of the Society reading room.

Were these extremely valuable items? I'd guess no. Could they be traced to the Society's collections? Maybe, maybe not — but if somebody wanted to identify me as light-fingered, they'd have to be able to prove it, so the odds were good that these items would show up in the online catalog, with definitive descriptions.

So someone was setting me up. Rich or Charles? Or someone else entirely? My security was laughable, but I didn't have much that anyone would want to steal. Who on earth buys locks to keep people from *leaving* stolen goods in their house?

But why would anyone plant stolen items here? Did anyone really think that trying to pin the Society thefts on me would work? One look at my bank account would make the idea laughable. No way was I pawning trinkets, valuable or otherwise.

I needed help to make sense of this. With surprising calm I went to my purse and fished out the card that Agent James had given me, which included a cell phone number. I punched it in, and he answered on the third ring. "Morrison," he said curtly.

I almost hung up then, but he'd already seen my caller ID. "Agent Morrison. James. I think I have a bit of a problem. Is there any way you could come over to my place?"

"This is related to the thefts at the Society?"

"I think so."

"We can't do it at your office in the morning?"

"No. There's something you need to see here."

"All right. Address?"

I gave him the necessary information and hung up. I supposed that I should be flattered: I call an FBI agent after hours and he takes me at my word that what I have to say is important. Now I didn't know whether to hope it actually was or not.

He arrived fifteen minutes later, which left me wondering just where he lived. He rang the doorbell and I let him in. "Thank you for coming. Would you like coffee?"

"Whatever. What is it you wanted to show me?"

I guessed that coffee was out of the question. He was a very direct man. "Okay, as you see, I'm not the world's greatest housekeeper, and I don't always look too hard at this place. But tonight I noticed something, some items scattered here and there that don't belong to me."

"What kind of items?" I had his interest now.

"Nice, small antique items. Items that would fit neatly in a pocket. Items that might have come from the Society's collections."

"Show me."

I pointed at the collection assembled on my table, noting where I had discovered the items. Or at least the ones I knew about. For all I knew, if I dug any further I might find lots more.

James gave them a cursory look, then said, "Maybe we should have that coffee now." He watched me with unnerving silence as I brewed coffee and poured two mugs.

"How do you take it?"

"Black."

It figured. I handed him one mug, added sugar to mine, then nodded toward the living room. He turned and sat down at my dining table, and I joined him. Without preamble I said, "I had two visitors last weekend: Rich Girard and Charles Worthington. It's the first time either one has been here."

James nodded, once. "I thought it might be something like that."

"Then you'd better tell me why."

He sipped from his mug as though he had all the time in the world. "Good coffee." He took another sip. "I think someone's trying to set you up, and that someone is going to drop a little hint suggesting that we should take a closer look at you. And you know, if we hadn't had our little chat at Marty's, I think that could have been a real problem for you."

I laughed incredulously. "Has somebody also deposited a million dollars into my bank account? Just to make me look really guilty?"

He shook his head. "No. Sorry."

"You mean you already checked? Then maybe I used my ill-gotten gains to buy a lot of gold and buried it in the backyard. Want a shovel?" I was really steaming now.

"Nell, calm down. I don't believe you had anything to do with the thefts. We've been checking everybody's records as a matter of routine." He paused as if searching for words. "If, say, your employer, whose record is spotless, suggested that you might have a motive for taking valuable and easily sold items from the collections, we would have to take that seriously. You certainly have had opportunity, and, surprise, we would have turned up suspicious items in your possession."

I was stunned. Charles? If he was trying to set me up, that meant that *he* was the one stealing things from the Society . . . which was ridiculous. He was the leader of a prestigious institution; he made a healthy salary; he had come with glowing recommendations from his prior places of employ. Why would he do it?

"Can you tell me about your relationship with Charles Worthington?" James asked.

Oh, hell. No way was it going to look good if I said I'd been sleeping with my boss. But covering it up wouldn't look good, either — somebody was bound to know something, or guess. Doris had. Even Marty had hinted at it. "We've been, uh, involved in a personal relationship since shortly after he arrived in town."

James nodded once, and I guessed that he had already known or figured that out. "Thank you for being honest. I had reason to believe that, but you've saved us both a lot of time."

"Thanks, I guess." I wondered if Marty had tipped him off. "Look, he was new in town, I offered to help him learn the ins and outs of the Philadelphia community, and things just sort of went from there. Apparently we aren't as close as I thought we were, though, if he's the one who planted the items. But why implicate me, and why now?"

"Because you know about the thefts, and he knows you weren't going to let it go easily. That's probably a compliment."

How nice of Charles to recognize that I had some moral fiber. "But if it was Charles, what did he hope to gain?"

James sat back in his chair and swallowed some coffee. "Let's look at this hypothetically. The thefts have been discovered and acknowledged in-house, but it's hard to pinpoint what has disappeared and when it happened. You've been there a few years, you've had plenty of opportunity, and your salary's not terrific. That makes you a good scapegoat. Absent any real proof, it's unlikely that there would have been any charges made — the Society has its reputation to consider, and they wouldn't want the publicity. But you would probably have been fired, security would have been beefed up, and the thefts would have stopped."

I could see his point. "But then Marty got pushy, so we had to go public, or semipublic, anyway, which meant Charles had to move quickly. So he tried to set me up to take the fall by planting this stuff. Is that what you're saying?"

"That's what I'm guessing."

239

"What about Rich?"

"As a suspect? Not a likely candidate — he hasn't been there long enough. Although someone could have pressured him into doing their dirty work, at least where the Terwilliger Collection is involved. He has a juvenile record for theft."

"I know — he told me when he was here." Did that make Rich honest, or was he just being devious and trying to throw me off? "But don't juvenile records get erased or something?"

"We can access those records," James said bluntly.

"What about Alfred?" I whispered. "Did Marty tell you . . ."

"That she thinks he was murdered? Yes, she told me. I took it with a grain of salt. The police dismissed it, and no matter what you want to think, they're good at their jobs. They found no evidence that his death was anything but an accident. I know, the timing is pretty suspicious, but there's no way that the investigation will be reopened, based on the physical evidence, or that the FBI would get involved in it now. The FBI's responsibility is the thefts." James looked at me with something suspiciously like pity. "But, Nell — if it's any consolation, based on what I've heard, Charles's whereabouts are pretty well covered for the time of Alfred's death. If it was murder — and I stress the *if* — he couldn't have done it."

I resumed breathing. "I really can't see Charles doing anything as messy as killing someone. I mean, I saw him that night, after the event, and he didn't act like someone who had just killed someone — at least as far as I know. It's not like I've met a lot of killers." I straightened my back and looked Agent Morrison in the eye. "All right, what do we do now?"

James grinned. "Good for you. I didn't think I'd have to hand you a box of tissues."

I managed to smile back. "I'll take that as a compliment. Do you have a plan?"

"The barest outline of one. Look, I'll be honest. It keeps coming back to the fact that we have very little hard evidence that any thefts have actually occurred, beyond a list put together by a man who is now dead, whose information is locked up in a computer system nobody else has figured out yet."

"Have you looked at his computer?"

"Not yet — our computer whizbang is working on another case at the moment. In any event, even when we do get to it, from what I've learned about your operations, it's going to be hard to prove anything. Now, don't overreact — we've only been looking at this for a few days, and it takes time to follow up some of these trails."

"But you've got to do something! The thief, whoever it is, could be looting the collections as we speak, especially if he thinks we're on to him. It's his last chance."

"We are doing something, Nell. Listen, I'm breaking about every rule in the book by telling you any of this, but frankly, I need your help — I need you on the inside."

I pondered that. "You mean, you want me to go back to work and wait for someone to drop the dime on me? Is that the right term?"

His mouth twitched. "Yes, it is. And yes, that's exactly what I want you to do. We wait and see. Look, I don't know how long he's been at this, or how good he is. Maybe he thought if the FBI found incriminating evidence in your house, we'd leap to the obvious conclusion and that would be the end of it. Certainly it would take the heat off of him and send us looking in another direction, which could buy him time."

"Time for what? To get rid of the evidence? To cover his tracks?"

"That's getting harder to do, thanks to you and Marty. And now we're watching for stolen goods that might have come from the Society, so he might lie low for a bit."

I was not convinced. If no one had noticed items from the Society on the black market by now, what would have changed? All I could imagine was more of our priceless collections disappearing, never to be retrieved. "I'll do whatever you think is best for your investigation — and for the Society."

"Thank you. Just hang tight. The fact that you found those items here in your house means that our thief is getting nervous, and that's good to know."

Well, at least I'd made someone happy. It sure wasn't me. "So how are we supposed to communicate? I can't exactly phone you from the office or even talk freely there — you've seen that. You want to call me here?"

"We can meet at Marty's, as long as you're discreet about it."

"Sir, I can be the soul of discretion."

"I'm banking on it." He stood up. "Thank you for telling me about this, Nell. A lot of people might have been afraid to say anything. I'm glad you trust us."

"And I'm glad you believe me."

"Don't worry. If we're lucky, we'll get this sorted out in a few days."

"Right." I stood, too, and followed him to the door. I knew perfectly well that it was going to take more than a few days to sort out what was missing and where it might have gone, but nabbing the culprit and stopping the hemorrhage was at least a start. "So I'll wait to hear from Marty about getting together? Or I'll let her know if I need to tell you something?"

"Exactly. Good night, now."

And he was gone, leaving me confused. And hungry — I went back to the kitchen and rummaged in the freezer until I found a half-empty container of ice cream. I ate it all. It didn't help.

CHAPTER 18

I slept badly: too much to worry about, too much caffeine too late. Wednesday morning I dragged myself out of bed before the alarm went off, and in the shower tried to scrub myself back to life, with little success. I dressed carefully, hoping to look like a responsible grown-up who couldn't possibly engage in felonies, just in case anyone was watching, and I fled for the train station to catch an early train. I had my orders from the FBI, and I was going to go to work.

Could Charles actually have planted stolen goods at my home? Could the man I had admired and respected — and slept with — do something like that to me, and I hadn't seen it coming? How was I going to be able to look at him today? Much less be nice to him? *Argh.*

I let myself into the building and made a beeline for my office. Once there, I scuttled behind my desk. I looked around at the familiar clutter — odd souvenirs, framed prints, posters, hanging calendars, and stacks of things to be done, and things that had been done but needed to be filed.

I jumped three feet when the phone rang. It was Doris.

"Mr. Worthington would like to see you. Now."

Damn, he's in early. "I'll be right there," I said sweetly.

I marched into Charles's office, shutting the door behind me. We stared at each other for a long moment. I didn't have a clue what was going on in his head, but I could feel my view of him shifting moment by moment. Before, I'd seen him as an attractive man, an able administrator, a considerate lover; now I was wondering if he was a felon and a liar. I hated it.

"Nell, I've had a rather disturbing conversation with that FBI agent this morning," Charles began. "I have to conclude that the FBI is looking at staff members' possible culpability in this theft matter."

"That wouldn't surprise me, Charles." I considered elaborating but decided to see how Charles would play this out.

In the end he opted for doing the right thing. His face softened. "Nell, of course I don't think you would steal anything from the Society. I know how much this place means to you."

"It does, Charles. I just hope this gets sorted out quickly. I wouldn't want to see these losses continue."

"I agree. But I think it's important at this juncture, while we are under such scrutiny, to be as circumspect as possible. It's not a good idea for us to meet behind closed doors — it might give people the wrong idea. The fact that we've enjoyed a relationship and concealed it might send the wrong message."

"Of course, Charles. After all, you never know who's watching or listening." Although I had a pretty good idea that Doris had very sharp ears. "If there's nothing else, I have a lot to do today." I stood up and took a fast two steps toward the door and yanked it open, in time to surprise Doris hovering nearby. She immediately turned away to shuffle some folders on her desk.

I smiled sweetly at her. "He's free now, Doris."

Back at my desk I mulled over what Charles had just said. He was right, at least according to his perspective: any appearance of concealment might send up red flags at the FBI, which none of us wanted at this point. But, I had to add, if he was

247

trying to cast blame on me, his distancing himself would be a strategic move. I supposed I could be disappointed that he hadn't decided to side with me more openly, but had I ever expected that?

The next surprise of the day was a phone call from Marty.

"You have time for dinner?" she began abruptly.

"What, tonight?"

"Yup. I want to run something by you."

"You've got a plan?"

"Maybe. You coming?"

"I wouldn't miss it. I'll be there at six thirty."

I survived the day by immersing myself in busywork. I left work a little past six and walked over to Marty's house. She answered the door with a look that I swear contained more than a hint of amusement. "Come on in. Want a drink? Sounds as though you've had an interesting few days."

"Thanks to you. I take it you've talked to James? And yes, I will have that drink."

"About what you found at your house? Yup, he told me. What did Charles do today?"

I took the full wineglass she held out to me. "Okay, Marty — who's running this show, you or Cousin Jimmy?"

She stared at me innocently. "Why, he is, of course. Or the FBI, anyway. Look, I had a legitimate complaint, and when nobody at the Society seemed interested in doing anything about it, I went to Jimmy. All quite aboveboard. But we're all working together on this, right?"

"Of course we are. But is everybody telling everything?"

She grinned. "I'd say it's on a need-to-know basis right now. I don't tell Jimmy everything."

"Did you tell him about Charles and me?" I demanded.

She had the grace to look ashamed. "Um, yes. I had to make sure where your loyalties really lay. And once I figured that out, I didn't want you to get caught in the crossfire, if Charles was involved. I thought Jimmy should know. Sorry, Nell. That is, if there's any reason to be sorry? I didn't think Charles would throw you under the bus."

"Don't be sorry, Marty. I thought we had more between us, but obviously I was wrong. And now I'm mad. I take it Charles doesn't know you're related to James?"

"Of course not. Why should he? And I don't think he realizes that I was related to Alfred, either. But I may have underestimated Charles."

We'd drifted to the living room, so I threw myself into a chair (without spilling my wine) and asked, "What do you mean?"

"James says you found items planted at your house not long after Charles had visited you, right?"

"Yes. What are you saying? You think Charles did it?"

"It wouldn't surprise me. But there's something that's been bothering me, and I'm trying to figure out how your little discovery fits with it. I've been to Alfred's place more than once, maybe a couple of times a year. He was a very meticulous person, orderly, methodical — that's what made him good at his job. Same at home: everything had its place. Now, Alfred did have a few nice things, and he was proud of them. Some of them came down through the family, and some of them he probably bought himself, since he didn't spend money on much else. Definitely not stolen. Since I knew about his little weakness, I made sure everything he had was on the up-and-up, and he kept his word to me. Anyway, since I'm just about the nearest relative Alfred had, when he . . . died, I had to go to his apartment that Friday, find his papers and stuff."

"And?" I wasn't sure where this was going.

"I didn't recognize half the 'good' stuff I found there."

"So what does that mean?" Although I thought I could guess.

"The stuff hadn't been there the last time I visited Alfred, so I'd bet it was planted there, just like at your place. Problem is, there's no way Charles could have been at Alfred's place. He was working the crowd throughout the whole gala, and then I gather you saw him not long afterwards." She paused, waiting for me to nod confirmation. How had she known? "There is no way that he could have gotten into Alfred's apartment, planted the stuff at his apartment, and made it to his own house in time to welcome you. It's just too tight a schedule, and I don't see Charles running around like that."

I definitely didn't like the sound of that. "So you're telling me you think that there was someone *else* who was planting evidence? And who might have killed Alfred?"

"That's the only way I can see it."

I fell silent, trying to make sense of what she had told me. "Or, if it was Charles, he had an accomplice?"

"That's a possibility."

251

I had one more question. "Did you tell James about the stuff you saw at Alfred's?"

"Yes, I told him when I told him about the Society thefts. I said before, I knew about Alfred's problem, but I wasn't sure if Jimmy did, and I didn't want him to get the wrong idea. I knew something was off the minute I walked into Alfred's place, and that's what I told Jimmy."

So James Morrison had had reason to believe that someone was setting me up before he arrived at my place. I wasn't sure whether I was reassured or disappointed.

"In case you're wondering," Marty went on, "I saw nothing in Alfred's apartment that I thought was relevant to his death, and I can't say whether the things came from the Society, although I'd say the chances are good they did. I don't want to see the Society get trashed publicly any more than you do. Question is, what now?"

I wished I knew. I was suddenly starving; I wasn't sure I was thinking well at all these days, but food wouldn't hurt. "Marty, do you have anything to eat? I don't think well on an empty stomach."

"Oh, right. I got Chinese. A lot of it. Come help me schlep it to the table."

I did, and then we concentrated on eating for a while. Everything tasted wonderful, and I kept helping myself until I had to undo the button of my trousers. Finally I sat back and sighed. "Much, much better. Thank you. Now, why don't you tell me about this plan of yours."

Marty grinned. "Tell me, how much faith do you have in the FBI to solve this?"

"A reasonable amount — I've never worked with them before, though. Or are you asking about your cousin? You know him better than I do."

"Jimmy's a bright guy, and he works hard. But he's also a government official, and that means he has to play by certain rules. He's already bending a few by talking to us, but I don't think he'd go much further."

"What are you getting at?"

"I believe that the FBI will ultimately track down the thief, and maybe even some of the missing stuff. That's their job, and it's what they're good at. I'm just worried that it won't be fast enough. The thief — Charles or whoever — may see what's coming and dispose of the evidence before the FBI can gather enough proof to act, and we'll never recover a lot of what's been taken."

"I agree, but what are we supposed to do about it?" I wondered how long our window of opportunity would stay open once the thief realized that his efforts to cast suspicion on other people had failed.

"I've got an idea." There was a curious gleam in Marty's eye. "First of all, do you agree that Charles is behind this, at least in part?"

For a moment I felt regret for all the lovely times I had shared with Charles — and then I remembered what he'd done today, deliberately putting distance between us and casting doubt on me to others. "Maybe not the murder, but yes, I do."

She raised her glass to me. "All right, this is how the story goes . . ."

CHAPTER 19

Marty settled back in her chair for what I suspected would be a long session. "You were around when the Society was looking for a new president?"

I nodded. "I was on the search committee, although I didn't have a vote."

"And Charles was by far the best candidate, right?"

"No question. We thought we were lucky to get him."

"Right. Well, it worked both ways. Charles found the perfect niche here. He was certainly in a position to know how lousy our cataloging was and how trusting the Society has always been."

"Well, that's hardly unusual. Besides — why would he care?"

"Because he knew what we had, and he knew he could get his hands on it and sell it without anyone noticing." Marty looked very pleased with herself. "I think he got himself the job here specifically so he could plunder the collections."

It took me a moment to process what she had said. "Marty, I'm not following this. You're saying that Charles planned to rip the place off when he applied?"

"That's my guess. Oh, he's done it very well — nothing obvious, and so far not much that's traceable, thanks to our crappy records. But, think about it — he's been in the business for most of his adult life. He knows who the rabid collectors are, including the ones who lie low. He can sell the good stuff without it ever going public, and nobody would know where it went. People can ask for a specific signature, document, whatever, and he can go shopping in the Society's collections and fill the order. But he knows his handy cash cow will go away as collections management improves. Sure, some of the missing items we can attribute to lousy record keeping, but I'd be willing to bet that the better part of that five million worth of stuff has disappeared from the Society's collections within the last two years. He's done really well for himself."

"But" — I stalled as I tried to wrap my head around this idea — "how could he get away with that? Wouldn't somebody blow the whistle on him?"

Marty shook her head. "Did they? No. I suspect that Charles knows his market, and he's bound to have been careful. He just exploited the Society's weakness. And I think you underestimate the collecting lust. There are some people who want something, and they really don't care where it comes from as long as it's theirs in the end. They aren't about to tell anybody. Problem is, I think that Alfred figured it out. After all, he was closest to the collections, hands-on."

"But then what? Did Alfred confront Charles? He had only just told us, and we know he didn't go to the authorities. Would he have tried to blackmail Charles or ask for a cut of the proceeds? And if Charles didn't kill Alfred, who did?" *If anyone,* I reminded myself. We had nothing that resembled proof, and maybe it *was* only a tragic accident.

Marty shook her head. "I don't know. I don't even know that Alfred ever had the nerve to talk to Charles, and anyway, I'd swear he was honest. He wouldn't think of blackmail. I think Alfred waited until somebody came to him — that would be you, Nell — and then he nudged you in the right direction. I bet he figured that if other people knew officially, then he wouldn't be at risk. Poor Alfred."

"Wow." I was stunned as I considered the ramifications of what Marty had said. Then another thought percolated to the top of my reeling brain. "But, Marty, *why* would Charles do this? He's at the top of his profession, he's got a solid reputation, a good income. What's his motive?"

Marty looked smug. "Money. And I don't mean personal gain — sure, he's got enough for himself. But I've got a theory. Want to hear it?"

I nodded. I was in too deep to stop now.

Marty draped her legs over the arm of her chair, making herself comfortable. "There's something else about Philadelphia that's tailor-made for his needs: a good supply of wealthy and unattached women. Charles wants money — more than the Society or any other institution can pay him. And I figure he wants to marry it."

I could only imagine the expression on my face as Marty continued. "So Charles arrives in town, settles in at the Society, and starts scoping out potential donors — particularly female donors. I know, that's what *you* do — but somehow I don't think you go so far as trying to seduce your targets."

"Of course I don't! Marty, how do you

know all this?"

She looked at me with embarrassment "He tried it out on me, when he first arrived. Oh, he's smooth, isn't he? Very charming, very polite. Takes you out to dinner, invites you to highly visible public events — exhibit openings, that kind of thing. Then he invites you to his oh-so-tasteful home and cooks for you — that's a sure-fire winner. He's very patient, and he waits until the right moment to make his move."

I stared at her, horrified. "And did you . . . ?" I was scrambling to remember when he and I first connected — and what I hadn't noticed. Or hadn't wanted to notice.

"No, we never got that far. Oh, I was flattered at first — I mean, I'm unattached, we shared common interests, he's good-looking, and I'm human. But, you know, I didn't really trust him. He was just too good to be true, too polished, too suave. So I started pulling back, and he got the message and withdrew gracefully. But . . ."

"What?"

"I suspect he might have looked into my finances, somehow. I don't have the kind of money I think he wants. So if I hadn't said no, I bet he would have found some other reason to retreat."

"But, Marty, maybe he actually was interested in you at first, and it just sort of faded naturally." I was clutching at straws, and I knew it.

"Nell, you really are an innocent. Once he'd tried it out on me and then dropped me, I started paying attention. You know — checking the society column in the paper to see who he took to which party, and so on. Thing is, I knew some of the other women, so I could ask around, at least a little. He made a little more headway with some of them, then backed out, always gracefully."

"Oh, damn," I spit out. "That's why my nightgown disappeared into a drawer — he was hiding it from . . . whoever the lady of the week was."

"Probably. He's discreet that way."

"Where did I fit in, then? It certainly ain't the money, and it ain't love."

"You were useful to him. He was the new kid in town, and he could use you to bring him up to speed on the Society, plus you had that useful donor database. He could pump you for information. Let me ask you — how many significant male donors has he cultivated in the time he's been here?"

I thought for a moment, then laughed ruefully. "None." I was furious — and embarrassed. How could I have been such a pushover? "I feel like an idiot."

Marty looked at me with sympathy. "Oh, come on, Nell. You knew he was dating other women. Didn't you?"

She had me there. I had to admit, I *had* known, at least as much as I'd wanted to know, which wasn't much. Sure, I'd seen the society-page photos that Marty had mentioned, but I'd told myself those evenings out with other women were part of his job, an opportunity to charm new donors. Charles and I had even discussed them on a few occasions. The truth was, though, that I had deliberately ignored Charles's other dates because I hadn't wanted to believe that those relationships were anything other than social, unlike our more intimate association. But Marty had seen right through him. "Well, . . . We didn't . . . I mean, we weren't . . ."

"Right. No strings. Now wasn't that convenient for Mr. Worthington?"

I didn't know whether to cry or to rage — and I was damned glad we'd been careful about protection all along. I gave up and laughed. "You are so right. And I thought I was being so casual about the whole thing."

"*Do* you care?" Marty asked carefully.

I considered that. "No, not about him. I think I was at least honest with myself about that. It's my pride that's suffering. I don't like to be made a fool of. But, Marty, I still don't understand why he did this. Okay, he stole so he could court women with even more money?"

"I think so, at least in the beginning. It takes money to woo the kind of woman he wants. You know, all those theater tickets, expensive meals. He's got a great house — with a big mortgage. And he has high-dollar tastes. Maybe in the beginning he did it just enough to give him the ready cash to impress his targets. But maybe once he discovered how easy it was, he got hooked. I mean, come on — at the Society he must have felt like a kid in a candy shop, with so many easy pickings. Plus he could thumb his nose at the institution. You must've noticed that Charles thinks he's smarter than everyone else? He kept proving it to himself, over and over." Marty laughed. "Don't beat yourself up. He's very, very good at this. Just not quite good enough for us." She had a wicked gleam in her eye.

"What do you mean?" I had to ask.

"You think we're going to let him get away with this? Where's your gumption, girl? He's been using you, in more ways than one. As for me, when he went after the Terwilliger Collection, he made it personal. He thought

I wouldn't notice? And then he has the nerve to try to pin the rap on you and poor Alfred, who never hurt a fly and who's dead so he can't defend himself. Are you going to let him get away with that?"

"No way."

Marty looked pleased. "All right, then, here's the deal. Let Jimmy and the FBI track down the artifacts and the money. That's what they get paid to do. But you and me, we can launch our own, sort of parallel, investigation."

"What, snoop around and see what women he's wooed? What's the point?" The idea struck me as vaguely repellent.

"Motive. Okay, maybe the law doesn't care about that, but without it, as you pointed out, Charles has no obvious reason to be stealing, and I'm sure the FBI has gone over his records by now. He's got a good life by most people's standards."

"And," I said slowly, "we'll be sparing some other woman the embarrassment, right? Because he's not going to stop now, is he? As long as he thinks he's getting away with it?"

"Exactly."

"How do we do this?"

"You can talk to your professional colleagues; I can talk to Philadelphia society.

That should cover all the bases. He's got to have been doing this for a while. And this is the kind of thing no woman is going to admit to the police or the FBI, even if they knew enough to ask."

"Wow. Marty, I have seriously underestimated you. You have a devious mind — and I'm damn glad we're on the same side. So what's the plan?"

Marty grinned at me. "The FBI is operating under the assumption that Charles has been stealing documents and artifacts from the Society, and most likely selling them, or maybe holding them for a bit, waiting for the right buyer to come along, under the radar. So they're going to set a trap for him. They're going to create a phony collector who is willing to pay big money for something specific — something that we know can be found in the Society collections. Their collector will put the word out on the street that he's in the market, and then the FBI will see who bites."

I stared at her as though she had gone mad. "Marty, how do you know all of this? And wouldn't Charles be crazy to try to take something else, now that everyone's watching?"

"Jimmy told me all about it because he needed my help. He knows I know the collections, and he wanted to figure out what the best bait would be. It had to be something big enough to justify the risk. And this is Charles, remember? He's arrogant, and he's sure we're not going to figure out what's what. He'll think he can get away with it — and the FBI will make sure the prize is tempting."

I tried to visualize how this would work. Then a sudden thought struck me. "You didn't say anything to James about the other thing — the women Charles has been seeing? Or his possible motive?"

"Nope. Jimmy's really only interested in the thefts — the *why* doesn't matter. You and I have a greater interest in the other part."

"It's not a crime to marry a rich woman, or at least try to. What's the point?"

"Because the thefts are all tied up with his motive. Of course he can't come to a prospective bride empty-handed, or he *would* look like a gold-digger — can a man be a gold-digger? Anyway, he's got to be able to play the game, and that takes money. Real money."

I could see the logic in that. "But how do you plan to prove that's why he's stealing?"

"I told you, I have an idea. If you're up for it. The rough outline goes like this: we find a rich woman willing to string him along, until he attempts to seal the deal by wowing her with his impressive stock portfolio or whatever — and we listen in, maybe even record the conversation."

I turned a quizzical eye toward Marty, and she laughed at my expression. "No, Nell, not me. Besides, he's already rejected me as not rich enough. But" — she smiled wickedly — "I know who he's cultivating at the moment."

"Another relative?" I asked.

"No, Libby Farnsworth, someone I went to school with. Well, her brother *is* married to another cousin of mine. But she's got the bucks, and the right profile. What's more important is that she's the type who'd love to play along. She's been updating me on Charles's current campaign, since she knows I know him and she knows I'm involved with the Society, and she's just been keeping him around to squire her to social events, so her heart's not going to get broken. Besides, she's got a devilish sense of humor, and I think this might appeal to her."

I pondered, for about three seconds. "I like it. We attack his ego from all sides in a pincer movement — he loses the girl *and* he gets nabbed as a thief. But — how long is this going to take?"

Marty laughed. "Oh, he's ripe for the picking. I think we could turn up the heat over the next week or so and pump him for all he's worth."

I wasn't so sure. "You think your friend can convince Charles that she's head over heels about him all of a sudden? And then what? She asks him for his bank statement? But isn't James keeping an eye on Charles's bank accounts? If he's got money, the FBI will find it."

"Maybe, maybe not. Poor baby — you really don't get it, do you? There's nothing simpler than to convince Charles that he's conquered another heart — who could resist him? — and besides, Libby's bankroll is more than worth it to him. And he knows her well enough to believe that she'd want to check out the financial side of things before she committed, love or no love. I think he'd take the gamble — he'd have to show her the money, one way or another. Charles can't imagine failing, because he thinks he's smarter than everyone else. He fooled you, didn't he? Didn't he turn on that famous charm and make you think you were the only woman in the world, even if it was only for about fifteen minutes?"

She was absolutely right. I thought I was

pretty smart, but I'd fallen for the line. Charm — ha! If he could bottle it, Charles would be a millionaire without even trying. The only saving grace was that I hadn't lost my heart to him — just my self-respect. I certainly didn't have anything to lose now, and I really, *really* liked the idea of sticking it to Charles. "Marty, I like it. Is it legal?"

"Do you care?"

"No."

"Atta girl! I knew you had it in you." Marty refilled my wineglass and then her own, and we raised them in salute. We were going to nail Charles to the wall, and I for one was going to enjoy it.

"So, what's the next move?"

"We're having lunch with Libby on Friday."

"In Center City?"

"No, Libby lives in Chester County."

"But Marty, that's an hour away on a good day! I can't take that kind of time for lunch on a workday."

Marty waved her hand, dismissing my concern. "Tell your staff you're doing some donor cultivation. Just don't mention who the donor is. Heck — it might even be true. I've been working on Libby for years for a contribution."

Why not? I decided. It wasn't as though

my job could get much shakier. "Just tell me where."

"Chef Henri's, in Wayne. Libby lives near there."

I gulped: I certainly hoped somebody else was going to pick up the tab, because the place certainly wasn't within my budget. "All right. Listen, I'd better go catch my train. Shall I meet you at the restaurant?" At least I knew where it was, having driven by it many a time and dreamed about it.

"Noon." Marty extricated herself from her chair and stood up. "Nell? Don't worry — we're going to see that Charles pays for what he's been doing."

"Marty, I think I believe you. And thank you for everything. See you at the board meeting tomorrow."

"I wouldn't miss it," Marty replied.

CHAPTER 20

I woke to a hint of morning sun and felt cheered, until the events of the past two days rose up like a tidal wave and washed over me, leaving me feeling like a piece of limp seaweed. No, that wasn't right — seaweed just lay there and got buffeted around by the large, impersonal ocean. Me, I'd been mistreated by someone I had liked and trusted — I'd have to come up with a better metaphor than seaweed.

Maybe it was just reaction. At Marty's the night before, I had been pumped up with righteous indignation at Charles, ready to march into battle. But that high was fading fast in the cold clear light of reality. I had no idea how we were supposed to sort out a multimillion-dollar theft — not to mention what might be a murder — and I saw no way that the Society was going to come out of this without at least some tarnish. I couldn't even be sure I'd have a job at the end of it, because this could be a death blow to the institution.

Come on, Nell, get out of bed and get moving. Wallowing in self-pity wasn't going to help anyone or anything. I took a shower and dressed. I fixed myself some coffee and sat in my kitchen, chewing on a stale English muffin, then left to catch the train.

As I rode toward Philadelphia, I pondered my position. Should I be thinking about looking for another job? And who would write me a letter of recommendation? I watched glumly as the towers of Center City loomed on the horizon, and grew steadily larger.

Tonight was the board meeting, which meant that everyone would be scurrying around with last-minute details. I still had no idea what Charles or Latoya intended to tell the board members about the thefts — if anything.

Luckily there was plenty of busywork to keep me occupied. I needed some information for the development report I was going to present to the board, and I needed to talk to Carrie about membership statistics.

"Carrie?" I called out.

She appeared in seconds and leaned against my door frame. "You need me?"

I thought she looked uncharacteristically

271

nervous; usually she was relentlessly cheerful. "I need updates on membership — you know, the usual. New members, nonrenewals, and so on."

"Oh, right, for the board meeting. I forgot. Listen, Nell . . ." She wavered in the doorway.

I gestured to her to come in, and I was surprised when she shut the door behind her. She looked scared. What was she going to tell me now? I wasn't sure if I could handle any more problems. Maybe she wanted to quit, which I really didn't want to hear. "Is something wrong, Carrie?" I asked gently.

"Well, yeah. Maybe. I don't know. It's about Rich."

That I hadn't expected to hear. "Rich?" I prompted.

"Yeah. We've been, kind of, seeing each other, I guess."

I was still puzzled. Did she think I would view this as a problem? Canoodling coworkers was not high on my watch list, and who was I to cast stones? Or did she know something about Rich that she thought I should know? "I don't have any objection to you two dating. Is that what you're asking?"

"Well, kind of. I mean, it's good that

you're cool with it. But he's been really worried that you'd think he was the one who stole those papers. No way he could do that! He really loves his job and this place. He's not a thief."

It was kind of sweet, watching Carrie come to the defense of her boyfriend. "Carrie, I agree with you — I can't see him doing anything like that. But since this is an FBI investigation, they have to look at everybody. Just tell him to cooperate, and I'm sure we'll get it all sorted out soon."

Carrie bounded out of her chair, and for a moment I thought she would try to hug me. She restrained herself. "Thanks, Nell! It's just been so crazy lately, nobody knows what to think." Her face clouded. "I'm not going to lose my job, am I?"

"Not if I can help it. Now, how about those numbers?"

"Right away!"

She opened the door and disappeared, leaving me troubled. Obviously the presence of the FBI was making itself felt among the staff, and if things went on this way much longer, we probably would see some resignations. One more problem the Society did not need right now. With a sigh I turned back to my report.

As the day wore on, I wondered if our

library patrons sensed anything strange about the atmosphere, but when I walked by the reading room to pick up a quick lunch, everything looked the same as it always did. Was it only me who had this calm-before-the-storm feeling?

The afternoon dragged, in part because most board members usually didn't arrive until after the doors had closed to the public, so I had nothing to distract me. As a long-term senior staff member, I knew them all, to varying degrees. Some of them I had worked with on various committees and knew fairly well; others tended to look right through me, as though I were part of the furniture. A few, like Marty, came in regularly for a variety of reasons apart from their board responsibilities, and we shared some kind of ongoing relationship. In any event, I was supposed to be present, visible, and available to schmooze, so I was in the lobby to welcome the arrivals (and direct them to the bar).

Doris usually spent the day or two before the meeting calling each member to remind and to wheedle them into coming, or at least saying that they would; we usually felt lucky if we got between fifteen and twenty attendees at any given meeting, but at least that would give us a quorum. This time was no different, and there were seventeen people milling around, clutching their information packets, by six o'clock. Charles usually waited until there were enough people to make it worth his while to circulate, and then made the rounds, oozing charm. He headed for the women members first, before turning to the craggy alpha elephants of the group. Maybe he had to flex his charm, warm it up, before taking on the bigger prey — or maybe he just liked talking to the women more. A random thought occurred to me, as I watched him work the room: had the financial contributions of the women board members gone up during his tenure, and if so, had they gone up more than the men's contributions? Interesting idea . . .

After Charles had made a full circuit of the room and a few stragglers had arrived, he caught my eye to signal it was time to get down to business. I was the official annunciator. Annunciatrix? I cleared my throat.

"Ladies and gentleman?" I waited a moment as the conversations ebbed and they turned their attention to me. "I think we should move on to the business portion of our meeting. If you'll all just go up to the boardroom?"

The group split, the older, frailer members heading for the elevator, the others taking the grand staircase. Marty made a beeline for the stairs, and I managed to catch up with her.

"Anything new?" I said in a low voice.

"Nope. I'm waiting to see how the meeting goes. If Charles tries to keep a lid on this, you may see some fireworks." We'd reached the top of the stairs. "Talk to you later." Marty squared her shoulders and marched into the boardroom, ready to do battle.

The second-floor boardroom was distinguished by a total absence of windows plus erratic ventilation, which made it a less than ideal place to hold anything, but at least there were no distractions. Doris had carefully laid out the last-minute supplemental materials at each place and added freshly sharpened pencils. She was already entrenched in her stiff chair in the corner, pen and pad at the ready, as the members trickled in.

At the head of the table, Charles called the meeting to order. When silence had fallen, he said, "Before we move into the business portion of this meeting, I need to say something about the unfortunate death of one of our staff members recently. I've spoken to all of you individually, but I want to say again that our registrar Alfred Findley was a valued member of this institution. He had made great strides in untangling the mystery of our record keeping, and he will be missed. Now, if we could turn to our agenda . . ."

We worked our way through the printed agenda, and I gave a brief summary of the gala, including our strong financial results, and fielded several compliments about how things had gone. As the reports wound down, I saw Charles and Latoya Anderson, who looked distinctly jumpy, exchange a few glances. Marty was watching both of them with an enigmatic expression. I assumed that there was some sort of statement in the offing, and I was curious to see how they handled the situation. The board members apparently had no inkling that there was anything out of the ordinary going on.

Finally every department head but Latoya had taken their turn. She and Charles shared one more glance, then Charles cleared his throat.

"There is an item of particular concern that has arisen since our last meeting, regarding collections."

A small ripple ran through the room, and

I wondered who else Marty might have told. Marty's eyes remained fixed on Charles.

"It has been brought to my attention that there are significant weaknesses in the way in which we track items from our collections." He raised a hand to forestall comment. "Yes, I know we have raised this in the context of our long-range plan, and that there have been discussions regarding electronic security measures. We have also enhanced our electronic cataloging. But I think we need to give serious consideration to some interim policy changes."

One of the older members, a blunt lawyer with a big-name Philadelphia law firm, interrupted him. "What're you saying? Something important gone missing?"

Charles sidestepped quickly. "I don't mean to imply that. But as we have moved forward with our cataloging project, it has become increasingly clear that we — and our predecessors — have been rather cavalier about our collections management process. I think Latoya will back me up when I say that we have made great strides toward correcting this, and Alfred Findley was a key part of that effort, but at the same time — yes, I must admit that we aren't always sure where a particular item is at any given time. And I'm sure you will all agree that it is imperative that our stewardship not be questioned, if we hope to keep attracting contributions of items of historical significance, as well as funding to support them."

Another member spoke up. "So what are you suggesting?"

"A multipronged approach. We need to make it clear that we do have effective internal systems in place. I would approach this as a public-relations issue — that, for instance, we refrain from issuing news releases saying that we have discovered a rare and wonderful treasure in our collections — because that implies that we didn't know it was there in the first place. Rather, we should say that the wonderful collections of the Society include such items as X, Y, and Z. Much more positive, proactive, as a statement."

There was a consistent, if slightly bewildered, nodding of heads among the group around the table. The board members still watched Charles expectantly as he continued. "Likewise, we can make use of our in-house publications in much the same vein. But I also think we need to make our security measures more visible to the general public."

"What do you mean? We've already decided that we can't afford surveillance, at least not right now. What brought this on, all of a sudden?" That came from one of the more reactionary members.

Charles gave a barely perceptible sigh. "I'm sure you know that security has been an ongoing debate among our peer institutions. Things do disappear. Our head librarian has reported on a regular basis that she had observed patrons slipping documents into pockets or even under clothes. In most cases, a quiet word to the offender has sufficed. There are, in fact, a few persons who are known to the staff for this behavior, and we keep an eye on them. But it is difficult to watch everyone constantly, especially when they have access to some areas where they know they will be unobserved. Every room has its blind spots. And our staff is limited. It is my intention to try to discourage this behavior by instituting more visible security mechanisms."

"You gonna do body searches?" One of the newer members threw this out; he had been recruited more for his checkbook than for his personal charm.

Charles gave this person a withering glance. "I am well aware that option raises serious issues — not least of which is reluctance among current staff members to undertake such activities. But I think that we need to make it known that this is a possibility. We need to post *our* rights more prominently — including the right to search all items and, yes, persons. We need to let the public know that we are serious about this and that we will prosecute offenders, not just send them on their way with a slap on the wrist."

As a general rumbling broke out among the people around the table, Charles raised his hand once more, asking for silence.

"I realize that you will need time to reflect on this and that we will need to draft more specific guidelines for your review and ultimate approval. But let me emphasize that I do think this is important and that we should act on it sooner rather than later. I would suggest that, at this time, we pass a general resolution to effect near-term improvements to collections security, and that we empower the Collections Committee to create and implement specific guidelines. I would like to see this done within the next two weeks."

In the glacial world of the Society, this was truly precipitous. I looked at Marty, but her expression gave nothing away.

"Moreover," Charles pressed on, "I would like to have these new policies in place as soon as possible, so that we can observe the results and make any necessary revisions at the next board meeting in three months. Do I have a motion?"

Somebody muttered, "So moved."

"Second?"

Two or three people said, "Second."

The members voted unanimously if unenthusiastically to support the measure.

"Doris, please note that the resolution has been made, seconded, and approved, and that the Collections Committee will meet to draft improved security measures."

Giving the responsibility to the Collections Committee made sense, and taking this action would mollify Marty. Plus it was a standing committee — trying to create a new committee at this point would just delay action. And I had to admit to myself that Charles's strategy was masterful: he appeared concerned without being alarming.

But a nagging little voice in my head was also noting that Charles had carefully distanced himself from any mention of the potential thefts, should they go public. He had made it look as though it was his adept management that had uncovered the problem — rather than his obliviousness or shortsightedness that had permitted it to occur. I glanced across the table at Marty and found her staring at Charles with a look that combined speculation and skepticism. She hadn't said anything yet, pro or con, but I had no doubt that she wouldn't hold her tongue if she found something she didn't like. As if she had heard my thoughts, she turned her gaze to me, but her expression did not change. I met her look squarely, but I really wasn't sure what she was thinking.

The meeting wound down quickly after that. I escorted some of the board members downstairs, and Charles stayed behind for a few minutes, then joined me in the lobby. It was getting late, and people were not disposed to linger. When the last person had gone, Charles and I were left alone. I found I still had mixed feelings about his strategy.

"So, Charles, you elected not to warn the board that we may have a serious problem?"

He regarded me levelly. "Nell, we aren't sure if there is a problem, or what the scope of it may be. I bought us some time to investigate more thoroughly, while at the same time implementing what may be the first in a series of new security measures. I don't think we need to stir up any panic at this point."

An irrational thought flashed through my head: *So when should we schedule the panic? What would be a good day?*

"Let me handle this, Nell," he went on. "I have things under control, and it seems Marty is on board with our plans. I think I have done what is necessary for now." He looked at his watch. "Is it that late already? I'm meeting a friend for dinner — I have to dash. Thanks for all your help, Nell."

And with that dismissive comment, he turned quickly and headed back to his office to retrieve his coat. I made my way to my office more slowly, thinking as I went. Something did not feel right. But what could I do about it? It wasn't my department, and Charles had made it clear that he didn't want me meddling in it. I sighed. I certainly had enough to do without going looking for problems in other departments.

I wasn't exactly surprised to see Marty waiting for me in my office. "I thought I hadn't seen you leave. So, what just went on in there?" I asked as I made my way around the desk to my chair.

"Charles is dancing around the issue and covering his own ass."

"That's about what I thought. Are you happy with that?"

"Wait and see."

CHAPTER 21

With the board meeting behind me — and with the memory of Charles's evasiveness fresh in my memory — I took stock. Agent James Morrison had his plan, Marty Terwilliger had her plan, and I was darn well going make some small contribution of my own to untangling this mess. It was all well and good to do everyone else's bidding, but my self-esteem was at stake. I had to make up for misjudging Charles the Snake, if only to myself. I had time to think on the train ride home — and came up with some ideas.

As Marty had suggested, I told Carrie that I'd be out the next day beating the bushes for contributions, which was close enough to the truth. Friday I pulled into the parking lot at Chez Henri a few minutes before my scheduled luncheon with Marty and her friend. I sat in my car trying to collect my thoughts. I had done a quick search of our donor cultivation records about Marty's friend Elizabeth Farnsworth, aka Libby. She was the widow of one of the great industrial magnates of Philadelphia and had inherited beaucoup bucks, although I seemed to recall reading that some of her late husband's children by an earlier marriage had tried to break his will. My impression had been that there was plenty to go around. I knew she had to be Marty's age, since Marty had said they had been at school together. I also knew that she had a nice townhouse in the city and a sprawling estate in the Chester County horse country. Charles had mentioned in passing that he had escorted her to an event or two. I had never met her, but I had made sure that the Society had a complete file on her, in case we ever had the opportunity to ask for a contribution from her. I would never have anticipated the contribution that Marty and I were planning to solicit. Oops — maybe that wasn't the best choice of words.

With a sigh, I got out of the car and headed for the door. I was waiting in the restaurant lobby, admiring its warm colors, earthy tiles, and the glowing light bathing the yellow walls when Marty and her guest arrived. Libby Farnsworth was much as I would have imagined her — relentlessly slender, deeply tanned, her hair artfully colored yet casually arranged. She wore her clothes carelessly, but the chunky gold jewelry at her ears and wrists was obviously real. Marty pointed to me, and Libby gave me a sharp look before extending her hand.

"I'm Libby Farnsworth. So you're our partner in crime?" Her handshake was firm and decisive.

"Eleanor Pratt — Nell. Guilty; or maybe I shouldn't say that under the circumstances."

One of the many hovering flunkies arrived to escort us to our table, located in a reasonably private corner, and with a flourish, handed us elegantly engraved menus. I tried not to look at the prices, and wondered how much room I had on my credit card. Since the meal appeared to be prix fixe, I decided to splurge on a glass of Chardonnay — the chef's taste in wines was legendary. Once the waiter had bustled away, the three of us sat back and contemplated each other.

"I guess we should get started." Marty looked positively gleeful. "Nell, I didn't have time to fill Libby in on the details — so you can help me out as we go. Libby, the FBI is looking at your boyfriend for grand larceny and violating God knows how many federal laws. Oh, and Nell, Libby already knows you're another woman scorned."

Great. Could I be more pathetic? I took a

swallow of the excellent buttery Chardonnay and almost forgot to answer. "Well, I certainly feel like a fool. Yes, Charles and I have been, uh, involved since shortly after he took the job at the Society."

"Come on, sweetie, he's been boffing you, right?"

I nodded but couldn't meet her eyes. "I didn't have any illusions that we were madly in love, or that it was going to go anywhere. But, looking back, I can see that he was using me all along, and I didn't even realize it. I made things a lot easier for him — and then he turned around and tried to pin the thefts on me. Marty told you about those, right?" I finally managed to look at Libby, whose glance combined amusement and sympathy.

"She sure did. Oh, Charles is a charmer, all right. Knows just what to say, and how and when. It takes a strong woman to resist the package. Kudos to you, Marty."

Marty sighed. "Wish I could say I saw through him, but he was the one who cooled it — told you, I'm not a big enough prize. Although I think he milked me for a heck of a lot of information about who's who in Philadelphia. No, I didn't feed him you, Libs — he can read the society column and a credit report. But I gave him a jump-start, so to speak."

Libby took a healthy sip of the large martini that had materialized at her place. "Oh, goody. He was getting a bit tiresome — although I must say, if he's really been doing what you say, it makes him much more interesting. Hidden depths and all that. What's the larceny deal?"

"Well, we think he's been making off with some valuable items from the Society, but the FBI's looking for proof of that, so don't worry about it. But we also know for a fact he's been running through the Blue Book widows for the last year and more. My guess is, he's angling for a new wife — someone who will support him in the manner to which he'd like to become accustomed. So we want to get him where it *really* hurts," Marty said with a sly grin. "And of course I thought of you, dear."

Libby cocked a well-groomed eyebrow at her and grinned as our first course arrived. While listening to the conversation, I admired the artful composition of the food on my plate, the lovely plate itself, and the silverware that flanked it. I even admired the crisply pressed napkin that more than covered my lap. Then I tasted the food. I stopped listening to the conversation and diverted all energies to my taste buds.

Amazing. I wondered if I was purring out loud.

When the second course appeared, it was more beautiful than the first course, almost too pretty to eat. It was with sincere regret that I turned my attention back to the other women.

"Libby, has Marty told you what we're thinking of doing?" I said.

Libby seemed oblivious to the wonders on the plate in front of her. "I gather you want me to seduce him and wrangle all his secrets from him, after I've, uh, softened him up?"

I had to laugh at her turn of phrase. "Well, more or less. Anyway, we'd really like to see if he'll talk about his assets — financial, that is."

"And maybe record him," Marty added.

Libby's eyes sparkled. "Ooh, does that mean I get to wear a wire? Like on TV?"

"I don't know the technology, but something like that," I said, glancing at Marty for corroboration. She nodded enthusiastically.

"And I'd be working for the FBI?" Libby asked.

I frowned. "Well, indirectly. They don't know about this, and we aren't exactly planning to tell them, but we'll turn over anything we find out to them."

"Don't worry — my cousin Jimmy is an agent in the Philadelphia office," Marty added.

"What, little Jimmy Morrison, the one who couldn't swim?"

"That's the one."

"Will wonders never cease. So now he's a G-man?"

"He grew up."

"I always wondered what happened to him. Government snoop certainly seems to fit."

Marty looked mystified. "What do you mean?"

"Don't you remember that time he spied on me and Arthur, oh, what's his name? We were exploring the, um, wonders of nature in the boathouse one summer. I must have been about sixteen, which would make Jimmy, what, nine? He got a real eyeful. Maybe that's how he got started on this FBI stuff."

Marty laughed. "I'd forgotten about that. So he won't hear anything he hasn't heard before, if we tape you and Charles?"

"Ooh, Martha, you are bad. But you're right. Nothing like keeping it all in the family, eh?"

As I swirled a piece of the excellent crusty

French bread around my plate to capture the very last of the extraordinary sauce, I contemplated the bantering women before me. I wondered if they came from another species. Growing up with both money and connections, they seemed to have a different view of the world than I did. Not that they were putting on airs, and they were both being quite open about what had gone on between them and Charles, and that club now included me. I decided that overall I liked them. After all, it wasn't their fault that they had been born rich. I could deal with that, as long as the fallout included meals like this one.

Dessert arrived, along with excellent coffee. Once again, I gazed in awe at the splendid composition on the plate before me. Was I really supposed to sully it with a fork? What a shame. But I managed. Libby and Marty were talking about various people I had never heard of. Yes, I could get used to this life . . .

Libby gestured imperiously to a passing waiter to refill her coffee cup, then said, "Okay, what specifically do you want me to do?"

Marty took the lead. "You've been seeing Charles on a fairly regular basis?"

She nodded. "It's not like we have a standing date every Tuesday or anything like that, but yes, I'd say once or twice a week, depending on the social calendar."

"Purely public dates, or have you met in private?"

"I've been to his place a couple of times, and he's been to my place in the city once."

"Where does he seem more comfortable?"

"His place, definitely."

"Have you taken off your clothes there?"

Caught by surprise, I stifled a laugh. Libby tried to look outraged but failed, and ultimately gave in to laughter. "Yes, Marty, we've done the deed there."

"You slut, you." The two old friends smiled at each other. "Well, if you spend time at your place, we could wire the place rather than you. If you have to go to his place, *and* if you take off your clothes, it gets more complicated to hide any microphones."

"So it's more than just your prurient interest, I gather. All right. Look, I'm not all that familiar with your high-tech doodads, but I can tell you, since I have reached a certain age, I prefer to preserve a bit of mystery. In other words, I wear a nightgown. Oh, by the way, Nell, that white silk number was yours?"

I stared at her. "Uh, yes."

"Charles thought he'd hidden it, but I'm a snoop. It's very nice."

"Thank you." I blushed, then decided it was time to divert the focus away from the physical to the technical. "Uh, ladies, what about these listening devices? We can't exactly call up James and ask to borrow a few."

Marty waved a hand dismissively. "My sister's eldest son is into that high-tech stuff. I'm sure he can set us up with what we need. I'll give him a call later."

I was not convinced but decided to wait and see. Then another thought struck me. "You know," I began slowly, "I'll bet *I* could get the bugs into Charles's place." I liked the idea. I could kill two birds with one stone: plant the bugs and break it off with Charles.

Marty stared at me. "I hadn't thought of that. But what'll you say to him to get you in the door?"

"Oh, I guarantee it'll be a conversation he won't want to have on the stoop." I gave a moment's thought to falling into Charles's bed again and gagged. No, not after what I had learned over the last few days; not after what he'd done, or tried to do, to me. But I could go and tell him that whatever we'd shared was over. "I think I deserve one grand farewell scene. Besides, Libby reminded me that I want my nightgown back. That way I'd have the perfect excuse to get into the bedroom — to collect the stuff I left there. I could probably stick a bug somewhere in there."

"What if he doesn't let you in?"

"Well, it's worth a try, isn't it? If he won't let me in, then Libby can take a shot at it. But I think he would be polite, at least. He's never been deliberately rude. And I'll bet he has a great farewell speech drafted already."

"Might work. But it's got to be soon. I'd better get those bugs, so we can figure out how they work."

Libby faced us. "Assuming we get the thingamajigs to work, what is it you want to hear him say?"

Marty grinned at her. "Well, it's going to look a bit odd if you drag him straight into bed and start trying to wheedle information out of him. String him along a little — turn up the heat bit by bit, let him think he's making progress. Then turn the tables and ask him about his intentions — which should lead right into discussing his financial standing. He's not stupid, he'll have done his homework, and he'd expect you to ask that kind of question. Get him to lay out his portfolio. Think you can handle that?"

"Not a problem." Libby stared over our heads, thinking. Finally she said, "But can I keep the heavy-breathing part to a minimum? I don't want to become a legend at the local FBI stag parties. You do trust Jimmy, don't you?"

"Oh, he's the real deal," Marty replied complacently. "His mother was horrified when he went to work for the government rather than his father's brokerage firm. But he's done quite well, from what I hear." She looked at her watch. "Well, ladies, I have to go help Cousin Althea start making her infamous fruitcake for Christmas — it has to be soaked in rum and mellow for a couple of months, which is the only reason anybody will eat it. Libs, I'll talk to you as soon as I get a line on the bugs."

I stood up, uncertain. "Marty, I need to talk to you — can you wait a minute?" Then I turned to Libby. "Libby, thank you for being willing to play along with this. We're both worried that the FBI may not find enough to nail Charles for the thefts, and this gives us some extra insurance."

Libby laughed. "Hell, I wouldn't miss it. This will be the most fun I've had in a long time. And we girls have to stick together, right? Marty, give me a call when you get the doohickeys. Nell, good to meet you, and I have a feeling I'll be seeing more of you."

Marty and I left her to deal with the check, although I had to wrestle with my conscience. Unfortunately my meager wallet trumped my heavy conscience. I hurried out after Marty. "Listen, I remembered what you said about talking to colleagues. I'm going to try to talk to some of my counterparts at the other places Charles has worked and see what I can find out. I figure they might be more likely to talk to me than to an FBI agent."

"Brilliant! Nell, I'm beginning to think you have a real talent for conspiracy. Well, I've got to run. I'll call you when I've got the equipment lined up, and we can go from there."

I watched her pull out of the parking lot. It was nice that she thought well of my skills, but I was beginning to wonder just what I had gotten myself into. How would *bugged a romantic tryst to solve a felony* look on my résumé?

CHAPTER 22

I didn't hear from Marty over the weekend. Monday morning in the office, I took a look at the plan I had come up with, decided it still made sense, and started to put it into effect. Armed with a large mug of coffee, I logged on to the Internet and reviewed the staff lists at organizations where Charles had spent time in the past twenty years or so. I remembered details of his CV from his interview, and I knew that he had been a busy boy, climbing steadily up the administrative ladder and then hopping from one place to another (bigger, better) one as soon as it was seemly. He had apparently done it very well, and the progression led quite naturally to the top post at the Society. I focused in on the places he'd worked within the last decade. High staff turnover in development is normal, so people I might have known in the past had moved on to other places, and I had to do a bit of tracking.

In the end, after an hour or so of trawling websites, I identified two women whose paths had crossed mine, either at fundraising conferences or at museum or library functions, and who I could legitimately contact with business questions. For the moment, I was going to assume that the word of the Society's troubles was not common knowledge, especially beyond the Philadelphia community. And I had a perfect cover story: I wanted to know about how our sister institutions handled their security measures. I was researching various state-of-the-art security systems, with the view of writing grant proposals to fund a new system for the Society, and I had heard that they had installed a blah, blah, blah. It would do to get my foot in the door, and it had the added benefit of being almost true.

The ones I knew best, and thought I could glean the most information from, were in Boston and in Washington, DC. I started with Diane Carpenter in DC. "Diane? This is Nell Pratt, from Philadelphia? I'm the development director at . . ." And so on.

And we were off and running. Five minutes of polite chitchat later, I had a date with Diane for the next day — on my tab, of course. DC was a two-hour train ride away, but it was worth meeting her in person, rather than trying to do this over the phone. I wasn't sure how my budget was going to stand for this, but maybe the FBI would reimburse me. Oops, the FBI didn't know about my own investigation. Well, maybe they would reimburse me if our little plan worked out. Boosted by my first success, and no less by the apparent viability of my cover story, I tried the second name on my list, Gail Wallace, and set up a meeting in Boston for later in the week. Surely one or the other would have some good dirt to dish. Otherwise I'd run out of time and money pretty fast this way.

I sat back in my chair and reviewed my strategy. It seemed likely to me that Charles might have done a little harvesting at various collections, sort of a dry run before tackling the Society. But what if he'd been going after the patronesses there, too? My contacts were both women, and who better to fill me in on the nonpublic aspects of Charles's activities? The ones that never made it to the personnel file; the ones that made the institutions very glad to give him a glowing endorsement, hoping fervently that he would become someone else's problem. This was one part of the investigation that I could handle much better than Agent James. I knew what I was looking for and how to ask the right questions. It felt satisfying to know that maybe I could pull my own weight and do some good.

The next morning, I caught an early train to Washington. I suppose I could have driven, but it would be easier to just get there, see Diane Carpenter, and come back again without worrying about parking or getting lost. I doubted she'd be willing to let down her hair to a comparative stranger, so the meeting would probably be short. I just hoped it would be sweet.

I didn't know Diane well. We'd chatted at various meetings over the past few years, but we were more acquaintances than friends. I knew she was about my own age and, like me, had worked at a variety of places in her career, but I couldn't recall any other personal data to save my life. Children? Pets? Hobbies? I spent the train trip trying to figure out how to steer the conversation toward in-house thefts and Charles Worthington's girlfriends, official or otherwise.

From the station I grabbed a cab to Georgetown. Diane was my counterpart at a small but exquisite library, whose collections and massive endowment made many of us in the business green with envy. Once inside, I made the appropriate reverent noises about the handsome building and impressive collections; it was easy to be sincere, since both were wonderful. She gave me the full behind-the-scenes tour, including the basements and the elaborate electronic control room that ran their security system, and I dutifully asked her to join me for lunch, which she accepted with tepid enthusiasm. I let her pick the place, and when we were settled and had ordered, I started my oh-so-subtle probing.

"If I may be direct," I began, "can you tell me if you installed your system as a precautionary measure or because of a specific incident?"

Diane fixed me with a cold eye. "Does this have anything to do with the call I received this morning from the FBI office in Philadelphia?"

I stared at her, hoping I didn't look like a deer caught in the headlights. I could play ignorant, or I could tell her the truth — or a modified version of the truth. I decided on the latter.

"Actually, yes, it does. What did they tell you?"

"Very little. They asked about Charles Worthington's tenure at the library. They already knew about our theft."

I looked blankly at her. Either this had been very carefully hushed up, or I hadn't done my homework very well. "Theft?"

Her expression shifted to disdain. "Yes. Several years ago, we lost a collection of Greek coins that were part of the original endowment from our founder. They never surfaced in the marketplace, and they were never recovered. So, to answer your original question: yes, that was what prompted us to invest in a more effective security system."

"I didn't know about that."

"I'm glad to hear that, because we made every effort to keep the incident quiet. It would not reflect well on us — as I'm sure you know."

I avoided her eyes. "What makes you say that?"

"I can put two and two together. You call out of the blue and want to talk about security systems, and then I get a call from the FBI? I have to infer that the Pennsylvania Antiquarian Society is having a problem with theft, too."

I considered my options. If I was frank about our theft problem, would she be? Did she have any information that could help me? It seemed worth a try.

"Diane, you're right. Like you, we've had

some problems, but we haven't gone public, and we hope it won't come to that. But we're just beginning to get a handle on the extent of it."

"Do you have any suspects?"

There was the sticking point. I decided to dodge it for the moment. "What makes you think that we would?"

She regarded me as though I were a bug under a microscope. I didn't like it. "To put it bluntly, your institution and mine share one obvious common denominator: Charles Worthington."

We looked at each other for a moment, like two boxers sizing each other up. Finally I said carefully, "Was Charles a suspect in your case?"

She maintained her stare a moment longer, then her shoulders sagged, and she took a drink of water before replying. Composed once more, she said, "There was no evidence to implicate him."

You're evading the question, I thought. "But the timing was right?"

She nodded. She didn't add anything.

I sat back in my chair. "Diane, I appreciate your discretion. I believe we at the Society find ourselves in a comparable situation. Like you, we have suspicions but no proof." I thought hard for a moment. "Is there anything else that you can add, that might help us now?"

She carefully aligned the silverware of her place setting. With her eyes on the table, she said deliberately, "Charles made a point of . . . getting close to people who could be helpful to him."

Luckily I had a pretty good idea of what she meant. "And would his, uh, relationships have helped him to gain access to the collections?"

Diane nodded. "He cultivated a close friendship with the chief librarian, who managed the collections. She left us after the, um, disappearance was discovered. I'm not sure if she's been able to find a comparable position — this was such a blot on her reputation, and word spreads, even without public exposure."

The food arrived, providing a welcome break. I didn't think Diane would be any more specific about what had happened, but she had told me what I needed to know. When the waiter had withdrawn again, I said, "Diane, I understand your position. What you've told me corresponds to what we have put together, and I think it will help. If we uncover anything that would lead to your missing items, I'll make certain to share it with you. And thank you for telling me — you could have just blown me off."

"Nell, you and I are part of the same rather small cultural community. We should be able to provide mutual support. I will be glad if I have helped you."

And we dug into our meal, while the talk turned to more neutral topics. An hour later, I caught the train back to Philadelphia, and as I watched the landscape roll by, I reflected that, if nothing else, I was building my network of colleagues. There were a lot of women in nonprofit development, and most were intelligent and committed. Unfortunately, some of them were gullible as well. And Charles knew exactly how to exploit us.

CHAPTER 23

When I got home on Tuesday afternoon, I had a message from Marty saying we were to meet at Libby's country place the next day, and giving me the address and some rather vague directions. Wednesday afternoon found me wandering the lovely lanes of Chester County, trying to find Libby's house. I'd looked at my maps and checked MapQuest, so I'd thought I had a general idea where I was going. The problem was, reality was quite different. For one thing, the places out here sat on more acres than I could guess at, and most boasted discreet and tasteful signs giving the name of the estate — but no numbers. It wasn't like I could stop somewhere and knock and get directions, because most of the homes had driveways that were miles long — I couldn't even be sure there was a house at the end of them. I swear I passed one estate that had its own landing strip.

I finally pulled into what I hoped was the right driveway, only fifteen minutes past the appointed time. I parked my car in front of the house, on a graveled drive that surrounded a lovely circle of enthusiastically blooming flowers — not a dead or wilted one in sight — and studied the building before me. It was actually quite modest by local standards, a handsome fieldstone colonial from the early 1920s, by my semi-educated guess. It looked to have at least six bedrooms (not including the servants' quarters, of course), a screened porch at one end, and a matching three-car stone garage. The front overlooked rolling hills and artfully distributed clusters of trees — and there wasn't another house in sight. Nice. *I could live this way,* I thought once again, *and I'd certainly like to try.* I tore myself away from the view and rang the doorbell.

Although I half expected a maid with a black uniform and frilly apron to appear, it was Libby herself who opened the door.

"Nell, glad you found us. Some people just give up after the first few wrong turns. Come on in — we're in the library. I thought it was fitting."

I followed her through the broad entrance hall with a magnificent sweeping staircase, and to the designated library at the back of the house. Marty was already there, and there was a buzz-cut young man next to her, who, at the sight of an unfamiliar female person, bounced to his feet and stood awkwardly, shifting from one foot to the other. One look at him and I felt old: he couldn't have been much more than nineteen. Still, it was the young ones these days who understood all the rapidly changing technologies, leaving us old fogies in the dust.

Marty stood as well. "Hi, Nell. This charming young man is my nephew Philip. He's an electronics wizard."

Philip blushed, and extended a hand, which I shook. "Phil. Hi," he said. That exhausted his social repertory.

"I made tea," Libby announced, waving her hand vaguely at a low table surrounded by easy chairs. That was something of an understatement: what looked to be a magnificent Georgian silver teapot was flanked by matching creamer and sugar, with sugar tongs in the shape of birds' claws, and I could swear the china was Royal Crown Derby. I itched to turn them all over and read the identifying marks, but that would be impolite, and besides, they were full. I sighed inwardly — maybe later. At least I could use them. I sat and added three lumps of sugar to my teacup — with the antique tongs, of course.

When everybody was settled with something to drink, and a plate of cookies (packaged, I noted, which made me feel better) had made the rounds, Marty took charge of the *meeting.*

"Nell, when we started talking about bugging, Phil was the first person I thought of. He has some toys to show us."

"Is it okay to talk openly in front of . . ." I nodded toward Phil.

"The kid?" Marty finished my question for me. "Sure. You can trust him."

Phil blushed.

But should he trust us? I wondered. "Good. Okay, before we get into all the tech stuff, I want to bring you up-to-date on what I've been doing. I figured that there were people in the business who might talk to me, even if they wouldn't talk to the FBI. And I don't think the FBI would be asking questions about Charles's, uh, amorous adventures."

Libby gave a snort. Marty nodded encouragement.

I took a swallow of the tea, which was lukewarm. Silver might be pretty, but it lost heat quickly. "So I talked to a colleague of mine in Georgetown yesterday, at an institution similar to the Society, and I've got a

310

chat lined up for tomorrow with another colleague in Boston. Diane pretty much confirmed what we suspected. I think we're definitely on to something."

"So tell us," Marty urged impatiently. Phil sat like a mouse at her side, nibbling on a cookie.

"First, there was a significant theft at her place, although they kept it quiet to protect the reputation of the institution. And it corresponded to Charles's time there."

"Yes!" Marty exclaimed, slapping her knee. "I knew it."

I went on. "Second, he apparently seduced the person in charge of the collections, and she lost her job after the theft."

Libby had been quiet but burst out now. "Why hasn't anybody put this together? How is it that he keeps getting bigger and better positions?"

I glanced at Marty before answering. "Probably because the women involved feel embarrassed or ashamed or stupid, and they'd rather not say anything — besides, who would they tell? They got taken in by a slick line and some nice suits, and then they got dumped when they were no longer useful, without even knowing why. There hasn't been any evidence to pin on him for the thefts, unless you count the fact that he was around for all of them. And since the institutions kept these things quiet, how would anyone know?"

"Jesus, doesn't anybody check references anymore?" Marty said in a tone of disgust.

"Marty, you should know it doesn't work like that," I protested. "He hasn't lied on his résumé. He's got a nice list of scholarly publications, speaking engagements, activities in national organizations — all the stuff you look for in a job applicant. And, as I said, the women he's used wouldn't want to say anything — after all, what harm has he done? Nothing illegal, as far as they know. And finally, as a board member you know the potential fallout if you say anything negative about someone and it gets back to him — you risk getting sued. I'll bet most places were glad to see the back of him, so of course they'd say wonderful things about him just to get him out of their hair."

Marty turned to her silent, wide-eyed nephew. "Phil, you are getting an invaluable education about the realities of the working world. I do hope you're paying attention."

I had a last point to add. "Oh, and one other thing — the FBI called Diane. That's both good and bad. At least we know they're thinking along the same lines we are and checking out Charles's history. But the downside is, if anyone at these institutions puts two and two together, the word of our thefts is going to get out. I more or less had to admit to Diane that we shared a problem."

Marty said promptly, "Good for Jimmy. I told you he was smart. But it sounds like we need to nip this in the bud, before it gets any worse."

Libby drawled, "So I still get to do my femme-fatale routine?"

"Looks like it, if you're still willing. Uh, ladies?" I didn't quite know how to approach this, but I thought I should at least mention it. "I did a little research. You know that taping a conversation is illegal in the Commonwealth of Pennsylvania without the consent of all the parties?" I knew I sounded like a priss, but I had been doing my homework on the Internet, and I thought they needed to know that. "In fact, bugging someone's place is illegal. Just so you know . . ."

"Oh, pooh," Marty said. "So what?"

"It means that anything we hear, we can't use as evidence. And the FBI will be extremely annoyed at us. And finally, Marty, you're dragging Phil here in as a co-conspirator."

Young Phil volunteered something for the

first time. "Excuse me, but there is an exception to that — if you record something you could normally overhear."

I burst out laughing at the image that conjured up for me. "Great. Libby, all you have to do is tell Charles that you have an ear infection that affects your hearing, so that he has to yell at you to be heard, and then Marty and I can stand on the sidewalk outside, holding a microphone up to the window. Can't you just see it? Real subtle."

Marty was trying to suppress her own laughter. "Ah, Nell, don't worry about it. We're not trying to gather proof for prosecution — let Jimmy do that. That's what the FBI is for. We just want to verify *why* Charles thinks he needs money — and stop him."

Poor Phil's eyes just kept getting wider and wider. I was not convinced, but I wasn't about to pull the plug. As long as Libby didn't feel threatened by this game of ours, I was willing to go along. I threw up my hands. "All right, I'm in. But remember, no court is going to be happy about this."

Marty turned to Phil again. "OK, whiz kid, show us what you've got."

He cast a shy smile around the group. "Aunt Marty said you wanted some trans-mitters that were small, easy to hide, but with good pickup. I forgot to ask how far you wanted to transmit — are you going to be close by? Do you want to listen in, in real time, or do you want something voice activated, that just records when somebody is talking?"

We exchanged glances — clearly we hadn't thought that far. "What's the potential range?" I asked.

"Depends. You could park in a car outside the house, or you could sit in a restaurant a couple of blocks away. The further you want to go, the more the stuff costs."

I hadn't considered what this might cost us. I looked at Marty. She waved her hand at me, so I guessed I didn't need to worry about that. I turned back to the young genius.

"I can't see Marty and me freezing our tails off in a car, listening in, and we'd be pretty obvious on the street. And it's not like we'll have to burst in and rescue you in the pinch, right, Libby?"

"I think I can manage to take care of myself, thank you," she said.

"So nearby would be good, maybe under a block. Can we record from there, too?"

"No problem," said young Phil.

Marty interrupted. "There's a nice, quiet restaurant the next block over, almost directly behind Charles's house. Would that work?" Phil nodded. "Nell and I can settle ourselves there and listen in." Marty fixed Libby with a calculating eye. "Unless, of course, you're planning to spend the night?"

Libby laughed. "I'll keep my options open. I wouldn't want to tip him off, now would I? Besides, he's great between the sheets. Wouldn't you agree, Nell?"

I tried to look sophisticated and worldly. "Um, yes." I avoided looking at young Phil. He was getting a varied education today.

She gave me one last look, then took pity and changed the subject. "So the plan is that Nell plants the bugs in Charles's house during their big breakup, then the next night you two sit in the restaurant and listen to him and me do some heavy breathing, right?"

Poor Phil didn't know what to make of this, and studied his shoes intently.

Marty spoke briskly. "More or less, Libs. Phil, we'll go with the recording device at the restaurant with us — what's that, a couple hundred feet? Now, where can we put the bugs? How many can we use? How do we attach them?"

The conversation got technical, but luckily Phil seemed to know what he was talking about, and in the end we decided that we needed two bugs: one in the living room and one in Charles's bedroom, each with a pickup range of ten feet, and each recording independently. Phil told us that he could get equipment that would record a sneeze on the street a block away, but we assured him that was probably overkill. He looked disappointed. Marty and I would each be equipped with unobtrusive earpieces and a small recorder, so we could sit at a table in the restaurant and not attract too much attention.

I looked around at the group. The tea and cookies were long gone, and it was getting dark outside. Inside we were hatching a plot to catch a thief. Ms. Farnsworth in the bedroom with the electronic bug — the old game Clue drifted through my mind. And Charles's career and reputation would be the victims, if all went according to plan. That was still a big *if.*

"Well, now all we need is a time line. Libby? You and Charles have anything scheduled?"

"Charles has tickets for the symphony on Friday, so we could come back to his place after," she said. "Phil? Does that give you enough time to get the equipment? And to show us how it works?"

He nodded. "No problem."

She turned to me. "Nell, how about you?"

"I'll aim for tomorrow night. The timing might be tight — I'm flying back from Boston in the afternoon, and you'll still have to show me how to plant the bugs and how the listening end works." If Charles was going to the symphony with Libby on Friday, I could probably count on him being home on Thursday night. I could show up on his doorstep for a good-bye scene, which would allow me to wangle the opportunity to collect the few personal possessions I had left there — the nightgown, some toiletries, a bottle of perfume. Which would give me a legitimate excuse to get into the bedroom — just where I needed to go. "If I don't make it back in time, Libby will just have to take them along and figure something out."

"Great. Phil, when can you get the stuff together?" Marty asked.

"I can pick 'em up tomorrow morning."

"If you can get them to Marty, I'll come by her place on the way back from Boston," I told him.

"Make it happen, sweetie," Marty said. "So that's the plan. I get the bugs from Phil, Nell plants them at Charles's place, then Libby does her bit on Friday, with us listening. God, I feel like we're the Three Musketeers."

Libby stood up. "Ladies, this calls for a toast. I've got some champagne in the fridge." She disappeared toward what I assumed was the kitchen. Marty and I looked at each other.

"The time line is pretty tight, and I don't know what we do if the gizmos don't work. I sure as hell hope we're doing the right thing," I said dubiously.

"Nell, you worry too much. We *are* doing the right thing. It'll be fine."

"I'll make it work," I replied, with more assurance than I felt.

Libby returned with a champagne bottle and flutes. When she had filled and distributed them, Marty stood up and raised her glass. "To the downfall of the mighty Charles Worthington!" We saluted her and drank.

Driving home after dark, a single glass of Libby's excellent champagne bubbling through my system, I hoped that this crazy plan was going to work.

CHAPTER 24

I caught an early flight to Boston the next morning — hard on the credit card, but I didn't have much time, and now I needed to be back in the afternoon in time for Phil's tutorial. I'd told Carrie to let people know I was researching security systems at our sister institutions, which was at least partially true. I was scheduled to meet with Gail Wallace at the Massachusetts Book Club, a private library in Boston.

On the short flight, I found my thoughts drifting to Charles. Thinking about him was like poking a sore tooth: it was painful but hard to stop. I had trouble being objective about him when he'd made me feel like such a fool. I didn't mind getting kicked around in my love life — I was a big girl, I had gotten involved with Charles with my eyes wide open, and those were the breaks. I could handle that. But when he started messing with the Society, undermining an institution whose sole purpose was to preserve and protect the remnants of the past, I got mad. Nell Pratt, guardian of the gates, keeper of the flame, protector of the departed, and their treasures and reputations. I was ready to fight for truth, justice, and the American way. *Don't mess with the Society, bub, or you'll have to answer to me.*

I dragged my mind away from Charles and back to Gail Wallace, who seemed to be a more likely candidate to share gossip than Diane had been. The last time I had seen Gail had been at a fundraising seminar a couple of years ago. After we had suffered through an endless series of droning discussions about database management programs, multipart mailings, and event planning, ad nauseam, punctuated by inedible meals in airless function rooms, a number of us had retreated to the hotel bar and swapped development horror stories until they closed the place. I remembered that Gail relished the telling of a juicy anecdote, especially if she had an eager audience. I was prepared to be eager.

I arrived at the library promptly at eleven. I played out my spiel, dutifully took notes about the security system vendors Gail had interviewed; we wandered through the building, noting the carefully concealed spy cameras, the limited means of egress, the process for tracking who was in the building and who had left. Even if she ultimately kept silent about any tasty gossip, I was learning a heck of a lot about institutional security, which I hoped would come in handy. As the tour wound down, I said, "Gail, that was great — exactly what I needed. How about I take you out to lunch, to pay you back?"

She grinned at me. "I thought you'd never ask. What do you feel up for?"

"Hey, it's your city — you choose."

"Expense account?"

I gulped. "Sure — but remember I work for a nonprofit, just like you."

"I hear you. Okay, follow me."

Gail led the way down Beacon Hill and into the Back Bay, and she guided me to a charming small restaurant on Newbury Street. Once we were seated, she gave me a long look. "You didn't get in touch with me just to talk about security, did you?"

"No," I replied. "There's something else, now that we're off-site."

"That's what I figured." She waved at a waiter and ordered a drink. I stuck to iced tea, but I hoped that alcohol would make it easier for me to direct her conversation along the lines I needed.

"So, Gail," I started again, "nobody's stormed your gates since you put in this wonderful magic electronic system?"

Gail was ogling a thirty-something banker type who was standing at the bar with some buddies. "What? Oh, no, it works just fine. We'd been having some little problems with things vanishing, but it stopped cold, maybe six, seven years ago. You know, if we could just pay our staff better, they wouldn't feel the need to walk out with our stuff."

"You have a problem with staff pilfering?" I tried to sound appropriately incredulous.

"Oh, don't play dumb. You mean you don't have the same problem?"

I thought I'd do just that — play dumb — to be safe. "Hey, that's not my department, that's collections' problem. I just use what they tell me in my proposals."

Gail snorted. "Don't ask, don't tell, huh? Well, babe, it goes on everywhere. Sometimes it's bigger and better stuff, that's all." Her glass was empty, and she signaled for another drink. Since the banker had ignored her come-hither looks, she shifted her attentions to a tweedier collegiate type a few tables away. I thought I had better get my questions about Charles in before Gail became totally inebriated, or her longing gazes snared some hapless male.

"Wasn't Charles Worthington running your place a few years ago?" I probed.

Gail dragged her gaze back to me, reluctantly. "Sure was. That's right — he's your boss now, correct? I could tell you a few things about ol' Charlie."

Exactly what I wanted to hear. I put on my best gossip face and leaned forward. "Ooh, spill it!"

"You plan to hit him up for a raise or something?"

No, Gail, I intend to feed him to the FBI as a felon. "You never know. But he's quite a charmer, isn't he?"

"Ha!" Gail's eyes wandered again. "Well, Barbara Kensington certainly thought so."

It took a few moments for my mental database to crank out just who Barbara Kensington was: the current director of the Book Club — and Gail's boss. I put on what I hoped was a shocked expression. "You don't mean . . . were they?"

Gail nodded vigorously. "Oh yeah, big time. All the time. You know Barbara?"

I shook my head. "I've seen her a couple of times, but I've never talked with her. But — she's got to be pushing sixty, and, uh, not exactly a babe." That was being kind: Barbara was short, shapeless, and plain as a post. She had an excellent reputation as a scholar and administrator, but no one had ever said she had a life outside of her job.

"Yeah, I figure that's why she fell so hard. You know, repressed virgin or whatever. Charles came along and swept her off her feet, sweet-talking her, taking her out, wining and dining — the whole nine yards. Hey, for a while there she almost looked pretty. It got kind of embarrassing; in staff meetings she'd give him these gooey gazes and defer to him all the time. For the love of God, she was practically simpering, which sure isn't her usual style. I swear, that man turned her brain to mush."

Gail had my full attention. "So what happened?"

She shrugged. "I don't know. One day they were all lovey-dovey, and then suddenly he was gone — had a new job somewhere else. Boy, was she a pain to live with for the next few months, even though she stepped into his shoes. Everybody at the place was tiptoeing around, scared to death of her. If you looked at her cross-eyed, she'd bite your head off."

"Wow," I said.

"Yeah, right." Gail focused on her empty glass in front of her. "But you know the worst part? He was two-timing her."

"Huh?" I was rapidly exhausting my witty

repartee.

She leaned forward over the table and dropped her voice. "I saw him in a restaurant one night — he didn't see me. He was with another woman, and he was dripping charm all over her, and she was eating it up with a spoon. Funny thing was, she wasn't a babe, either, kind of middle-aged and plain. A lot like Barbara, come to think of it. What is it with this guy — he goes for pathetic older women?"

Yeah, like me, I reflected grimly. "Maybe he was just doing a little donor cultivation?" It was the best thing I could come up with. It's what I'd told myself, after all.

"Right," she snorted. "Very up close and personal. Say, has he been working his way through the society dames of Philadelphia?"

I wasn't about to say anything. "Got me. I don't run in those circles. He's certainly been a big help with our fundraising — our last president was a disaster. Had no tact and no social radar at all. Hey, shouldn't we think about ordering food? I'm starving."

She looked at me. "Oh, yeah, sure."

The food was good, and Gail ordered another martini. After declining dessert, I was trying to figure out how to make my escape without insulting her — although I wasn't sure she'd notice if I wasn't there —

when she fixed me with a bleary eye.

"That Charles — he sure was something."

She looked almost wistful, and I had a sudden, awful thought. "Were you two . . . ?"

"Yeah. It was great while it lasted." Her gaze sharpened as she looked at me. "You?"

I sighed but figured I owed her a nod.

Gail raised her glass to me. "Welcome to the club." Then she drained the glass.

I wondered how much of this conversation she would remember. Since her glass was officially empty, I convinced her that it was time to go. Luckily there were taxis cruising on Boylston Street, so I got her into a cab and pointed in the right direction. I stood on the pavement, watching the cab disappear, and felt sad and foolish. And then mad. Charles was a cad, a rat, a scoundrel . . . I couldn't find an adequate vocabulary, even dipping into Dickensian adjectives. But no way was I going to let him get away with it any longer — and I had the means to stop him.

I caught my plane back and after retrieving my car from the lot, I took off for Marty's house in the thick of rush-hour traffic. Phil was already there when I arrived, and Libby arrived soon afterward.

Phil had brought us an amazing array of

tiny toys and was delighted to show us how they worked. We spent an hour playing with them, interrupted only when Marty sent out for pizza. Marty's row house was large enough that we could test varying distances, and the reception was excellent from anywhere within the building. We also made sure we knew how to activate the recorder, since we might have only one chance to get this right, and we didn't want to blow it because we didn't know which button to push.

The bugs were simple — tiny disks with sticky stuff on one side. I could keep them in my pocket easily and stick them on the underside of something with no problem. That was the least of my worries.

Shortly before eight I stood up. "I'd better get going. Wish me luck, ladies."

"Go get 'em, Nell!"

Chapter 25

It was dark when I left Marty's house and drove slowly toward Charles's, and traffic had thinned out. I went around the block a few times until I began to wonder if the police would think I was casing the place. There was only one light on downstairs. I certainly hoped he didn't have another woman there, but I didn't think even he could find another dupe that fast, especially if he thought he had Libby on his line. Finally I parked, walked with heavy feet to his stoop, and rang the doorbell.

He opened the door quickly. I stood on the step below him, looking up at him. Casually dressed, by his standards — which meant he'd taken off his silk tie and his collar was unbuttoned — he looked tired. But he still looked good, even though I knew what a rat he was.

"Hello, Charles."

"Nell. What brings you here?" His voice

gave nothing away.

"May I come in?"

"Of course. Please. Can I get you anything?"

"A glass of wine would be nice." I needed a little liquid courage but had no intention of staying around past the first drink.

"I'll just be a moment." He disappeared toward the kitchen. I prowled around the parlor, running my finger along the (dust-free) tops of the eighteenth-century tables, reveling in the patina that comes only from years of hand polishing — all the while looking for a good place to stick my first bug. I settled for the underside of the end table next to the elegant damask-covered settee. When I straightened up quickly, I noticed a folder on the side table. Charles was still in the kitchen — I heard the pop of a wine cork, the clink of glasses. Idly I picked up the folder and opened it. Inside there was a hinged mat (acid free, I noted), which when opened revealed an old deed, its brown ink still legible. I tilted it toward the light to make out the signature: William Penn. *Oh my.* I perused the text briefly — it looked like a deed for a piece of property in Bucks County. A small piece of Pennsylvania history, over three hundred years old.

Charles returned, bearing two glasses. I

held up the folder. "This is marvelous, Charles. Is it new?"

He smiled. "Yes — I saw it in a catalog for an auction in New York, and I just had to indulge myself. It was a bit expensive, but it seemed so appropriate to bring it back to Philadelphia, don't you think?"

"Of course." I set down the deed down gently, out of harm's way, before taking one of the glasses from him. He took my elbow and steered me gently toward the damask-covered settee.

"You look troubled." He took a sip, studying my face. "This isn't really a social call, is it?" he said quietly.

"No, Charles, it's not." I took a sip of my own wine, then inhaled. "It's been a hell of a few weeks, hasn't it? With Alfred dying like that, and now the FBI coming around."

I might have been imagining it, but I thought I saw a flicker of relief pass over his aristocratic features.

"A tragic thing, Alfred's death — and of course, your finding him. He was a good man. We'll need to start the search for his successor as soon as possible."

"Of course. But I didn't really come to talk about Alfred, either. Charles, Alfred's death made me think about my own life. I mean, the man lived for his work, and he had no life outside of the Society. I don't want to find myself in that position."

"Nell, what are you trying to say?"

For a moment I wondered if he was afraid that I was going to ask him to take our relationship to a higher level, and I hurried to disabuse him of the idea.

"Charles, I have truly enjoyed our time together, and you're a wonderful man." *That's right, lay it on thick.* "But we've always been honest with each other." *Like hell we have.* "I think I need to move on, find someone who's willing to make a greater commitment to me, to a life together."

Before he could protest, I help up one hand. "No, Charles, I'm not trying to pressure you into anything. You've never made any promises to me, and I've never kidded myself that we had anything more than a casual relationship. And that was fine, until now. But now I need something different."

I looked at him to see how he was taking it. I couldn't see any signs of devastation. "I wanted to tell you face-to-face, because I don't want this to jeopardize our working relationship. I love the Society, and I think I've done good work there. I would be delighted to keep working with you to make it all that it can be." *As soon as we clear up that little problem of the dead employee and the thefts.*

He smiled with just the right degree of sadness. "You have indeed, and I don't know what I would have done without you to advise me. And you're a very wise woman, Nell. Of course I'll regret that we won't be as close as we have been, but I respect your wishes and your honesty." He raised his glass in a mock toast; I responded in kind.

For one last time I looked at him, really looked. He was still elegant, very much in control of himself. I felt a stab of regret: in a different universe, maybe we could have had something real. But I knew now what lay beneath that polished facade, and he didn't move me. I drained my glass and stood up.

"Thank you for making it so easy for me. Oh, if you don't mind — I'd like to collect the few things I left here? My silk night-gown, for instance?"

"Of course. They're upstairs. Let me get them for you."

I moved quickly to beat him to the stairs. "I'll go — I know where everything is, and I might forget something. I won't be a minute."

I dashed upstairs and began collecting my things, starting with the nightgown. Along the way I stuck a second bug beneath his mahogany night stand. I took one last glance around. I was going to miss the elegance of this place, I realized, far more than I was going to miss its owner. As I came back down the stairs he met me at the bottom, offering a pristine shopping bag for the odds and ends I was clutching — Brooks Brothers, I noted.

At the door, I turned and said quietly, "Good-bye, Charles," kissed him on the cheek, and slipped out without any further fuss. I at least was a class act. I managed to remember not to skip with glee as I walked down the block away from his house toward the restaurant where Marty was waiting.

Marty was seated at a booth at the rear of the restaurant, a knit cap pulled low on her head — her idea of a disguise, I guessed. She must really be enjoying this. I slipped into the other side of the booth.

"Mission accomplished. Did you test it?"

Marty looked around at the few other patrons in the nearly empty restaurant. Nobody showed the slightest interest. Then she pulled a small box out of her bag, plugged in a set of earbuds, and handed it to me. The red light was blinking, so I assumed it was on and recording. I put on my own earbuds. She studied the buttons on the small recorder, hit Rewind, then Play. I gave Marty a thumbs-up — the transmission, apparently from the living room, was crystal clear: at first I could hear footsteps, the rustling of papers, the chink of a glass as Charles set it down on a table; and then I heard myself and Charles. After listening for a minute, I pulled the earbuds off. I sounded unbearably sanctimonious, at least to my own ears.

"Perfect. Phil picked well." I took a sip of coffee. "Marty, were you listening?"

She nodded, shamefaced. "I was — just to make sure it was working. You did a good job, very smooth. I certainly would have believed you, and I'd give odds that Charles did. I'll bet he's feeling very grateful to you at the moment. He should be all primed and ready for Libby. We'll have to remember to tell her to be very sympathetic and stroke his wounded ego." She cocked her head at me. "Are you all right?"

I nodded firmly. "Yes, I am. Give me a little longer and I'll feel damn good."

CHAPTER 26

Marty and I debriefed Libby over a hasty lunch on Friday. We met in a hole-in-the-wall restaurant near the public library. It all felt very cloak-and-daggerish, and faintly ridiculous.

"He's all yours," I told Libby. "I let him down gently, but no doubt there are a few pinpricks in his massive ego."

"He's a man, isn't he?" Libby said complacently, spearing the good stuff in her salad. "He just got dumped. I will be appropriately attentive. He won't know a thing."

I sighed and prodded my salad. "You know, I still feel like an idiot. I can't have meant anything to him, other than a source of information and the occasional roll in the hay. I just didn't want to see it."

Libby regarded me with a mixture of sympathy and exasperation. "Oh, Nell, don't feel bad — I've just had more experience at manipulating men than you have.

Anyway, I never pretended to myself that this was serious, but he's a very presentable escort, and he's very easy to be around. So attentive, you know?"

"I know," I said glumly.

"All the equipment working?" she said around her full mouth.

"Like a charm." I turned to Marty. "Marty, what does Phil think we're doing? I do hope he's not going to get into any trouble over this."

"Nonsense. He's just a kid who's good with gadgets, and he's thrilled to have a chance to show off. Besides, he wouldn't rat on us — I'm paying half his tuition at Penn. We're not going to get caught. And if we do, Jimmy can fix it."

I certainly hoped she was right. I also hoped we wouldn't need any "fixing."

Libby finished chewing and drained her Bloody Mary, signaling the waitress for another at the same time. "So, tonight's the night. He's picking me up at seven."

"You know what we need to hear?"

"Well, if I play this right, I nudge him into declaring that he wants to spend the rest of his life with me," she began. "Then I convince him that, despite being hopelessly besotted, I still retain a few shreds of common sense, and I'm not about to support him, and I'm sure he doesn't want to be just a gigolo, since his job at that tacky little place downtown certainly doesn't pay enough. So, what are his plans? And if I'm as good as I think I am, he'll spill."

She winked at Marty. "I made my second husband — you remember Aston, don't you, Marty? — sign a prenup, and I demanded full financial disclosure. So there's a precedent on record, and Charles should know that if he's done his homework. I could do no less with Number Three."

"Maybe. But remember that he's got to trot out his ill-gotten gains somehow."

"Exactly. He's got to prove he's worthy of my affections." She looked at us both and laughed. "Don't worry so much, you two. I have my ways. I'll get him exactly where I want him."

"Just make sure it's not the kitchen floor, please — we only covered the living room and the bedroom."

"Check. Oh, I'm *so* glad you got me involved in this, you two. I haven't had this much fun in years. I never thought I'd get to do something so exciting — too bad it's a one-shot deal."

On Friday night, I hung around the Society doing mindless paperwork, until it was time to meet Marty. At eight thirty, the two of us were seated at a table at our restaurant, the one in proven range of our transmitter. We ate some forgettable food — which might explain why the place was half empty — and I went to the bathroom three times, because I didn't want to have to go in the middle of the action and miss something important. Marty's sizable tip had ensured that we could hold the table as long as we wanted. Now all we could do was wait.

At ten fifteen, the little light on our receiver flickered, indicating it was picking up something. Marty and I exchanged startled glances across the table. We each donned our earbuds, like two warriors arming for battle. It was show time.

Footsteps. Giggles. Murmurs. More footsteps. Marty and I were still as stone figures, staring into oblivion, trying to visualize what was happening. Someone took off a coat; there was a clank of hangers in the hall closet (Charles was a fanatic about hanging up clothes).

"A liqueur?" Charles's voice. He came across well, his tones smooth and mellow — maybe he could consider a job in radio broadcasting. From his jail cell.

"Fabulous, darling." Libby's alto purr. "I'll have some of your lovely Cognac."

The clink of glasses, more footsteps.

Rustle-thump: they were on the settee. I followed them in my mind. A discreet gurgle — Charles pouring into the crystal snifters. My, these bugs were sensitive.

"There you go. What shall we drink to?"

"To many more lovely evenings like this one, my sweet. Thank you for that fabulous dinner — I never know what to choose, because it all sounds so wonderful. You picked just the right dishes. You know me so well, Charles." Libby was troweling it on.

That's right, Libby, throw yourself into your role.

Rustle, pant. "Oh, Charles, what you do to me . . . I can't get enough of you." Oops. Marty's and my eyes met, then slid apart quickly. Things were going according to plan, but what we had talked about in the bright light of Libby's library didn't seem quite the same as sitting like a pair of perverts and listening to the reality of it. I hoped fervently that Libby could extract what we needed from Charles and we could sign off before things got too hot and heavy.

"Elizabeth, darling, you know you have the same effect on me, as you can see." *Oh, ick.* "Elizabeth . . ." His voice was husky, and the following silence was filled with more heavy breathing. *Come on, Libby — get on with it.* Then Charles spoke again. "I think we should consider becoming more than just lovers." Aha! The first salvo. And Libby hadn't even had to make it herself. Marty and I held our breath.

A new waiter appeared at our table. Marty and I didn't even look at him, but we both waved him away frantically. He retreated, bewildered. Okay, we were crazy ladies, but we tipped well.

Libby spoke in her lazy drawl. "Why, Charles, what do you mean?" *Come on, Libby, don't overplay it.*

"Darling, I've never met a woman like you. You are amazing — smart, funny, and sexy. Damn sexy." There followed another interlude of inarticulate sounds. Then Charles's voice again, heavy, rough.

"Marry me, Elizabeth. We could have a wonderful life together."

"Oh, Charles. There's nothing I'd like more. But . . ."

Slither — the sound of silk. And was that a zipper?

"But what? You're free, I'm free. We love each other. What more is there?"

"Oh, Charles, I do love you. But . . . I'm afraid. Of what other people might think. That you're marrying me for my money. You know — you're so handsome and successful, but I'm . . . a little older than you

341

are, and I know what my mirror tells me. People will talk. I know I shouldn't care what they think, but I do." I looked at Marty again, and I think we both would have burst out laughing if we weren't afraid of missing something. Libby certainly had a flair for this.

"Let them talk. You know what you feel, and what I feel. It's no one's business but our own. Who are they to matter?"

"Oh, but, Charles, they do. You haven't been here very long — you don't know what a provincial town Philadelphia can be. And it's my home — they're my friends."

A brief silence. Was Charles weighing his chances? Would he play the next card? I didn't dare breathe.

"Elizabeth, I know it's in poor taste to talk about such things, but I want to assure you that I'm not without resources. You wouldn't have any reason to be ashamed." *Come on, Charles, come on. We want details!*

"Well, darling," Libby began, with just the right note of skepticism, "I know you have a nice home and nice things, but . . . that's not the same as *money*. After all, you work." The contempt in Libby's voice when she said "work" was perfectly calibrated.

A silence that seemed somehow colder. Maybe Charles wasn't used to meeting any resistance to his wooing. Finally he chuckled — an odd sound from him. "You're perfectly right, my dear. I must be honest with you. I don't flaunt it, but I assure you that my net worth is in the seven-figure range. Do you need to see documentation?"

Ah. Well, there we were. He had the money.

"Oh, darling. I'm sorry — I didn't mean to imply that you were taking advantage of me. And I'm so relieved. But a girl can't be too careful. I had to ask."

"And I respect you for it. I wouldn't have it any other way."

"Thank you, Charles." Another interlude as Libby soothed Charles's wounded pride. Marty studied her nails. I refolded my napkin several times and wondered if I still remembered how to make an origami swan. After a few minutes, I broke the silence.

"Well, we're halfway there," I whispered. "Charles is claiming to have a lot more money than James seems to think. Do you think Libby is going to get any more, or will she get swept away by passion?"

"Don't worry about Libby — she's very focused. She's just paving the way."

Right. From what I was hearing, that part was going very well. No words emerged for a while, although I wouldn't say things were silent. Finally Charles spoke.

"Wouldn't we be more comfortable upstairs?"

"Brilliant idea."

The settee creaked as it was relieved of the weight of two bodies. Footsteps padded away, presumably toward the stairs. Then the sounds faded . . . and resumed again, from the bedroom transmitter. I hoped Libby planned to do a little talking before launching into any other activities.

There was a squeak as they sat on the bed. "Oh, Charles, marriage . . . it's such a big step. I've been there before, as you know, and so have you. So many details — children to tell, houses to sell. My place in the city, this place, my country house. That house might be much more comfortable for the two of us. Unless, of course, the commute would be too much for you? But then, you wouldn't need to keep working at all, would you? At that tatty little place?"

Another silence. From what I could hear, Charles was removing his clothes, one piece at a time, and hanging up each piece. Shoes neatly aligned in the closet, pants on their hanger, shirt and socks in the hamper. Libby, on the other hand, was not moving.

Charles spoke again. "Darling, you have on far too many clothes. Here, let me help

344

you." Which he proceeded to do, stopping to hang up Libby's dress along the way. "There, much better."

"Oh, Charles."

"Darling."

Marty signaled the hovering waiter. "Could you get us, uh, some ice water?" She looked at me, and I nodded emphatically. "And some coffee?"

I didn't know whether I should remove the earbuds, out of respect for what we knew was going on, or whether to worry about missing something crucial. After a couple of minutes, I was convinced that they were beyond words, at least temporarily. I dangled the earpieces around my neck and looked at Marty.

"Maybe she's waiting until . . . after?"

Marty nodded. "That makes some sense. Men're a lot more likely to talk then, don't you think? All their defenses are down. Unless, of course, they just fall asleep." She looked at her watch. "How long . . ."

"Fifteen minutes," I said promptly. "I'll put a five on it."

"I'll take twenty minutes," Marty snapped back. "You may know Charles, but I know Libby."

"We're awful, aren't we?" I giggled. She smiled her agreement.

It was, in fact, eighteen minutes before the rhythmic noises of the bedsprings ceased. There was heavy breathing again, and then it slowed until it approached a normal rate. I handed Marty a five-dollar bill. "You were closer."

"Oh, Charles," Libby cooed, "that was wonderful."

I swallowed a laugh.

"You bring out the best in me, darling," he replied, his voice rough. "And we could be doing this much more often, if you marry me."

"Oh, Charles, I'm so tempted. But wouldn't you be bored?"

"Sweetheart, you could never bore me. I'd love to grow old with you. But . . ."

"Yes, Charles?" I wondered if it was possible to hear eyelashes fluttering.

"May I be honest with you?"

"Of course, Charles." *That's right, Libby, don't overdo it. Nice restraint.*

"Elizabeth, I want to be worthy of you. So I want to share something with you, something I've never told another woman. I don't believe my career is over — I never pretended that being president of the Society was the highest pinnacle. No, I want something more. I want to leave my mark in a bigger way."

346

Marty and I exchanged a glance, and she cocked one eyebrow at me.

"And I'm sure you could, Charles, but whatever do you mean?"

Marty and I stopped breathing.

"Elizabeth, I have a plan, something dear to my heart, something I've been thinking about for a long time, since the beginning of my career. I'd like to share it with you, and I'd like you to be a part of it."

"Tell me, Charles," Libby purred.

"I want to create something new, a multi-disciplinary center for the study of American history — sort of a nexus where all the resources come together: museum-quality artifacts, original sources, modern references, state-of-the-art technology, the best academic minds, young scholars in training. Nothing like this has ever been done. Each discipline has been locked into its own narrow concerns, afraid to step outside of their box. I want to break out of the box, create something new, bold, exciting. Can you see my vision?"

"You make it sound wonderful, Charles. But — what does this mean?"

Charles's voice swelled with a different kind of passion. "A new center, combining the best of the old and the new. Right here in Philadelphia. And where better? This is where our country was born, and the great leaders walked our streets, talking together to shape this nation. We have everything we need right here — but it will take someone with vision to pull it all together, and I believe I am that person. And you can be part of it. We would be an incredible team, darling. What do you think?"

"Charles, I think that's a wonderful idea. And I can see how excited you are. Mmmm, very excited. Come here."

I pulled off my earphones again and inhaled deeply, as did Marty.

"Oh . . . my . . . God," I breathed. I had known that Charles was ambitious. He was, at least once upon a time, a good historian, an honest scholar. He never falsified anything on his résumé — the search committee checked his academic degrees and his references, of course, and some of the board members asked around. But this? I certainly hadn't seen this coming. "We were right, but we didn't see the big picture. Charles isn't doing this just for the money — the money is a means to an end. He's doing it to build a national shrine to Charles Worthington. Is this even possible, or is he crazy?" I looked at Marty in appeal.

"It looks to me like Charles wants more than the leadership of a small and fusty place like the Society," Marty began slowly. "He wants a bigger stage — an institution that would shape the direction of modern historical interpretation, with himself at the head. And, as you well know, that would take money. Lots of money. That explains a lot." She stopped and looked at me to see how I was reacting.

Actually, I felt as though my head was full of Jiffy Pop. Little kernels of doubt that I had nudged out of the way when Charles and I were seeing each other now started popping, expanding rapidly. "So he's got whatever money he collected along the way, from all those objects he stole and sold at his last few jobs, not to mention some or all of the five million dollars' worth of items he's skimmed from the Society's collections. But five million plus whatever won't be enough, so he's going to marry the rest of it."

"*And* give himself an entree into top society in town — the ones with money. That matters, too, around here."

"Hell and damnation. He certainly took a long view when he planned. He's smart, but he's also rotten. Do you think we've got enough on tape?"

"I know I don't want to listen to any more, that's for sure. I'll give the guy credit

— he's got imagination." She paused. "And stamina."

I started giggling and then gave up and laughed out loud. "I do hope Libby is enjoying this as much as we are."

"Libby always manages to get what she wants. Good person to have on our side. From what we've heard, I'd say she's having a wonderful time." She punched the Off button on our little box and sat back. "Well, I'm starving now, but I'm pretty sure they closed the kitchen down a while ago — they only let us stay because I gave the staff a whopping tip. What say we adjourn to my place and call Jimmy?"

"Marty, it's midnight!"

"Oh, fine, you wet blanket. I guess it can wait until morning. I don't think Charles will have the energy to do any more harm tonight."

CHAPTER 27

I went home, but I couldn't sleep. I hated the Charles we had uncovered — user, thief, and apparently megalomaniac with delusions of grandeur.

I still couldn't see where Alfred Findley had fit in. The stakes were higher than I had thought, and Alfred's meddling would certainly have been a threat to Charles's grand plans. But Charles had a good alibi; I was even part of it. And Alfred's murder seemed carelessly planned. Unlike everything else Charles had done for, what — decades? — it seemed almost spontaneous, although the murderer had gotten away with it so far. Of course, Charles had enough money to hire whatever muscle he needed . . . and there were the pieces that Marty had seen in Alfred's apartment — somebody had to have planted those.

Marty called at eight Saturday morning. "Jimmy's coming by at ten. Can you get

351

here by then?" She sounded subdued. Maybe she hadn't slept, either.

"Sure. I'll meet you at your place." I was already ensconced in one of Marty's armchairs when James arrived. Marty went to fetch him at the door, and they were talking intently as they came down the hall to the back of the house. He stopped dead when he saw me, sprawled comfortably.

"James, how nice to see you again," I said amiably, raising my coffee mug in salute.

"Nell," he said neutrally, his eyes wary. "Marty, you didn't mention Nell would be here."

Marty laid a hand on his arm. "Now, Jimmy, don't get huffy. We have a little surprise for you. Here, I'll take your coat. Get yourself some coffee and sit down."

He gave me an enigmatic look, then finally shrugged and took off his suit jacket, loosened his tie, poured himself a cup of coffee, and draped himself on one of Marty's chairs. "Good boy," Marty said. She glanced briefly at me before beginning. "We have something we want you to listen to. A recording we made, of Elizabeth Farnsworth and Charles Worthington together."

James put the cup down and sat up straight again. Uh-oh, Mr. Agent Man was back. "Wait a minute. That's your old pal

Libby, with Charles Worthington? You recorded them?"

"Yes, we did. Charles didn't know about it, but Libby did. She's been dating Charles for a while, and she was happy to go along with this. Yes, I know that it will never be admissible in a court of law. Don't give me a lecture, Jimmy — we're trying to help. And I think we've got something pretty big."

He stared at us, one at a time, then shook his head. "I don't know what you think you're doing, but I do know you're messing with a federal investigation. That is *not* a good idea."

"Jimmy, just shut up and listen, will you? You can figure out what you want to do to us later."

She pushed the Play button on the recorder, and the familiar sounds of Libby and Charles issued forth, loud and clear. I watched James's face as he listened intently, albeit with a growing look of distaste. His expression brightened when we got to the part about Charles's net worth. As the happy couple decided to go upstairs, Marty pressed Stop.

"So, what do you think?" she asked brightly.

He thought for a moment before speaking. "I think that you have some excellent sound equipment there. I think this is all entirely illegal and I shouldn't be listening to it. And I think we'd better look a little harder at Charles's financial records — there must be a dummy organization or an offshore account, or something where he's been hiding the extra money, because it's not in any of his regular accounts."

Marty reached for the machine, but James grabbed her hand. "You can't mean there's more?" He looked pained.

"Jimmy, if you could see your face. Yes, there's more — his motive. Just listen." She started the tape again. No fast-forward for Marty: she was going to make her unfortunate cousin listen to every sigh and squeaking bedspring. After a certain point, I found I couldn't look him in the eye any longer, and made an in-depth study of the state of my cuticles. When I sneaked a peek at James's face, it was an interesting shade of red, but he was still paying close attention. And when Charles launched into his grand scheme, his expression hardened.

The tape finally ended. Marty shut off the machine with a crisp snap, sat back in her chair, and looked at her cousin. "Well?"

I was beginning to appreciate the old-fashioned term *apoplectic*. Poor James looked as though he wanted to explode. He took a couple of deep breaths, without looking at either of us, before he attempted to speak.

"Martha Terwilliger, I don't know whether to arrest you, strangle you, or kiss you. And you, Nell — I'm sure she dragged you into this, but you're still an accomplice. Don't say I didn't warn you. I don't know how many laws you've broken. We are not having this conversation. I am not here. Got it?"

Marty and I nodded meekly, avoiding looking at each other.

He wasn't finished. "And I'm willing to bet Charles Worthington has broken a few laws we hadn't even thought of. Wait until our lawyers get hold of this."

He took a sip of coffee, then resumed in a calmer tone.

"All right, what does this nonexistent recording tell us? One, Charles has, or at least claims he has, substantial assets that we have not yet located. Two, we know why he has been amassing his little nest egg. Could he really do what he described?"

"I'll take that one, Marty." I decided it was time to stake my claim in this conversation. "I think the short answer is yes. I don't know if you could put a dollar figure on it; a lot depends on whether he can acquire an existing building or needs to build one, what kinds of collections he wants to put together — just how big and ambitious his goals are. He'd need a lot of money — tens of millions. But the more money he brings to the table, or controls directly, the more control he'd have over the whole operation."

James looked at me, bewildered. "But he's already head of the place — isn't that enough?"

I shook my head decisively. "Not for Charles — he's thinking bigger. I've been giving it some thought, and I'm guessing that he figures he can make the Society's reputation and its financial situation appear so compromised that if word of the thefts got out, he could swoop in and act as a savior — offer to absorb the collections, the library, maybe even the staff, into his new organization. Can't you see it? He wouldn't have to kowtow to a board or suck up to outside donors, or at least not as much. He'd tell the citizens of Philadelphia that he's doing them a great favor, saving a big chunk of their heritage — when all the time he set them up just so he could feed his own ego." I was working up a good head of steam.

"Mmph." James didn't offer any additional comments. "Tell me, whatever made you get Libby involved?"

Marty said promptly, "Luckily she's his latest conquest — at least that's what *he* thinks — and she was happy to help. But we figured he was acting according to pattern; he tends to use women, as Nell found out, for inside information, to make his job easier, and, yes, for money. He's done it before. Nell talked to a couple of women who confirmed it, one way or another."

James regarded me as though I were a specimen under a microscope. "Ah, yes, your colleagues in Boston and Washington."

I grinned at him. "They both said pretty much the same thing. There were some thefts around the time Charles was at their institutions, as I'm sure you know. What they might not have told you is that he'd also charmed a number of strategic women and then dropped them when they were no longer useful to him. And he was very careful — he kept his thefts off the radar for a long time."

James didn't say anything. After a few moments, he stood up. "Well, you've given me a lot to think about."

Marty was on her feet quickly, blocking his way to the door. "Oh, no, you don't. We showed you ours, now you have to show us yours. You must have found something on the thefts, or you aren't half the man you claim to be."

James looked a bit smug. "Yes, Martha, we are about to close the jaws of the trap. That's all I will say, but you can expect news shortly."

She tried to outstare him, hoping for more specifics, but he had clammed up. He looked at me. "Nell, would you see me out, please?"

In the vestibule, his coat on, he turned to me and launched into a lecture. "Are you crazy? I know my cousin is a loose cannon, but I thought you might have enough common sense to at least stay on the right side of the law. What on earth were you thinking?"

I fought a fleeting impulse to apologize, and then I got mad. "Hey look, pal, this is my career, my credibility on the line. Unlike Marty, I don't have a nice rich family to fall back on — I work for my living. The longer this drags on, the less marketable I become, especially if the Society sinks under me. And you all at the FBI have no imagination! You never would have stumbled on the way Charles uses women, not in a million years! And it was even worse than we thought!" I felt the sting of tears behind my eyes, and now I was mad at him *and* at myself. "Well,

I've had enough. Sure, Marty and I bent a few laws, but we got the goods, didn't we? We figured out the *why* for you — now all you need to do is work out the *how* and prove it."

I stopped, since I had nothing left to say, and I was either going to spit at him or burst into tears. "So get out there and do it, damn you," I ended feebly.

James stood perfectly still, staring at me. I had no clue what he was thinking. I knew what *I* was thinking: that I looked like a fool. He started to raise a hand, then dropped it. Finally he spoke.

"Nell, I'm sorry. You're right. I hadn't thought about how this affects you personally, and I can understand your frustration. But you have to look at it from my end, too: I need to build a case that will stand up in a court of law, that can't be challenged, and you're not making that any easier. I appreciate what you've done, but, please, can you two stay out of it from here on out? I promise, this will all be over soon." For a moment he looked as though he wanted to say more but then apparently thought better of it. "I'll be in touch."

CHAPTER 28

I closed the door slowly and walked back to Marty's living room. Marty looked critically at me and added, "You know, I think he likes you. Most people, he would have chewed their heads off. Yours is still attached. More coffee?"

"Great." I refilled my cup. "Now what?"

"For once I think I'll go along with Jimmy. We've given him all the information he could possibly want. Let him take care of it."

I felt curiously deflated. Was that really how this was going to end? And hadn't we lost sight of Alfred's death, in all of our plotting and scheming? Neither the police nor James seemed to care about that.

I laughed bitterly. "You know, before this whole mess started, I never realized how much we all depend on the basic honesty of our patrons and staff. We've always assumed that they respected the collections, wanted to preserve them — not rip them off for their own selfish ends. I really feel betrayed, even apart from the job thing. Naive, wasn't I?"

"I don't think so." Marty studied her own coffee, swirling the liquid around the cup. "Or even if you were, it doesn't mean you were wrong. It does take a special kind of person to care more about something abstract, like history, than about their own needs. Hey, I've worked with you for years now, since long before Charles came on the scene, anyway. I've never known you to cut corners, to fudge anything — basically, to do anything that didn't benefit the Society. I know you sure don't do it for the money. I have to figure you do it because you *do* care. So, if you have to be a little naive, if you have to believe in the best of other people, then I guess it goes with the job. It's a good thing, Nell."

I was a bit stunned. I hadn't known that she had paid me that much attention. "Marty — thank you. I don't know what to say. I've just tried to do my job, and I really do love the place, and the people are great, and, yes, I really do feel it's a privilege to handle some of the things I've had a chance to. And that's why it makes me so mad that somebody like Charles — somebody in a position of power — doesn't. But . . . I guess I never expected anybody else to notice. And I've got to say I misjudged you, and I'm very sorry."

Marty laughed. "Yeah, I know, you thought I was a lightweight who just liked sticking her nose into things. It's not the first time. Actually, you can hear a lot more that way."

I laughed. "I'll have to remember that. Well, then, what about this little FBI trap? Has James told you anything more about it? What's the bait?"

"You remember that Bucks County collection that was left to the Society a couple of years ago? That guy who had a strange house museum, and who'd never changed anything in the place?"

I nodded. "Yes. I worked with the executors to see that there was enough money to catalog the materials."

"But it hasn't happened yet, right?"

"Right. They finished probate maybe a year ago and delivered the stuff to the Society, and we stuck it in storage boxes on the fourth floor until we could get to it. We were going to advertise for a student intern to work on it next semester."

Marty cocked her head at me. "So nobody really knows what's in all those boxes?"

"Not really. I looked at some of the stuff right after the man died, when it was still at his house, just to get an idea of the scope, how much space we'd need, things like that. It was a real hodgepodge — junk like his Aunt Minnie's diaries, which talked mainly about the weather, mixed in with some really good items like detailed eighteenth-century records of the construction of the first house on the property, which architectural historians would love to get their hands on. I don't think the man ever threw anything out, and he was the last of his family."

"I've been through it," Marty said.

I looked at her quizzically. "What? When?"

"Not at the Society. His sister was married to my aunt's husband's brother, so I spent some time at the house. Since he never married and never had children, and had this big place on the river, he used to hold family reunions every now and then when I was growing up. He loved to show us his treasures when we were kids, and I was one of the few who cared. And when I got to college, I asked if I could use some of his documents for my undergraduate thesis. Why do you think he ended up leaving all the stuff to the Society?"

"Marty, are you related to *everyone* in the

five-county area?"

"Maybe half, or at least the families who've been around a couple of hundred years. Anyway, bottom line is I know what's in the collections now at the Society. So I pointed Jimmy to a couple of real gems. Like some William Penn letters, and the original land grant for the old man's property, signed by the founder himself."

"Wow. I had no idea."

"Thing is, I know who else was poking around the collections."

The gears in my mind were grinding rather slowly. "You mean — Charles?"

"Yup. I ran into him up on the fourth floor recently — he was rummaging through the boxes. He gave me a nice song and dance about familiarizing himself with the collections, and I bought it at the time. I think we ended up having lunch together that day. Maybe he thought he could distract me with his charms."

There was a little bell ringing somewhere in my head. William Penn . . . "Marty," I said slowly, "when I was planting the bugs at Charles's place, there was a deed on his desk signed by William Penn. I asked him about it, and he told me he'd picked it up at an auction in New York. I didn't think much about it at the time, but it sounds as though it could have come from that collection."

"Would you recognize it if you saw it again?"

"I think so. You don't get to handle original Penn documents that often. And I remember that the purchaser's name on the deed was the same as one of our major donors."

"That's the one. So that would make two of us who would recognize it. Anyway, to get back to the FBI side — Jimmy's been working with some of his colleagues in the New York office. They've got more people there who work with art thefts, dealers, collectors, and such — and besides, they're somewhere that isn't Philadelphia, which is good. They've got somebody working with them who's put out the word that he wants an autograph piece from William Penn and is willing to pay big for it. All very low-key, word of mouth, that sort of thing."

"That kind of stuff really goes on? And is it legal?"

"You really are an innocent, aren't you? Of course it goes on, all the time. And there are various dealers who are willing to act as go-betweens without asking too many questions — for the right price, or finder's fee. The FBI knows who they are, but they don't usually hassle them, because they're reasonably small fish, at least by their standards. We're not talking about Rembrandts or Impressionists here, we're talking about letters, diaries, little stuff. It's a whole lot easier to trade in, especially below the radar. And, as we've already proved, a whole lot harder to identify and track. Anyway, our undercover collector in New York got a discreet message — from someone in Philadelphia."

"No! You think Charles is selling that deed?"

"Already has. Charles moves fast. He knew you'd seen it, and he probably wanted to get it off his hands ASAP. The collector in New York will be watching for it, and he'll let Jimmy know when it arrives."

"He wouldn't just stick it in the mail, would he?" I was worried about that poor, fragile, three-hundred-year-old piece of paper.

"He's probably got a courier service, if he does this regularly. I bet the faithful Doris Manning would know."

"You're right. She handles all that kind of stuff for him. Heck, she even picks up his dry cleaning." I grimaced.

"I wonder if she's in the office today?"

"Maybe, if Charles asked her to be.

Should we call her?"

"Let me. She's more likely to answer the phone if it's a board member."

Marty got up and went to the kitchen to make the call. She was gone a couple of minutes, and when she came back she said, "She's there. She said Charles was in earlier and, in her words, 'left some work' for her. I didn't dare ask any more."

"Well, if the Penn deed is going out today to the guy in New York, at least we'll know where that is. I hope there's nothing else in that shipment."

"Amen. Anyway, when that arrives, Jimmy should have what he needs to make his move on Charles — if we haven't given him enough other stuff. The fact that you saw it closes the circle, from the Society to Charles to the FBI's collector."

"But James doesn't know some of it officially."

"There is that. But cheer up, Nell. Charles's days are numbered."

We raised our coffee cups to each other in mock salute.

CHAPTER 29

I had a lot to think about on the way home from Marty's, so I started by making yet another mental list. One, I'd been flattered and touched by what Marty had said about me. I did care about the Society, and I tried to do a good job — it was nice that someone had noticed. Two, I'd been a fool about Charles. Looking back, I realized that in fact he had gotten a lot more from me than I had ever gotten from him. I'd been the perfect dupe. I had believed that whatever our personal relationship might be, at least he respected my professional abilities. Wrong: he'd assumed I was both blind and stupid and tried to frame me. *Great judge of character you are, Nell.*

But the nagging voice inside kept coming back to the big Number Three: who killed Alfred? We didn't seem any closer to an answer, and we were woefully short of suspects. Had Charles actually hired someone to do the deed? Was he working with someone else inside the Society? Had Latoya felt threatened by Alfred's insistent reminders that things weren't where they were supposed to be, and silenced him? Heck, for all I knew, Felicity Soames had grown tired of playing watchdog and whacked Alfred. All of the above seemed equally unlikely.

At least James would have enough evidence now to arrest Charles. That was a plus. All he had to do was collect the proof from his sham collector in New York, completing the chain of evidence, and reel Charles in.

But when was this going to happen? How long would it take the Penn deed to reach the New York buyer? Sunday I was reluctant to leave the house in case I missed a phone call from James or Marty, so I stayed home and cleaned things I'm not sure I had ever cleaned before: the tops of high cupboards, under the refrigerator. I scrubbed the grout lines of the tile in the bathroom with a toothbrush. Then I made lists of my CDs, my books. I labeled and filed all my photographs. I updated my address book.

In between I fidgeted, staring at the phone, willing it to ring. Naturally, when it finally did, I jumped a foot and snatched it up quickly.

"Hello?" I said breathlessly.

"Is this Nell?"

"Doris? Is that you?" She was the last person in the world I would have expected a call from on a Sunday. Why was she calling me?

"Yes, it is. Charles asked me to call you. He said there's something here at the Society that you need to see."

My brain was working slowly. "What is it?"

Doris sniffed. "I'm afraid I can't say. He just told me to call you and ask you to come. We'll be waiting for you here." She hung up before I could protest.

Well, that was certainly interesting. I tried to work out who knew what at the moment. Charles didn't know that I knew he was behind the thefts. Maybe he had collected all the things he hadn't already sold and concealed them somewhere in the Society building, and he was inviting me to share in his big discovery — *Aha, the lost is found!* To someone who was not in the loop on this, it would sound quite plausible. Well, I could play along.

But I wasn't going to be stupid about it. I picked up the phone and punched in Marty's home number — no answer. I dredged up the business card James had given me and tried that. Someone in the office answered, but James wasn't in. I left a message for him to call me and gave both my home phone number and my cell phone. Then I called Marty's phone again and waited for her voice mail to pick up so I could leave a message.

"Marty? It's Nell. I just got a call from Doris at the Society. She said that Charles told her to call me and ask me to come in, but she didn't say why. I figure I might as well go in and see what it's all about. Heck, maybe he's ready to confess. I'll give you a call when I know what the story is."

There. At least somebody would know where I was. I took an extremely quick shower, dressed, and went out to the car: trains ran so rarely on weekends that it was far faster just to drive, and on a Sunday, parking in the neighborhood of the Society wouldn't be a problem.

But I had guessed wrong. Apparently there was some sort of Center City holiday event going on, and I ended up parking a couple of blocks away. I walked back to the Society and let myself in with my key. On the third floor the offices were dark, except for Charles's suite. When I walked in, Doris was waiting primly behind her desk.

371

"Hello, Doris," I said. "Where's Charles?"

"He's downstairs in the basement. He asked me to wait up here and take you down when you arrived."

"Okay, lead the way." I followed her back to the elevator, and once inside, she keyed in the basement level. "What's this about?"

She remained facing forward, waiting for the elevator to hit bottom. "I don't know, but he said it was important that you see something." The elevator doors opened. "This way."

Doris led the way through the warren of cluttered rooms in the basement. I had never spent much time down here, except for a few occasions when I needed to estimate the scope of a collection. Plus the Society had been making a concerted effort to remove vulnerable items from this area, because the below-ground rooms were damp, and they were also affected by the steady rumbling from the subway trains that ran directly beneath our building. What remained was a jumble of broken furniture, unused display cases, and outdated electronic equipment. Doris kept going, down the long central corridor; she opened one of the doors at the back of the building. I could see lights on in the room beyond.

Doris didn't stop but marched into the

room, and I hurried to follow, mystified. She pointed at an open door to a small room at the back. "Charles is in there." She turned and looked at me expectantly.

I went to the door and peered in. And then something slammed me in the back. I fell forward into the space, and the door swung shut behind me with a solid clang, and I was in the dark. And, apparently, alone.

CHAPTER 30

It took me a moment to figure out what had happened. Doris had just locked me into a very small dark place in the basement, and Charles was nowhere around. I picked myself up off the floor, turned around, and sat, my back against shelves. Then I clamped down hard on the incipient panic attack.

I was not claustrophobic; I was not afraid of the dark. Good. So now it was time to use my brain and think. For starters, I knew where I was. Despite not having spent much time down here, I knew every corner of the building, since I had written more than one grant proposal begging for money to upgrade our lovely but aging 1900 building. This was the former wine cellar, an artifact of the glory days when the Society was run like a gentlemen's club, and those gentlemen liked to have a place to lay down their vintage port, the perfect accompaniment to perusing old documents. Needless to say, the space had not held wine for a very long time; now it held miscellaneous crap. It was located in the farthest corner of the basement, far away from any human traffic, and, as I knew well, it was well insulated.

As the product of an earlier, simpler era, it also had no internal light switch . . . and no ventilation. I squashed another moment of panic and tried to keep my breathing slow and even. I forced myself to look carefully around — any pinpricks of light visible through a crack? Nope. But no doubt Doris had turned off the lights in the room outside, and there were no windows in there, either. It felt cold in the room but was probably only around fifty-five degrees Fahrenheit; big deal — nobody froze to death at fifty-five degrees, although they might be uncomfortable. It was the possible lack of air, not the temperature, that was a bigger problem, I thought. It seemed unlikely to me that the room was hermetically sealed, and even if it had been once, the heavy metal door had warped from its own weight over the years, so it was letting in a little air. And anyway, weren't there plenty of stories about miners trapped underground in air pockets, who survived for days? All I had to do was avoid strenuous exercise and breathe slowly, slowly . . . easier said than done, of course, when trapped in the dark in a basement where nobody ever came.

Now, what did I have to work with? I had carried my purse with me to the basement, so I did a quick mental inventory. I had my keys, with a mini-flashlight on the keychain, but I wasn't sure how old the battery was and how long it might last — best to keep that in reserve. A half-empty box of Altoids — oh, goody, sugar. Kleenex, Band-Aids, my wallet — sure, like I was going to work my way out of here with a credit card. Not likely. Cell phone.

Cell phone! I grabbed it out of its little pocket, flipped it open, and pushed the button to turn it on. *Come on, come on,* I urged it. Its small screen provided a surprising amount of light, though maybe it was just in contrast to the absolute darkness around me. Finally it woke up and started searching for its service area — and found nothing. And then I remembered that I was in the bowels of a concrete-and-reinforced-steel structure, surrounded by metal shelves, in a room with a theft-proof metal door, with a subway track running beneath me. Of course it wasn't going to find a signal. Reluctantly I shut it again, conserving its light — I might want it later, if only for a little company.

What now? I pulled out the flashlight and flicked it on, so I could survey my dungeon. The feeble beam swept over more metal shelving, stacked with old books, outdated piles of Society publications, and miscellaneous junk. Unfortunately, no former visitor had left a handy sledgehammer for me to use to batter my way out. Nor a pry bar, nor anything else that might have an impact on the sturdy walls and door. I swiveled the light toward the door; no interior handle or keyhole. OSHA would be appalled, but the building had been constructed in a different era. And I didn't know how to pick a lock anyway — another skill I had been meaning to acquire.

Think, Nell, think! That's what you're good at! . . . Yeah, you and Butch Cassidy, and look where that got him. I made myself as comfortable as I could against the shelves. I had left Marty a phone message. Good for me. But I had no idea where Marty was and when she might listen to her messages. Assume the best case: she came home, immediately played her messages, and heard that Charles asked me to meet him here. So, eventually she'd expect me to report back about what he wanted. But when? Would she start calling me later today? Would she wait until tomorrow?

Again, best-case scenario, she would get worried late in the afternoon when I didn't answer at any of my numbers, so she'd start checking around. She'd call the Society, but no one would answer. Say Marty could track down Charles; he would profess ignorance of the whole thing. I had mentioned Doris in my message to Marty, so maybe she would try to find Doris — who would also profess ignorance, and who knows what phone she had called from. But Marty had my message, and if both Charles and Doris stonewalled her, she would know something was wrong. The problem was, how long would it take her to figure all this out?

Maybe she would call James. But didn't agencies have to wait until an adult had been gone forty-eight hours before getting involved in a search? Still, at least Marty and James knew what was going on, what was at stake. They would have to be concerned when I disappeared and didn't show up again. Certainly by Monday, when I didn't appear at work, right?

But Monday was a day away. Did I have enough air for that long? And how long would it be before somebody did a full search of the building? Nobody ever came down to this corner of the basement; there was no reason to come down here, maybe not for weeks. Maybe some future renovation would reveal my rotting corpse — or would I be mummified by then? How long did that take?

Stop it, Nell, I scolded myself. I decided to assume the best of all possible worlds: that Marty would worry sooner rather than later, that she'd demand that the FBI and the Philadelphia police do something immediately (and that she had enough clout to make that happen), and that they would be thorough and look in every nook and cranny of the building, and they would find me soon. Very soon.

I thought about looking at my watch to see how long I had been sitting here, trapped, but that would be a waste of precious flashlight power, and it had probably been no more than half an hour anyway. *So, Nell, let's examine the curious question of why Doris locked you in the wine cellar.*

What did I really know about Doris Manning? She was at least ten years older than I was, and had worked here ever since Charles had started. Had he brought her with him from an earlier job? I couldn't remember. She was very good at her job, and she was in a position to know everything about the building and operations. She had never married, and she obviously worshipped Charles — it was clear every time she looked at him. It was something of a joke among the rest of the staff. Although to be fair, Charles did nothing to encourage her; he just accepted her adoration as his due. She would do anything for him . . .

Like kill?

Oh my. I started to run the mental video of the gala. Had I seen Doris then? She had been invited, of course, but she was such an invisible sort of person that no one paid her much attention. She could have been there throughout, or she could have slipped out and done almost anything — including kill Alfred. He knew her and would've had no reason to be afraid of her. Doris could have asked him to check something in the stacks, maybe for a member, and he would have followed her willingly. Even eagerly — anything to get away from that party he hated. And it wouldn't have taken much strength to whack Alfred on the head with something heavy or to shove him into the metal bookshelves. Based on the push she had given me, I had no reason to question Doris's strength. And nothing ever ruffled her — she would have walked calmly away from Alfred's cooling corpse and gone about her business, without a hair out of place.

But *why?* What possible motive could she have to kill Alfred? But for that matter, what motive could she have to lock me in here? It had to come back to her adoration of Charles. No doubt she would have picked up some whispers of missing documents. We all knew she tiptoed around the place eavesdropping on conversations. Maybe she'd overheard me talking with Alfred. Heck, for all I knew, she was Charles's fence. Somebody had to arrange for negotiations with those under-the-radar collectors, and I knew for a fact that Charles was clueless when it came to computer programs, let alone mailing packages. Doris always handled it all for him. The more I thought about it, the more it made sense to me.

The question I really didn't want to ask myself was, what did Charles know? He couldn't have known how much Alfred knew, because Alfred hadn't told anyone except me, and then Marty. Even so, what had Charles thought when he heard that Alfred was dead? Did he never once consider that faithful Doris might have been involved? Or had he carefully avoided even thinking about it?

Which at the moment was moot. How the

hell was I going to prove any of this, locked in the basement? Knowing Doris, she would purge all records of anything remotely incriminating, if she hadn't already. By the time anyone found me, all the evidence would be long gone. Did she know that Marty knew the whole story? I went around and around with my reasoning. If I had really loved Charles, how far would I have gone along with his schemes? Luckily I would never have the chance to find out: the only thing I had done right lately was to dump him. At least *my* moral compass seemed to be working. I wasn't so sure about my brain.

When I had said good-bye to Charles, I had said I wanted something more in my life than he was willing to offer. I guess what I meant was *someone.* I had opened my mouth and that was what had come out, unscripted. Did I believe it? I did. I thought of Alfred, all but caressing Cassandra, his computer, and gathering his little trinkets in his small apartment. Or Doris, giving everything she had to her low-level job and worshipping the man she worked for, who took her slavish devotion as his due without giving her a second thought. What did I want? I liked my job, loved history and tending the bits and pieces of it that had survived. But I had to admit, it would be nice if there was someone who cared about me. Someone who would notice if I went missing for a few days — or forever.

I don't know how long I sat there in the dark, just thinking. I might have shed a few tears about the abysmal mess I'd made of things. Every now and then I worried about the air, but there wasn't a lot I could do about it. There wasn't enough room to get comfortable, but I thought I remembered that the air would be better down low. Or maybe that was in case of fire. Still, I might as well lie down and conserve energy. I put my purse under my head for a pillow, wrapped my wool jacket around me, and curled up in a fetal position to wait.

CHAPTER 31

I must have slept, because the next thing I knew, the tiny room was flooded with light, and somebody was feeling for a pulse in my neck. Startled, I lashed out.

"Are you all right?" Ah, the gravelly voice of Agent James Morrison. *Thank God!*

I stopped flailing. "Yes. Yes! Get me out of here." Back to light and air and freedom — *please!*

Strong hands reached in and hauled me to my feet. Upright, I found that my legs had gone to sleep, and as I fell forward, James's arms came around me to hold me up. The sudden shift from total darkness to light blinded me, so I buried my face in his chest and kept my eyes shut. I was also sucking in great gasps of air, which made it hard to talk. And I was shaking from cold, and shock, and reaction. While I waited for the storm to pass, I took a quick inventory: breathing — yes, and getting better; legs —

rubbery; brain — definitely fuzzy. Finally, I felt I could breathe normally and I pried my eyelids up. James was still holding on to me, and Marty was dancing around the pair of us anxiously. I didn't have any desire to move.

"Nell, are you all right?" His voice rumbled in his chest, under my ear. "Are you hurt? Do you need a doctor?"

"I'm okay, really," I managed. "What day is this?"

"Monday. Morning." He stepped back enough to look at my face, his hands still on my arms, holding me up — and I still needed holding up.

My brain was beginning to come back to life. "Marty, I didn't know when you'd get my message, or what you'd do about it." Reluctantly I peeled myself away from James's broad chest so I could stand on my own two feet. "We have a lot to talk about. But right now I want a bathroom and food, in that order."

"You sure you're all right?" James used his now-free hand to tilt my chin up and look in my eyes. He looked worried, and that made me feel warmer.

"Yes. And I think I've figured things out, but I don't want to talk about it until we can sit down and do it all at once. First things first."

"Then let's get you upstairs." James escorted me to the door and toward the elevator, his hand still on my arm. I didn't complain. I made a beeline for the nearest restroom, leaving James standing uncertainly in the hallway, and ignoring the startled looks from the one or two staff members around. Inside I did what was necessary, then contemplated my reflection in the mirror. I splashed water on my face and ran my fingers through my hair. *Not bad, Nell, all things considered.* A bit pale, maybe. My clothes looked like they had been slept in, which they had. I checked my watch: eight thirty. I picked a few bits of brittle old paper off my slacks and pulled my jacket into place.

When I emerged from the loo, my saviors were waiting in the hall, looking anxious. I announced, in no uncertain terms, "Food now, and lots of coffee. Then talk."

"The Doubletree," James said with authority. Good choice — it was right down the block, which was about as far as I thought I could walk at the moment. He held the heavy front door of the Society open for me and Marty, then shortened his stride to accommodate me as we walked the half block toward Broad Street. Once inside, he commandeered a table in the dining room and ordered one of everything on the menu while I gulped down a full glass of water. Coffee miraculously appeared before I finished the glass, and I added sugar to my cup and started on that.

I was beginning to feel human again. "While we're waiting for food, please tell me how you figured out where to find me."

Marty answered first. "I was out all day yesterday, and I didn't get home 'til late, so I didn't check my messages until this morning! I'm *so* sorry about that. And I had my cell with me, but it wasn't even turned on — I keep forgetting about it. When I finally heard your messages, I started calling you at home and on your cell, and you didn't answer, and that didn't seem right. Then I called Charles."

That was one call I would like to have heard. "What the heck did you ask him?"

"Oh, I was cool. I asked if he'd seen you or talked to you yesterday, and he said no, he had his kids this weekend, and they'd been out sightseeing or some such."

"Did you believe him?"

"Yeah, because I could hear a computer game in the background. So I said thanks a lot and hung up, fast. Then I called Jimmy."

I glanced at James — he was still watch-

387

ing me as though he expected me to keel over any minute. "And what did you think?"

"I thought we should track you down. Tried the GPS on your phone, but no luck."

"I know — I tried to call out, but, surprise, there's no reception in the basement of the building. So then what?"

"Marty said you mentioned Doris, so we tried to call her — no answer. So the two of us got together and headed over to the Society."

Hot and plentiful food appeared. I started forking up scrambled eggs almost before the server had set down the plate. With a full mouth I mumbled, "How did you get in?"

"I've got all the keys." Triumphantly Marty held up a loaded key ring. "And I do mean *all* of them. They were Daddy's keys."

I swallowed. "And you remembered the wine cellar?"

"Eventually. We started with the third floor — damn, I was scared we'd find you where you found Alfred. And then we looked in the upstairs stacks, although there's no place there to hide a human, dead or alive. We even looked in the dumbwaiter that runs between the floors. And when we didn't find you up there, we started for the basement. Remind me to tell the board we really need to do something about the mess down there. And, yes, I knew about the wine cellar because Daddy used to talk fondly about the good old days, when the building was new. Not that he was old enough to remember, but his father must have told him. Then it took me a while to figure out which key opened it, but I did, and voila! There you were, thank goodness. Okay, your turn."

The food on my plate had vanished, and I started in on the pastries in the center of the table, with another cup of coffee. "I had plenty of time to think yesterday, or last night, or whenever it was. I told you Doris called me at home and said that Charles had found something at the Society that I really needed to see. I thought he was going to try to make us believe that he'd located the missing items, or at least some of them, so I decided to go along with it. But something didn't feel right — that's why I called you, Marty. I figured somebody should know where I was going."

"Thank goodness!" Marty actually looked humbled.

"So I let myself in and went upstairs. There was nobody around except Doris, who was waiting for me. She said Charles was downstairs, and she took me down to the basement."

"And no Charles?" There was a hint of steel in James's voice.

"No. Doris headed straight for the back room downstairs, where a light was on. She said Charles was waiting in there for me, but when I went to look, she gave me a shove and locked the door behind me."

We all fell silent, contemplating the awful what-might-have-been. I didn't stop eating, however. I had three meals to make up. When the last of the pastries had disappeared, I said, "Well, before I went to sleep" — *or passed out,* I thought — "the conclusion I came to was that I really don't think Charles knew I was there. I think it was all Doris's idea. And I think she may have killed Alfred."

James managed to look both bewildered and frustrated — no easy feat. Marty just looked mad. "Doris, that spineless drip?" she said. "Why on earth do you believe that?"

"Think about it. She knew all about the wine cellar. In fact, I'm willing to bet there's not much she *doesn't* know about the Society — she's a snoop. And I know she was the one who pushed me in there; there was no one else around, and nowhere to hide in that room. And as you've noticed, she has a nasty habit of listening in on

390

conversations. Let's say she happened to overhear Alfred and me talking about the missing items, and she decided to nip the problem in the bud. Alfred probably trusted her — he had no reason not to — so maybe she came to him during the gala and told him she needed his help in the stacks, whatever, it doesn't matter why. So he followed her, and all she would've had to do was get behind him and hit him with something, or even just shove him so he hit his head on something, and that would be that. It wouldn't take a lot of strength, would it, James?"

Now he looked grim. "No, not really, if you hit him in the right place. And left him there to bleed to death. Either the scalp wound or cranial bleeding would have done the job, and she knew nobody was going to come poking around the stacks that night. Did you see her at the party?"

I shook my head. "Not that I recall, but she's kind of an unnoticeable person. She just fades into the woodwork, if you know what I mean. I don't think anyone would have noticed whether or not she was there."

"Say I buy that," James said slowly. "Why would she kill Alfred, and try to kill you?"

"Because she's in love with Charles, and she knows what he is up to." That silenced both of them. I noted that neither one of them was arguing with me. "Marty, you've seen the way she looks at him. Is it so hard to imagine that she would kill in order to protect him? I don't think she has much else in her life. Alfred was a threat to everything she cared about. And so was I, because Alfred confided in me, and then I wouldn't let it go. Maybe she would have gone after you next."

"Do you think Charles knows what Doris did?" James kept his voice level.

I answered slowly. "I don't know. He may have guessed about how she felt about him, but he probably found that convenient. Do I think he asked her to do his dirty work for him, or that he knew or guessed what she was doing? I can't say. But if he did figure it out, after the fact, no doubt he realized that to implicate her would only throw a spotlight on his own activities. Maybe he even worried that she'd give him up in order to save herself if it came down to it. Maybe he hoped the police would just chalk Alfred's death up to an accident, which is exactly what they did."

We all fell silent, working through the various ramifications of what I had said. Finally James broke the spell. "I think we need to have a conversation with Doris. And with

Charles."

I nodded. "I think you're right. But do we bring the police in now?"

He regarded me levelly. "I think we'll have to, but let's talk to Doris first. I am obligated to point out that the only crime we have any evidence of at the moment is Doris's attempt to kill you, and even that isn't clear — it would be her word against yours."

We stared at each other for several beats. He was right: if I accused Doris, there was no way to be sure that a charge of attempted murder would stick, and there was still no guarantee that we could prove she was Alfred's killer. And frankly I wasn't sure that the Society could recover from the double whammy of a murder plus grand larceny splashed across the headlines. While my construction of the plot had seemed perfectly logical when I worked it out in the silent darkness of the wine cellar, I wasn't sure if it would stand up under scrutiny. But there was one way to find out.

"Let's go talk to Doris."

CHAPTER 32

Back at the Society, Marty, James, and I hurried up to the third floor. I was not surprised to find that Doris was not at her desk; Charles wasn't at his, either. I retrieved Doris's address; she lived within walking distance in nearby Society Hill. "What if she's not home?"

"We'll deal with that when we come to it."

It took no more than fifteen minutes to walk the mile or so to Doris's address. I was torn between the need to find out if I was right about what had happened, and the reluctance to confront Doris. We walked up the two flights of the nineteenth-century brick row house, now apartments; Doris's apartment was on the top floor. James rapped authoritatively on the door as Marty and I hung back. Inside, there were footsteps; the peephole darkened briefly, and then multiple bolts were shot back. The door opened.

Doris was neatly dressed, every hair in place. She took a long time studying us: first me, then James, then a quick look at Marty. Then she stepped back. "Come in, please. Can I get you some coffee?"

I squashed an urge to giggle. Doris, my would-be murderer, was pretending this was a social occasion. But then, I wasn't sure what the proper etiquette for an accusation of murder might be. I decided to let James handle this — he had a lot more experience than I did.

He stepped into the short hallway. "No, thank you, Ms. Manning. We need to talk with you. You weren't at work today."

Doris sniffed. "Miss, if you don't mind. Mr. Worthington gave me the day off. I'll be happy to talk with you." She turned on her heel and led us to a small living room, its windows overlooking the street. We distributed ourselves among the chairs. "What did you want to talk about?" Very cool and unruffled. I felt a tingle of alarm.

James began. "Can you tell us what happened yesterday afternoon at the Society?"

She glanced at me. "Of course. Mr. Worthington asked me to call Miss Pratt. He wanted her to see something he had discovered in the basement. I called her, and she arrived an hour or so later."

"And then what?"

"I escorted her to the basement."

"Where was Mr. Worthington?"

"I can't say."

"He was not in the building?"

"No, I don't believe so. I expected him to meet us there."

"Had you seen him at all yesterday?"

Doris shook her head.

"Talked to him?"

"Well, I must have, wouldn't you say?" She looked at James as if challenging him.

He took a different tack. "After you led Miss Pratt to the basement, what did you do?"

"I went back upstairs. I had some paperwork to finish up."

"You must have finished it, since you didn't go in to work today."

"Charles was kind enough to let me take the day off."

"Where was Miss Pratt when you left yesterday?"

"Still in the basement as far as I'm aware. May I ask why you would like to know?"

"Are you familiar with the room that used to be a wine cellar, in the basement?"

"Not to my knowledge. I seldom go downstairs — there's more than enough to keep me busy upstairs."

"So you were not aware that Miss Pratt spent the night locked in that wine cellar?"

Doris's eyes darted briefly to me. "Why would I be?"

I stared at the woman in front of me: prim, self-contained, sitting tidily on a straight-backed chair, her legs crossed at the ankles. Was she a very good actress? Apparently she was. But something about Doris Manning was off. She had shown no surprise when we appeared at her door, and little curiosity about why we were here. I decided to cut to the chase. "Doris, you knew I had a relationship with Charles, right?"

For a brief moment her eyes flashed with venom. Then the shutters dropped again. "That's none of my concern."

"Did you know about the other women, too?" I pressed.

"I know that Mr. Worthington meets many women in the course of his duties as president. On occasion he has asked me to make a dinner reservation or send flowers."

"Did you know that he made a pass at Marty and is now dating a friend of hers? And that he's been involved with other women — multiple women — at every place he's worked in the past ten years?"

Doris was now glaring openly at me. "Why should that be of any interest to me? He's my employer. I don't intrude upon his personal affairs."

I sat back in my chair. "Of course you don't. But he depends on you, doesn't he? You're a great help to him, and you're an important part of the Society's organization."

"I try to be of service," she said. "It is, after all, my job."

And how far did her devotion go? I was getting tired of this. "Doris, cut the crap. Yesterday afternoon you pushed me into the wine cellar and locked the door. I think you hoped that it would be a good long time before anybody found me." When her expression didn't change, I realized that she wasn't going to alter her story, and I had precious little proof to back up mine. But then an idea occurred to me. "Doris, I'm going to bring charges of attempted murder against you, and against Charles. If he asked you to, uh, remove me, then he's equally guilty under the law, and he'll be arrested, too."

I could see that shot had hit home. For all I knew, she was perfectly willing to be a martyr, but she wasn't about to let Charles be dragged down with her. Not after she had gone to such great lengths to help him. "No! Charles didn't know."

"Know what, Miss Manning?" James said.

"About . . . what I did, yesterday."

"And what was that?"

Doris lifted her chin. "I did push Miss Pratt into the wine cellar. And I knew that she wouldn't be found for days, if not longer."

James said carefully, "You admit that you attempted to kill Miss Pratt?"

Doris nodded vigorously, dislodging a piece of her precise coiffure. "Yes. I did it. But Charles knew nothing about it. I never even talked to him yesterday — you can check the phone records. You're with the FBI, and you can do that, can't you? You'll see, it wasn't Charles, it was me. All me." There was a thread of hysteria in her voice now.

I stared at the woman. Someone I had known, had worked with, for years. Whose obsession with the boss I had laughed off, dismissing it as trite and pathetic. She must have hated me. I shivered and wondered just what else I had missed along the way.

But there was still one other matter. I wasn't sure what my standing here was, but I had to know. "Doris, what about Alfred?"

She swung her gaze at me, eyes wide.

"What about him?"

James shook his head at me, but I ignored him. "How did he die?"

I could see that Doris's hands were trembling, and she clasped them in her lap. "It wasn't Charles," she said stubbornly.

"You don't have to tell us what happened, Miss Manning. You can have a lawyer if you want one," James warned her.

Doris shook her head vehemently. "No. You have to know it wasn't Charles. Alfred, he . . . found out things. He was going to tell someone — I know he told you, Nell — and that would mean disaster for the Society. It would hurt Charles, wreck his career. I couldn't let Alfred do that. So I had to stop him. He couldn't tell."

"What happened, Miss Manning?" James's voice was gentler now.

Doris nodded. "I told him I needed his help to find something in the stacks. He didn't ask any questions — I knew he wanted to get away from that party. He hated parties. There was nobody around upstairs, not in the hall, not in the stacks. We went inside, and I pointed toward a shelf, and when he turned to look, I picked up the step stool and I hit him with it. Just once. He must have heard me pick it up, because he was turning, and then he fell back against the shelf and hit his head. He fell on the floor. He was bleeding. I waited to see if anybody had heard anything, but nobody came. He was unconscious, and when his breathing changed I knew he wouldn't last long. I went back downstairs to the party."

Doris's calm, even tone sickened me. She'd just described murdering someone, watching him die, and she didn't seem to feel a thing.

Then she turned to me again. "Why couldn't you have left it alone? Alfred was nobody — he had no right to interfere. What did it matter, a few bits and pieces of old paper? The Society would survive. Charles would make sure of that."

Marty finally spoke up. "Alfred was my cousin, and he was a good man. And at least he was an honest one, which is more than you can say for Charles."

Doris stood up abruptly. "How dare you!" And she sprang at Marty, claws out. James stepped in and held her back, and she turned on him. "Don't touch me! Take your hands off me!" She was sliding into full-blown hysteria, and it was all James could do to restrain her. Over his shoulder he said to me, "I think we could use a little help here. Can you call the police?"

I was happy to comply.

I went downstairs and out to the front steps to make the call, and stayed there to wait for them. I wanted to get out of that cramped apartment and away from Doris. I sat on the brick steps until the first police car arrived, and I wasn't surprised when Detective Hrivnak stepped out.

"You again? What is it this time?"

I debated very briefly about taunting her, but mainly I wanted this to be over. The fact that she was here meant that she or someone had taken my mention of murder on the phone seriously. "Top floor. You might need a hand — there's a hysterical woman up there, and she's trying to confess to Alfred Findley's murder."

Hrivnak eyed me incredulously but headed up the interior stairs, followed by a uniformed cop. I remained where I was.

Marty came down shortly and sat down beside me. "Well."

"Yes. Well. Should we have known?"

Marty shrugged. "I don't know. I hope not." She lapsed into silence.

Finally two officers guided a still-struggling Doris out of her apartment and down the stairs, followed by James and Detective Hrivnak, talking with each other. "I'll come by in a few minutes, Detective.

There are some other things you need to know," James said.

"Right. Make it sooner rather than later." She nodded wordlessly to Marty and me, then climbed back into her car and followed the black-and-white to wherever they were taking Doris.

James turned to Marty and me. "I'm going to have to go with them and explain things. Nell, why don't you go home? You look like you're about to fall over. I think we can hold her for Alfred's murder alone, unless you want to press charges."

I shook my head. "No. Let's keep this simple." I shook my head again. "That was really unnerving. Doris has always been so cool and collected, and then she just fell apart. I can't believe she really killed Alfred. But — what about Charles? What are you going to do about the thefts now?"

"I think we can wait until tomorrow for that. At the moment he doesn't know we're on to him, and he has no reason to disappear. If he gave Doris the day off, he won't expect to see her until tomorrow, most likely. We can deal with him in the morning. Good enough?"

"You're the expert. If you're going to arrest Charles, can I be there?"

"I think you deserve that much. Look, I've

got to get over to the police station, but let's say we meet at the Society tomorrow morning."

"All right. I'll let you in, say eight thirty? Before the rest of the staff shows up."

"Fine. Go get some rest, Nell." He headed down the stairs, leaving me standing in the hall with Marty.

"Well," I said.

"Exactly," Marty replied. "He's right — you look done in. You okay to drive home? Or you want to stay with me tonight?"

"Thanks, Marty, but I'm okay. I'd really just rather be in my own place." I wanted to slink back into my cave and hibernate. I had a lot to process. I shook my head in disbelief. "What an unholy mess. And tomorrow isn't going to be any better. Marty, what's going to happen to the Society?"

"I won't kid you — it may be rocky for a while. But I think Doris was right — the Society will survive. We've survived this long, and damned if I'm going to let it go under on my watch."

"I'm glad to hear that. Walk me back to the car?"

We made our way slowly back to my car, now decorated with a couple of parking tickets. I drove home carefully, where I fell into bed and slept for twelve hours.

CHAPTER 33

The next morning, I lay in bed trying to sort out what had happened the day before and what was going to happen today, and what it might mean to me and to the institution where I worked, a place I happened to care about quite a lot. Funny, wasn't it, that a crumbling building filled with a lot of old books and papers could lead to such drama. But in a perverse way it made me feel better — the place, or at least its contents, were worth fighting for. If I hadn't cared about it, maybe I would have brushed off Marty's accusations of theft as the rantings of a crank, and ignored Alfred's findings, much as Latoya had, and things would have gone on just as they always had.

And maybe Alfred would still be alive.

But I had taken Marty's complaint seriously, and I had talked to Alfred, and I had sent the whole thing tumbling down. How would we put it back together?

Well, lying in bed wasn't going to help. I hauled myself upright, took a shower, and stood in front of my closet. What does one wear to an arrest? I decided a sober black jacket and wool pants would be appropriate, with a silk blouse in a rich but subdued burgundy. I put on my grandmother's pearls, then took them off again — this was not a social occasion. I put on my good leather shoes and some real gold earrings. The appropriate outfit to help the FBI arrest a criminal.

I decided to drive into the city, since I had no idea how or when this day would end. I made it without mishap, parked in the expensive garage next to the Doubletree Hotel, and walked briskly to the corner. I was early. I spied Marty approaching and nearly laughed: her outfit was a mirror image of mine, as though we had enlisted in the same army. As we stood there, I saw James approaching.

James was accompanied by another agent — a Morrison-in-training, as it were. He was younger, and smaller in all dimensions, but he was doing his darnedest to emulate his associate's stance and demeanor, all the while hanging back a respectful two feet.

James introduced us to the second agent, Agent Tuttle. Then he turned to Marty and me. "You are here as a courtesy, and I'd prefer it if you don't speak. I don't expect Charles to react violently, but Agent Tuttle is here just in case." The young agent tried to look menacing and failed. "Are you ready?"

Marty and I looked at each other briefly, then nodded. On the stone steps of the Society, I fished out my keys and opened the door. The lobby was still dark, but I didn't bother with the lights before leading the way to the elevator.

We rode up the elevator in silence. When we reached the third floor, the men got off first and strode toward the executive offices, Marty and I trailing behind. No one was in. Would Charles appear? Why wouldn't he? When we reached the outer office of the president's suite, Doris's desk was pristine — not a stray paper in sight. Wordlessly, all four of us sat in the stiff visitors' chairs to wait for Charles.

We didn't have long to wait. I could hear the whine of the balky elevator, although the carpeting in the hall muffled footsteps. And then Charles appeared in the doorway. There was a moment of absolute silence. At the sight of us, he paused and surveyed the group before speaking.

I watched his face. He was not a stupid

man, and he had to know the game was up. But he chose to play the gracious host.

"Gentlemen, ladies, to what do I owe this visit? Please, come in."

In his office, James took a small step forward. "Charles Worthington, you are under arrest for the theft of historic items from the Society. You have the right to remain silent . . ." He ran through the familiar litany. Charles did not respond, did not move, but maintained a pose of studied dignity until James had finished. Then his eyes flickered toward me, briefly, as though contemplating his options, weighing the odds. I met his gaze, and he was the first to turn away. He turned back to James and finally spoke.

"I see. Well, I suppose I should contact my lawyer, if I may?" He raised an eyebrow.

"Of course. You can tell him to meet you at FBI headquarters on Arch Street."

Charles went to the door. Little Agent Tuttle sprang to follow him, but Charles went only as far as the doorway, and I realized he was looking for Doris. Her absence appeared to surprise him. He came back, then extracted his wallet from a pocket and searched for a business card. "May I?"

James nodded. He left Tuttle keeping an eagle eye on Charles as he made his phone call, and drew Marty and me into the outer office. "Right now I want to get him processed, and that should take a few hours. Shall we meet for dinner?"

I nodded on behalf of us both — I wanted answers. He looked at me, and I thought I saw a hint of a smile. "How about that restaurant with the great reception? Say, seven?"

"OK. Oh, what can I tell the staff?"

"I would hold off on making any official announcements, although I'd guess they'll notice that both Charles and Doris are missing. But I'm sure you can stall for a bit. Tell them Charles has been called away and Doris is out sick or something."

Marty nodded. "A day or two won't hurt. Of course, I'll have to inform the board, but that can wait until tomorrow, too. Maybe we can hash out a story at dinner. And, Jimmy? Try not to make us look too stupid, will you?"

"I'll do my best, Martha. See you later." Then he headed for the elevator, and Marty and I were left standing there in the hallway.

"So, now what?" I really was at a loss.

"Get back to work, I guess. Good luck, Nell."

I have no idea how I got through the day. I

sat at my desk and looked busy, took care of trivial follow-up letters, and updated the database, all on autopilot. A few people drifted by, but nobody asked anything about Charles's dark office or the more noteworthy absence of his fierce door warden Doris. It was as though everyone sensed something was wrong, but no one really wanted to know what it was, and I wasn't ready to tell them anything — not until I knew what Charles would say. At the end of the day I sat listening to the familiar sounds of the place shutting down for the evening — people heading for the elevator in twos and threes, doors closing, lights going out, and then quiet. And then I listened to the old building, and heard . . . nothing. The building was rock solid. It had been standing here for over a hundred years, and it wasn't going anywhere. That thought cheered me.

I made it to the restaurant with five minutes to spare. Marty was not there, at our table, but James was. He had a glass of clear liquid in front of him, which I feared was club soda, which meant this was still business.

I dropped into the seat opposite him. "Hello. No sign of Marty?"

"No. But she's not known for her punctuality."

"But she makes up for that in tenacity," I replied.

That drew a laugh from him. "That she does." Then the smile left his face. "I think Marty took Alfred's death hard, whether she admits it or not. I have to admit, I always thought Alfred was a weaselly little wimp, but Marty used to hit me when I said anything like that. She's very protective of underdogs, which explains half of her charitable activities."

"Sounds to me like you all had an idyllic childhood," I said wryly, trying to attract the attention of a waiter, any waiter, so I could get something to drink.

James raised one masterful hand, and a waiter materialized instantly. "White wine?"

He'd remembered. "Chardonnay, if they have it." The waiter nodded, then scurried away toward the bar.

The wine arrived in seconds. I took a healthy mouthful, then sat back, closed my eyes, and let it glide down my throat. Better. In fact, it tasted too good if I was planning to drive home tonight. Regretfully I opened my eyes and helped myself to a piece of bread. I looked up to see James studying me.

"What?" I said, more sharply than I might have intended.

"You still look tired."

Actually, I had no idea what I looked like at this point. I dimly remembered making a brief stab at applying makeup before I rushed to get to the city this morning. "I got plenty of sleep. But it's not every day that someone tries to kill me." James, on the other hand, looked as he always looked. "You look like you eat criminals for breakfast."

The smile was back. I wondered where he'd been hiding it all this time. I knew *why* he was hiding it, because the smile transformed his face from stern to boyish. For an instant I could see the happy kid running around with Marty and the gang, instead of the strong arm of the law. The smile disappeared, and with it the boy, leaving the monolithic Agent Morrison again. I sighed, involuntarily.

"Just doing my job, ma'am."

He looked up, past me, and I turned to see Marty making her way toward our table. She settled into the chair next to mine, dropping into it with a sigh and peeling off her coat. She'd shed the serious-woman armor of earlier and was back to her slightly offbeat casual wear, leaving me feeling overdressed. She looked tired, too.

James raised a hand again, and the waiter

popped up to take Marty's drink order. Apparently the FBI agent radiated an innate authority that trumped the big tip we'd given the week before, because the staff here certainly hadn't responded to us like this. Of course, we had been acting like two crazy ladies, which might have had something to do with it. "We should order," James said when Marty's drink arrived. We placed three orders for pasta and made meaningless small talk until the food arrived. When the waiter had retreated again, James cleared his throat. *OK, here it comes,* I thought.

He said carefully, "Charles Worthington was arraigned in federal court today on charges of conspiracy, theft, and receipt of cultural objects under Title 18, U.S. Code, Section 668, theft of objects of cultural heritage. The charges are subject to fine and imprisonment of up to ten years. Charles Worthington has refused to comment on the charges and has retained counsel."

"The Penn document?" Marty asked. When James nodded, Marty sighed. "What does that mean for the Society? What're the chances of recovering the stuff that's gone?"

James looked at her, not without sympathy, then said, "Marty, I just don't know. We may never know the full extent of the thefts from the Society. We're talking with

Charles's lawyer, and we may be able to cut a deal to recover at least some portion of the stolen items. Would the board accept something like that?"

"You mean, we get something back? I guess. The board will probably be happy to make all this go away as quickly as possible."

The food was helping: I could feel my mind revving up. Marty still looked depressed.

"And Doris?" I asked.

"At the moment she's undergoing psychiatric evaluation, to determine if she is in any shape to be charged. If she knows anything about the disposition of the items, we'll find out what we can."

That didn't inspire great hope in me. "I wonder if she kept any records?"

James concentrated on his food for a long moment. "If there is a plea bargain, Charles would return what he could to the Society, or identify where it went, and make financial restitution for some portion of the rest. It would probably be only a fraction of what he got away with, but it would stay out of the press. Marty, is that good enough?"

"Hell, I don't know. You can't put a price on our good name, but there's no point in dragging it through the mud publicly. I just hope Major Jonathan's correspondence isn't gone forever. Can you give me a few minutes alone with Charles to see if I can beat that information out of him?" When James glared at her, she held up both hands. "Joke. But I'm going to do my damnedest to track those down, whatever happens."

"James," I interrupted, "what about the other institutions where Charles had worked? Don't we have an obligation to notify them about any of this?"

"I'm not a lawyer, so I really can't say for sure. Of course if they get wind of this, they're free to file suit on their own. But from what you've told me, it sounds as though they're all in the same boat. If they admit they lost stuff, they'd look foolish, and they'd suffer for it."

"Damn. This doesn't seem right, somehow. We've got the bad guy in our sights, but we can't go after him because we'd all be too embarrassed." I sighed. "I know, I understand it, but that doesn't mean I like it. At least Charles will never work for a museum again — right, Marty? The board is not about to give him a glowing recommendation after all this."

"No way!" Marty said firmly.

I stifled a laugh. I looked down: my bowl was empty, my stomach was full. I felt about a hundred percent better than I had when I arrived.

"Marty, what do we do about the Society now? We don't have a leader — well, practically speaking. Who's next in line to take over? How will we handle day-to-day operations?"

Marty swallowed, then said slowly, "I can't say we've ever had to deal with something like this — as far as I can recall, we've always had an orderly transition, with someone waiting in the wings. I think the first step is to call a special board meeting — at least get the Executive Committee together. And get our lawyer there. And our insurance carrier. Jimmy, can you be there?" He nodded. "How about you, Nell? Since you started this whole thing, you should be there, too, to fill in any blanks."

"Sure."

Marty looked at her watch — it was after ten. "Too late to call them tonight — I'll get on it first thing in the morning, see if I can get a quorum together in the next day or so. We need to start doing some damage control here."

"Sooner rather than later," I agreed. "Listen, can I tell the staff tomorrow that Charles has been asked to resign? I know they've been picking up rumblings, and they deserve to know what's going on. I don't have to go into the details."

"Good point. I say yes." Marty stood up. "Guys, I'm beat. I'm going home. I'll talk to you tomorrow. And thanks, both of you." She wrapped her coat around her and headed out, leaving James and me alone at the table.

I realized I felt good. The buzz from the wine had not quite dissipated and I was well-fed; Marty no doubt would apply her considerable energies to sorting out the mess at the Society. Charles would be disgraced, even if only in his own eyes, and I felt proud of having ended our stunted relationship with a shred of dignity. The Society could move forward, somehow. I wasn't quite sure what form it would take, but I felt hopeful for the first time in days.

And most important, we had solved Alfred's murder.

It occurred to me that James hadn't said anything for a while. I looked at him to find him studying me again. I tilted my head at him, in question.

He gave an apologetic half smile. "Sorry — was I staring? I was just thinking that you've handled yourself well. You sure you don't want a job with the FBI?"

That made me laugh. "I'll consider it, if

things don't work out at the Society. But I know I can be useful there while all this is shaking out. And I'm glad we found Alfred's killer. I always counted Alfred as a friend. I respected his abilities, and I never wrote him off as unimportant, although I know a lot of other people did. Funny how he and Doris — two people who most of the staff never gave a second thought to — came so close to bringing the place down." I sighed.

The check materialized, and James slipped out his credit card.

"So, dinner's on the FBI?" I asked as I gathered my bag from the floor and stood to put on my coat.

"No, on me." He reached to hold my coat as I slid my arm into it.

I stopped for a moment and looked him straight in the eye. "Thank you — for everything."

He didn't say anything immediately. Then he nodded. "Where's your car? I'll walk you to it."

We didn't have much to say as we walked to the parking garage, but it was nice to feel safe on the streets of the city after dark.

It didn't take long to get to the garage.

"Well, this is it," I said. *Really bright comment, Nell.*

"All right, then. Take care."

For an awkward moment, I wondered if we were supposed to shake hands or something. In the end, I just turned and walked toward the stairs of the garage. As I entered the stairwell, I caught a brief glimpse of him, standing where I'd left him, watching me.

CHAPTER 34

The next morning when I arrived I posted signs on the entry doors announcing a quick staff meeting — déjà vu time. I waited for the troops to gather in the boardroom. People appeared quickly, no doubt apprehensive about the rumors that had been swirling around over the past few days. Gossip travels fast in a small place.

When it looked as though everyone was assembled, I began to speak. "I know you all want to know what's going on, but I only want to say it once. Is anybody missing?" People turned to look at each other and shrugged as one. "All right. I'll give you the short version, and then you can ask questions. Charles Worthington has resigned from his position as president of the Society, effective immediately. There will be an ad hoc board meeting tomorrow to formally accept his resignation and to begin a search for his replacement." I debated briefly whether to tell them about Doris's role in Alfred's death and decided against it. Let Alfred rest in peace, at least until the press got hold of Doris's arrest. "Any questions?"

Of course there were. The impromptu meeting with the staff eventually ended only because we knew there were patrons lined up at the door, fuming, and we couldn't afford to antagonize any of our supporters. Nobody mentioned anything about missing documents, not that many people knew about them. Had we really managed to keep that quiet? Or would staff members seek me out one at a time to get the real story? As I had told Marty, our staff were good people, by and large. I hoped they would stick around through whatever was coming, because we needed them, now more than ever. I hoped that they had enough trust in those of us who were left to be patient, and we wouldn't be seeing a mass defection. I would be saddened to see some of these people go, and they were important to the Society if we wanted to keep operating as usual through the stormy days ahead.

I wasn't particularly happy about the lack of leadership going forward. I remembered the search process from the last time and shuddered. If attracting qualified candidates and making a decision had been difficult then, what was it going to be like now, with Charles's abrupt departure? But that wasn't my problem: Marty was dealing with the board, and I knew she could handle whatever questions they pitched at her.

She'd managed to assemble the board in record time, or at least enough of them to make decisions. I don't know what she told them to get them to show up at the Thursday meeting, beyond the bare facts of Charles's defection. Since they shared some liability for what went on at the Society — and a fair number were lawyers — she had probably had to tell them more than that. In any case, they had all promised to come to the meeting.

Marty had asked me to be there, too, so I had dressed carefully, putting on my grandmother's pearls again, and keeping them on this time. As I walked through the lobby, then the catalog room, I got more smiles than frowns from the busy staff members, so I assumed that they weren't in panic mode. Yet.

The meeting had been scheduled for late afternoon, to accommodate professional schedules. Just before four, I wended my way to the boardroom on the second floor. It looked as though most people had already arrived. Marty was clearly in charge, back

422

to her former no-nonsense self, and when she spied me she came over quickly.

"Nell! Glad you're here — we've got a lot to get through. Jimmy's coming to explain the legal side of things, and then the board is going to have to vote on a couple of things. I think it'll be all right, but you never know. Listen, there's something —"

She was interrupted by the arrival of the board chair, Lewis Howard, followed closely by James, and the three of them conferred as a few stragglers wandered in. Marty directed one last comment to the chairman, who cleared his throat and called the meeting to order. People drifted to their seats, sat down, and looked expectantly at him. I took a seat against the wall so I could watch the proceedings, since I didn't have an active role in the group.

"Gentlemen — and ladies," the chairman began, casting a conciliatory smile at the few women in the gathering, "we meet today under extraordinary circumstances, in the face of a crisis that threatens to undermine the very foundations of this noble establishment . . ."

I'd seen Lewis Howard in action before at many board meetings. He was a Philadelphia lawyer with a long record of distinguished service, and he tended toward pomposity. Still, he was a noble figurehead for the Society, and he wasn't entirely past his prime. He waxed eloquent, alternately outraged, apologetic, and hopeful. He stopped orating only when Marty, seated next to him, gave him a nudge, and then he turned the meeting over to James.

Agent James Morrison stood. He began with a brief announcement of Doris's arrest, then segued into a crisp and concise summary of Charles's depredations of the collections and outlined the plea bargain that Charles had indeed requested. He touched on what we could hope to recover, and he gave a time line for expected events. The board members looked uniformly stunned.

As James wrapped up, he glanced briefly at me, but I couldn't read his expression. He returned to the assembled group. "Any questions?"

Marty had apparently done her work well, and there were few. The chairman asked if he should contact our insurance agency, and they agreed to meet at another time to review those details. Another member asked about issuing a public statement, and I cringed, but the majority voiced variations of the opinion that the less said, the better, and I breathed a sigh of relief.

James nodded to the group around the table. "If you don't need me for anything else, I've got a lot of paperwork waiting for me. Feel free to contact me if you wish." No one spoke, and he picked up his coat and headed for the door — where he paused, caught my eye, and winked. Winked? What was that about? And then he was gone.

Marty leaned toward the chairman and whispered something. He nodded, and she stood.

"I think we've covered most of our agenda, except for a few loose ends. First and foremost, we must officially remove Charles Worthington as president of this institution. He has tendered his resignation, but our attorney says that his alleged behavior certainly violates the terms of his contract, so I think that we may feel free to terminate him for cause." I was faintly amused when I realized that this meant Charles would receive no severance pay or related benefits. "Do I hear a motion?"

"So moved," three people were quick to answer. It was seconded in short order, and the motion was passed unanimously.

Marty spoke again. "That brings us to a second, related issue: how we intend to replace him." Her eyes swept the group. "I have discussed this with all of you, and I believe that we are in agreement?" Heads nodded. "I propose that we appoint Eleanor Pratt as interim president, to assume active day-to-day management of the Society."

Wait a minute! She wanted me to take over? For a moment I was speechless. She was grinning at me.

I found my voice. "Uh, excuse me, did I hear you correctly? You want *me* to run the Society?"

There were plenty of other eyes on me now. Marty looked around the table and then back at me.

"Yes. We've talked about it, and we all agree that you are the best choice, at least for now. You know this place, how it works. You've worked with the board. You were crucial to uncovering the thefts and to pushing for a more thorough investigation. And the staff like and trust you — they'll support you. It's going to be difficult for a while, but we really need someone like you at the helm."

My head was spinning. Part of me was screaming in panic: *No, I like the job I have, I don't want the responsibility, I couldn't possibly be any good at it . . .* And then the spinning stopped and was replaced by a great sense of calm. I had a flashing vision of what this place could be, of what I wanted it to be. And with that came a flood of ideas, things I had wanted to implement, experiment with, and how I could define strategies, work with the board . . . It was an extraordinary opportunity, and I'd be an idiot not to seize it. I looked Marty in the eye.

"I'm honored by your faith in me. I would be delighted to accept."

I was stunned. I had never been particularly ambitious, and I'd been happy to work with the people who ran the shop wherever I was. I was a good and dependable lieutenant. But . . . this?

But, I realized, it made sense. A president represented the place to the public, managed the staff on a macro level, and asked for money. I could do that. Heck, at least if I asked for money as president, I'd have more clout than I did as development director. That was a big plus right there.

Marty and Lewis Howard were both looking at me, so I guessed I was supposed to say something. I stood up and made my way to the head of the table. As I gathered my scattered thoughts, I looked out at the board, at people whom I had known for years, had worked with on events or committees. And I knew they were upset by what had happened — or what they knew about it. They'd never hear all the details, but they didn't need to. What they wanted to hear now was reassurance, comfort, hope. I could do that.

I cleared my throat and spoke. "Thank you for your confidence in me. We are all here because we care about history, about preserving the evidence of the past so that this generation and future generations don't lose sight of where they came from. We all know that the course of history is seldom smooth, and that applies to the Society as well.

"A few weeks ago we were happy to celebrate our one hundred twenty-fifth anniversary. While the events in the past weeks have been profoundly troubling, they in no way change who we are, what we do. We are lucky to have identified the problem and found a solution quickly, and I want to believe that this will make us stronger in the future. I think I can guarantee that we'll be taking a long, hard look at our security procedures." A laugh rippled through the group. I smiled. "I have a lot of ideas about what we can do, but this is not the time or the place to discuss those. I'm sure we'll be seeing a lot of each other in the coming months. But for now, I want you to know that we can and will weather this, as we have weathered problems in the past, and continue to serve our mission. And thank you for giving me the chance to be part of it."

I would have sat down, since my knees were a bit wobbly, but I didn't have a chair at the table. Luckily, Marty stepped forward and resumed command — for now.

"Welcome aboard, Nell. You know you can call on all of us to help you, and we know that, no matter what, you have the best interests of the Society at heart."

She looked around the table again. "Well, I think we've done enough for today. I'll be in touch about the next meeting — we can't afford to wait until the quarterly meeting to address a lot of these issues, but I think we can relax. Go home and try to figure out what's happened, and how we can keep it from happening again. And we'll deal with whatever publicity comes along, and the fallout from it. Thank you all for coming on short notice. This meeting is adjourned."

There was a moment of stillness, and then people stood and began gathering their belongings. About half of them approached me, shook my hand, promised to help however they could. I could sense their relief. I nodded, smiled, said things I'd never remember. Time enough to sort things out later — right now I had to avoid looking like a scared rabbit — I needed to project confidence and assurance. I was in charge; they'd said so. That would take getting used to.

Finally everyone had straggled out, and only Marty was left. I didn't know whether to hug her or kick her.

"You sandbagged me, you know," I said.

"You handled it beautifully. I knew you would. Admit it — you're happy about it, right?"

I grinned grudgingly. "I think I will be, when I have a chance to think about it. How did you sell the board on me?"

"Nell, don't put yourself down. You've done a good job here, and, as I said, people trust you. We need continuity, stability more than anything else right now, and you can provide that. You've got more common sense than most of the staff and half the board. And you really do care about this place. You're the best choice, and the board agrees. Don't worry about the long run — this is temporary, but you do a good job, you'll be around for a while. Madame President — I like it."

"One more thing, Marty. I think as my first official act I'd like to establish the Alfred Findley Memorial Fund for Collections Management. I think you'll be making a substantial contribution to it."

"Fair enough. Now let's go celebrate!"

ABOUT THE AUTHOR

Sheila Connolly has been nominated for an Agatha Award for the Glassblowing Mysteries she writes as Sarah Atwell. Under her own name, she is the author of both the Orchard Mysteries and the Museum Mysteries. She has taught art history, structured and marketed municipal bonds for major cities, worked as a staff member on two statewide political campaigns, and served as a fundraiser for several nonprofit organizations. She also managed her own consulting company, providing genealogical research services. In addition to genealogy, Sheila loves restoring old houses, visiting cemeteries, and traveling. Now a full-time writer, she thinks writing mysteries is a lot more fun than any of her previous occupations.

She is married and has one daughter and three cats. Visit her website at: www.sheila connolly.com.

We hope you have enjoyed this Large Print book. Other Thorndike, Wheeler, Kennebec, and Chivers Press Large Print books are available at your library or directly from the publishers.

For information about current and upcoming titles, please call or write, without obligation, to:

Publisher
Thorndike Press
295 Kennedy Memorial Drive
Waterville, ME 04901
Tel. (800) 223-1244

or visit our Web site at:

http://gale.cengage.com/thorndike

OR

Chivers Large Print
published by AudioGO Ltd
St James House, The Square
Lower Bristol Road
Bath BA2 3SB
England
Tel. +44(0) 800 136919
email: info@audiogo.co.uk
www.audiogo.co.uk

All our Large Print titles are designed for easy reading, and all our books are made to last.